C000271206

Simon Petherick was originall
Office of Information in Lor
government propaganda. For several years he ran
the rock music season in London's Hyde Park and
subsequently headed up the Queen's Dressmaker,
Hardy Amies, in Savile Row. He set up his own literary
publishing company which he ran in Soho for seven
years. He is the author of a number of fiction and non-
fiction titles. He lives in London and Cornwall.

Fiction

The Last Good Man
English Arcadia
The Damnation of Peter Pan

Non-Fiction

The Power of the Mind
The War in Plymouth

Like Fire Unbound

Like Fire Unbound

A novel about London

Simon Petherick

TSB
London and New York

First published 2021

Published by TSB, an imprint of:
Can of Worms Enterprises Ltd
7 Peacock Yard
London SE17 3LH
United Kingdom

www.canofworms.net

ISBN 9781911673026

9 8 7 6 5 4 3 2 1

Typesetting: Tam Griffiths

Cover: David Grogan, Head Design
www.headdesign.co.uk

Printed and bound by CPI Group (UK) Ltd,
Croydon, CR0 4YY.

The Forest Stewardship Council® is an international non-
governmental organisation that promotes environmentally
appropriate, socially beneficial, and economically viable
management of the world's forests.
To learn more visit www.fsc.org

London consoles those whom
it is about to consume.

Peter Ackroyd, *London: The Biography*,
on the custom of offering a bowl of ale
to a man before he was hung.

Chapter One

This is a story I want to tell you about London. It's
an hour before the dawn and Evie Sangster is on the
47th floor of the Pelican Tower on Bishopsgate sipping
a Bloody Mary in a fancy all-night restaurant and
waiting for the sun to come up on this Monday
morning. Evie is thirty-five years' old and she has been
in prison twice in her life although she is by no means
a bad or even reprehensible person. The last time she
was locked up was three years ago when she did five
months in Holloway, the year before the Chancellor
of the Exchequer George Osborne announced that he
was going to close the women's prison down and sell
off the land for housing. In 1955, they hanged Ruth
Ellis in Holloway, after she was convicted of murdering
her lover David Blakeley outside a pub in Hampstead,
and now they're still arguing about what houses to
build and whether or not to include a Women's Centre

in the redevelopment which, if they do, they will inevitably call the Ruth Ellis Centre.

Evie got five months for encouraging a retired NHS surgeon from Weybury called Mr Abbas to invest his life's savings in a scheme to build water refining units in Malawi, which collapsed without any water being refined anywhere, leaving three and a half million pounds of investment written off. Evie wasn't the only one who had encouraged people to invest their savings in the Malawi water refining project but, thanks to an ill-advised email with her name attached to it, she was the only one the government prosecuting barrister managed to prove had actively encouraged Mr Abbas to invest. Everyone else who promoted the scheme and earned massive commissions from the investments they secured, managed to rinse their online histories in time; Evie was just unlucky.

When she was in Holloway, she got to know an older woman called Joy Franklin who was in for shoplifting. Joy was forty-six and had been caught stealing a tatty piece of evening jewellery from a discount accessories store in Westfield, which she coveted because her daughter Jade was going to be twenty-one and she wanted her to have a birthday present she would remember. The judge said she was sentencing her "with reluctance" but this was the second time she'd been in front of her in a year so she was going to have to go down for six months. Joy lived in a five-storey council block off Edmonton Green and Evie had spent yesterday evening with her, waiting up for Jade to get back so she could make her parole meeting in the morning. Jade's just come out of Chelmsford where she did another two-month spell for repeated antisocial behaviour and she's already missed one parole meeting since she's come out; if she misses this morning's, they might send her back in. They have to be at the parole office in Tottenham for nine o'clock.

'Stop looking at your phone for a minute, Jade,' Evie says to the girl sitting beside her. 'It's about to happen.'

The girl ignores her and remains crouched over her Samsung on the red leather banquette. She's thin, has a shaved head except for a surprising dyed red Mohican tuft, and blotchy cheeks. She wears stonewashed jeans that are ripped above and below the knees, silver Nike sneakers which are tucked underneath her, and a red gingham shirt.

When Jade had finally turned up at her mother's at one o'clock last night, Joy had been asleep in her bedroom.

'Go to sleep, Joy,' Evie had said to her friend at midnight. 'I'll wait up for her.'

'You don't need to, girl,' Joy had said. 'She's my kid. I can look after her. You're the one wants looking after. State of you.'

'What do you mean, state of me?' Evie had replied.

'I'm fine.'

'Yeah, of course you are. Won't listen, will you? Bloody stubborn.'

'I'm not –'

'It's all right,' Joy had interrupted, wearily. 'I'm not having a go at you. But you know I'm right – you can't just keep trying to sort everyone else out, love. You've got to think about yourself. Anyway, wake me when she gets here? I'm the only one who can talk to her.'

But when Jade swaggered through the front door of the flat clutching a half-empty bottle of supermarket vodka, Evie didn't wake her friend. Instead, she grabbed the bottle off the girl, pushed her into an armchair and leaned her weight on her pathetic frame. She put her face close to the girl's.

'If you don't go to that fucking parole meeting in the morning, I swear I'll stick a knife in you.'

She has quite a physical presence, Evie. When she was growing up out east on the outskirts of Southend, she hung around with some tough kids which is how she got into a fix the first time. Her dad is a big fellow, runs his own business fitting out shop interiors, drives a Mercedes open top. Evie got her big-shouldered frame from him, and his resilience too. Her mum is retired now but she used to be a social worker for Southend Council and has always felt the pain of not being able to keep her daughter out of harm's way. Her parents still live in the rambling old house out on the marshes looking down over the Thames estuary where it dissolves into the North Sea.

Although she's all smart now, with her designer jeans and Manolo Blahnik heels and her carefully layered auburn hair with the touched-up roots, Evie is still pretty strong and she literally took the wind out of Jade by leaning on her last night. Jade is an addict, what she does eat is rubbish and her frame is like a teenager's. She knew when Evie pressed her face into hers that there wasn't any point in trying to get away; all addicts are stupidly cunning and think they can lay low until next time, and Jade just thought she'd have to submit tonight and then after tomorrow's parole meeting she could do what she liked again. Besides, she liked Evie; Evie looked after her mum and Jade wished she could look after her mum but she just never seemed to be able to.

Although Jade is only twenty-four she's already made quite a mess of things and at the moment she's lurching between cheap vodka, weed, Xanax and Diazepam, a combination which makes her unpredictable and often belligerent. Joy has no idea how to help her daughter off all this gear apart from keeping a close eye on her and making sure the front door is always open. Evie though, because she's been around addicts for years but never been one herself – she's much too disciplined for that, Evie, which we'll come to soon enough – knows how to handle them. Once she got some tea down Jade she just let her talk and Jade blathered on in her mum's front room, drinking tea and making roll-ups and telling Evie funny stories about her mates and Evie laughed with her while Joy carried on sleeping in the bedroom next door. When it got to three-thirty in the morning, Jade was showing no signs of slowing down, so Evie suggested they take the 149 bus down to the City to watch the sun come up from this posh restaurant she knew which was at the top of a skyscraper and stayed open all night. Once they'd done that it wouldn't be long before the parole meeting back in Tottenham so it would kill the time. She left a note for Joy telling her not to worry.

So at four in the morning they were sitting on the top deck of the night bus as it juddered down the A10 High Road through Stamford Hill and Stoke Newington and Shacklewell. Even at that time the bus was two-thirds full with Kurds and Somalis and Turks trying to snatch a bit more sleep on the way in to early-morning cleaning jobs and the shift stacking in the clothes warehouses in Whitechapel. Up here in north London in the middle of the night the street lights flicker because the private company the Council appointed to run them can't be arsed to fix them. There was an ambulance with the back door open and as the bus passed you could see a pair of legs sticking out the back in the pool of fluorescent light. There were a group of kids outside an all-night fried chicken shop and one of them chucked an empty nitrous oxide cannister at the bus and it bounced off the window. Evie and Jade sat in the front seat and Evie kept the girl talking because she'd started to flag a bit.

'Next weekend why don't you and me take your mum out to Southend and stay with my folks?' she said. 'They'd like you and it would do your mum good to have a bit of sea air.'

'Yeah, sure.'

'Bring your friend Mikey, they won't mind. They like having people there.'

'Maybe. Mikey's, you know...'

'Well ask him anyway.'

'All right.'

'You'll like this place, Jade. It's full on.'

'Why?'

'It just is. It's on the 47th floor and we'll go up in a glass lift and the restaurant is open all night with windows all around it so we can get a table and watch the sun come up.'

'I'm not really hungry, Evie.'

'You'll just have some eggs. I'll get them to make you some eggs.'

'I don't like eggs.'

'Toast then. I'll eat your eggs.'

'Eggs are gross. They're, like, baby chickens or something.'

'You don't have to have any.'

'I'm vegan anyway. Do they do peanut butter?'

'Probably but is that vegan?'

'Course it is. Nuts, isn't it?'

'I'll get my mum to make you a vegan Sunday roast next weekend.'

'Whatever.'

They got off the bus outside Liverpool Street and started walking up Bishopsgate. Silent passengers headed off towards office blocks and Evie watched as one let herself in to a cavernous, brightly lit foyer where a uniformed man sat unmoving in front of a computer screen at the reception desk. She watched the woman walk past the man without exchanging any words and the last she saw of her she was standing in front of a lift.

Now they've been sitting in the restaurant for about half an hour. Jade's still crouched over her phone, some uneaten toast on a plate in front of her. Every so often she reaches over and takes a drink of Coke from the glass beside it. Evie is lying back against the red leather banquette looking out through the floor-to-ceiling glass walls at the whole of east London suffused in monotone greys which are just beginning to silver here and there as the far horizon visibly lightens minute by minute. The restaurant is the usual stuff:

wooden floors, chrome and glass tables, red leather seats, a long zinc bar edging the open plan kitchen where scarcely-trained chefs from Spain and Romania are turning out the all-night signature dishes. The place is pretty busy, two tables with Chinese business people, a few late-night couples, some suits. A couple of suits at a nearby table have been casting glances at Evie – her clothes are really good these days and her hair is expensive. She has quite a tiny mouth which isn't beautiful but it's cute and just serves to highlight her brown eyes. There's something about those eyes: it's like they're crowded with meaning that is even lost on Evie. The prospect of the younger girl beside her with the shaved head and the tattoos and the broken skin probably puts the suits off from making a play. She'd have given them short shrift anyway, the morning display is about to start.

'Look up Jade, it's coming.' It doesn't matter that Jade isn't interested, at least she's safe here with her.

How many times has Evie been up here to see this over the last few months? Quite a few. It's a mystery to her why she's drawn to it, but she is. She uses this restaurant during the day every so often when she has someone to pitch but she tends to come on her own for the dawn show. She scans the still-grey landscape out in front and now that we're almost at five-thirty it's changed from a pin cushion of street lamps and car headlights to a more obvious layout of roads, houses, factories; hundreds and thousands of buildings stretching out for miles all around her, heading up north east towards Chelmsford, straight ahead of her a direct line out to Southend and her mum and dad; over to the south east she can just see the outline of the Queen Elizabeth Bridge straddling the Thames estuary, its four white fingers now showing their lines in the first light.

'Come on,' she whispers.

Then the first sight of sun, an improbably sudden slim disc of orange which breaks into the pale sky above the urban skyline way out east. It's so instanta-neous you feel like it's somehow audible, as though it's crashed into our world with a terrific noise and now at once the world is different and everything is different and life has changed gear, has speeded up, has roared into being. Evie stares at the horizon and the sun visibly grows in front of her and as the disc becomes a burning segment she can sense the explosions and fierce flares on the surface, the flames and shooting eruptions rippling its molten shape. She is gripping the edges of the leather bench and is sure that she can feel the heat of the rays upon her face as they now spill out and race down the roads and streets of east London to turn it into a living landscape where millions of people are still innocently asleep in their beds or maybe looking out from the deck of a warehouse bay at the end of a night shift or parking a Japanese car outside a terraced house and switching off the Uber driver app. For some it's the end, for others it's another beginning but right now she feels like she's the only one who is bearing witness to this terrible scene as the sun muscles half of its appalling weight into the world and sits for a second as a perfect semi-circle of malevolent fire.

When Evie looks down at Jade, she sees that the girl has fallen asleep, her mobile phone stuck between her thighs and her head resting uncomfortably at an angle on the red leather.

*O*n the morning of Saturday 1ˢᵗ September 1666, the winds were still light in the City of London. The gales that would arrive that night, which were to have such a terrible effect upon the metropolis, were still located out on the French side of the channel, causing havoc amongst the English ships gathered outside Boulogne to challenge the Dutch. But in Pudding Lane, just a gentle breeze stirred the fetid air in the narrow street as Lily Cadyman, maid to the baker Thomas Farriner, stepped out of the low shop door. Instinctively she lifted her skirts so they would not touch the blood flowing down the street from the hog butchers at Eastcheap, then she remembered that there was no killing on the Saturday so there was no need to step so carefully.

The young woman turned right to walk up the slope of the lane. What little sky was visible between the extended wooden top floors on either side was a surly grey, the almost permanent layer of smog sealing the streets from any glimpse of late summer sunlight. Lily hurried along: her master's daughter Hannah had slapped her face the day before because she had taken too long on an errand. Today she had an hour to walk to Master Doleberry's Apothecary in Fleet Lane and be back in *time to take the biscuits out of the oven. Hannah's father, the baker, was suffering in his digestion which made him bad-tempered and Lily was to pick up another bottle of London Treacle from Master Doleberry.*

The lanes were busy and noisy as usual as Lily tried to keep up her pace. The clang of metal being hammered in a workshop, the tired call of a flower seller, an angry exchange between two women over a bottle, the endless bells competing from different church spires. Lily limped, born with a deformity on her left foot, a fault she knew would keep her from a marriage. But she could walk well enough, and what could a man really do to help her? In her eighteen years, she had learned survival at least.

She disliked visiting Doleberry's shop because it stood in the eaves of the Fleet prison, and each time she visited she winced to hear the cries from within that foul building, the shrieks of madmen, the suffering moans from the deep underground cells. The smell of the gaol too was enough to make her stomach turn and her heart fear. But Doleberry was Miss Hannah's particular favourite of the many apothecaries scattered about the City and she was sure it was his London Treacle which had kept them all free of the plague which had taken so many lives that summer.

'Make sure he adds Malaga wine to the recipe,' Hannah had called from upstairs as Lily had been preparing to leave. 'Tis that which gives it the strength.'

'*That and the opium,*' *Lily muttered to herself. She disliked the Treacle but took a spoon each day under the Farriners' orders. And it was true, their neighbour Thomas Fludd had succumbed to the plague only three days before and he it was who had scoffed at the medicinal rituals next door.*

A shout from above caused her to dart under the overhanging eaves of a building as a bucket of slop was emptied from a top floor window, splashing noisily onto the cobbles in the middle of the narrow street. The stink of the slops stayed in the air briefly and she pinched her nose until she passed the oyster barrows on Fish Street Hill. A crowd was gathered around the barrows so it must have been a fresh delivery. Perhaps there would be fewer people on the way back and she might have time then to purchase some – Mister Farriner was partial to his oysters. She had no time for queuing now, not if she was to avoid another slap. But the oysters might buy her some temporary grace from her employers.

Lily waited at the entrance to Great Eastcheap for a carriage to squeeze through the throngs of people, then she joined the crowd and headed down to Cannon Street which would take her towards Fleet Lane via St Paul's. The street was a raucous hubbub of shouts, laughter, threats and street-sellers' calls and the air was thick with smoke from the furnaces which the glassmakers used to fashion their goods in these parts. This time she covered her mouth with a rag from the pocket of her dress and then she thought about her mother whom she would visit tomorrow, it being Sunday. Lily feared she had not long to live. She was forty-three now and the week before when she had visited her in the room in which she lodged in a house beyond Spital Fields her mouth had been black and her breath stank like the grave. She planned to siphon a little of the London Treacle before she went to bed tonight so she could give it to her tomorrow. It might help.

Chapter Two

Often when the train from Totnes edged into Paddington Station a few minutes after nine o'clock on a Monday morning, Henry Stirling felt a build-up of internal pressure so great that he could hear the blood racing around his skull, hammering pumping rhythms into his forehead and making his striped Thomas Pink shirt stick to his fleshy chest in furious perspiration. Today is no different. As the train shudders past the melancholy concrete of Trellick Tower in North Kensington, he stands up from his seat in the centre of the quiet carriage, and is frustrated beyond all reason to find his path to the door blocked by a tall elderly woman who is struggling to pull her coat down from the overhead rack.

'Let me get that for you love,' he says, trying to reach over her but she waves him away.

'Thank you, young man,' she replies primly, 'I am

quite able,' and he is obliged to watch in utter despair as other passengers take notice and stand up too, reaching for cases and pulling on jackets, leaving him trapped in the centre of the carriage while the vicious old crone fumbles around for her gaudy mackintosh and the aisle fills up with the pale, long-distance commuters who, like him, have travelled up from the south west and are once more about to do battle with London. It's week three of the heatwave, the hottest spell in London for thirty years and the shabby train's aircon-ditioning is already unable to cope with the temperature, so the combination of the muggy warmth of the carriage and his traditional Monday morning stress has reduced Henry's shirt to a soggy flannel.

Henry is sixty-two and is a splenetic, rotund, pin-striped emblem of all that this modern city sets out to destroy. He carries a cream Burberry gabardine over his left arm because there have been warnings of thunderstorms breaking the heatwave and his hand is gripping the seat handle so tightly that his knuckles shine damp and white. In his right hand he clasps the battered old brown Cleverley briefcase which contains a copy of the *Financial Times*, a messy collection of papers relating to his current transactions, a set of house keys for the Totnes house he moved to with his wife twenty years ago, another set for the flat in Ealing where he stays during the week, a third for his office in the City, a pack of spare ink cartridges for his Mont Blanc pen and an apple.

Henry is about as ill-equipped to deal with London at the end of the second decade of the twenty-first century as the despairing lions pacing around their ersatz Gujurati-themed enclosure in London Zoo. His face, blank and rigid now as he accepts that he will be standing here in the centre of the hot carriage for several more minutes while the slow shift of passengers empties onto the platform, is centre-pieced by a comically misshapen nose which he broke one too many times playing rugby as a young man. He has a curiously structured thatch of brown hair which makes you think of the word "perm" and his neck bulges over the tight collar which is tied with a nylon Saracens Rugby Club tie. He has small brown eyes and delicate lashes and his teeth are slightly too pointed to be able to achieve a recognisably friendly smile.

Henry is intelligent, knowledgeable, quick-witted in conversation and built of the same kind of stubborn persistence which some Londoners still refer to as "the Dunkirk Spirit". His primary failing, once you accept and then disregard his uncouth mind, his deep and innate misogyny and his laughably short fuse, is his clinging to that most uncontemporary of emotions, hope. Henry has hope running through him like the letters through a stick of rock. Without hope, there is no sense at all to Henry Stirling; with it, there is only the relentless course of tragedy.

On the rare occasions when Henry's wife Celia takes him out to dinner with friends in Totnes, she explains him by saying, "Henry does something awful in the City." Henry, if he is in a good mood, will further this by explaining patiently that it is only by the activities of men like him in the City of London that the good people of Totnes are able to enjoy the finer things in life such as Kundalini Gong Workshops and Tibetan raffia classes. If as is more often the case in recent years he is in a bad mood, then his lip and left eye will twitch and his skin will moisten beneath his nose and he will mutter incomprehensibly a series of imprecations against the town which even after twenty years he regards as a temporary weekend posting.

Henry moves as one with the human swarm from Platform Seven down into the Underground, and soon he is standing on the concrete behind the yellow stripe waiting for the Bakerloo line to take him to Oxford Circus, where he will change onto the Central for Bank. He stares at the 48-sheet advertisement on the other side of the track and wonders why anyone would want to have "that #FridayFeeling" every day of the week, as the makers of a disgusting-looking probiotic juice drink would have him believe.

The Bakerloo train is very full and he has to squeeze in, the wall of heat and body odour assaulting him as soon as the doors open. At Oxford Circus he marches quite spritely now through the tunnels from one line to the other and, despite the temperature, pleased with the look of his new co-respondent shoes whose black and white brogue leather and tassled laces reflect in his mind the bold approach he takes to all aspects of life on this earth. A group of young men walking towards him wearing skinny, shiny *Top Man* suits and scuffed grey loafers start to snigger while one actually calls out once they have passed, 'Nice shoes, mate!' as his companions laugh like hyenas. 'And fuck you too,' he calls out, not turning round but imagining smashing his fist into their dumb, puny, virginal little faces.

Henry walks down Queen Victoria Street once he's out of Bank station. High above him is the *Coq d'Argent* restaurant overlooking the City and, out of a self-imposed superstition he doesn't like to dwell upon, he glances up at the viewing platform from which, over the years, a number of people have killed themselves by jumping. It's only a glance and all he catches is the glint of white sunshine reflected off the metal railings, then he's marching on, stout but vigorous, his humour bleak since the unpleasantness at Oxford Circus and as he veers right into Watling Street he grimly places bets with himself on which of his faithless team will have failed to get into the office yet. He knows about Evie, she texted him earlier, but which of the three guys will have phoned in with a Monday morning stomach complaint? Useless, shiftless bastards.

Halfway down Watling Street he stops by a fading green door, jabs a code into the intercom and steps into a scruffy lobby with one wall taken up by pigeon-holes randomly filled with letters and parcels. He grabs the envelopes from the hole marked "Stirling Global" and climbs two flights up carpeted stairs, catching his co-respondent shoes on a loose carpet runner halfway up. He bangs the grey door open and walks swiftly past two young men, sitting at laminated desks, who are clearly enjoying a joke. They immediately stop and one says, 'Morning Henry,' which he ignores, choosing instead to hurl his briefcase against the far wall where a much older walnut-coloured desk with a claret leather top is covered with piles of papers and a cheap black PC with yellow Post-it notes stuck around its edges. The briefcase falls open to the floor and the apple rolls out and Henry kicks it, corners the desk, sits down on the old swivel chair and boots up his PC.

'Where the fuck is Darren?' he asks, without looking up.

A woman with a blonde bob held together with hairspray sitting behind a desk in the opposite corner exchanges glances with the two young men and then says:

'Darren says he'll be in at lunchtime, he has to go to the dentist for an emergency filling.'

'Tell him not to bother.'

'Going to the dentist or coming in?'

'Both,' Henry shouts, looking up. 'God Almighty, Jean, Mickey Mouse wears a Darren fucking Hegarty watch! I get up at five o'clock in the sodding morning, I spend a hundred and twenty bloody quid to sit in a steaming cattle truck for three hours and still that Irish bastard can't make it to work before me and he lives in bloody Farringdon.'

'I'll make you a coffee,' the woman says, standing up and straightening her pleated skirt. She goes out and now the room is silent. After a couple of minutes, one of the young men places an earpiece and microphone apparatus on his head.

'Is that Mister William Cecil? Good morning, Mister Cecil. Rufus Carter from Stirling Global, we spoke last week. Yes, that's right. Don't worry, Mister Cecil, I – yes, absolutely, what time will you be back? Lovely, I'll ring you then. Enjoy your swim.'

He takes the headset off. His voice betrays the relaxed confidence and privilege of the public schoolboy.

'These old bastards have the life of Riley. Going to the swimming pool at 9.30 on a Monday morning.'

Henry looks up.

'Is he interested?'

'Seems to be.'

'He either is or he isn't, Rufus. Seems to be doesn't cut it.'

'He will be, boss.'

'Good lad.'

The tension in the room relaxes as Henry leans down to pick up his briefcase from the floor. He sits it on his lap and begins to pull paperwork out.

'Your boys embarrassed themselves on Saturday, Jimmy,' he says, rifling through untidy sheets of A4. 'First game of the season too.'

The second of the two young men scowls. 'Shameful,' he says. 'I was out of the bloody ground with ten minutes still to play. Another bloody waste of money – three grand, the season ticket now.'

Henry laughs.

'We only managed nil-nil,' he says.

And so begins another week at Stirling Global, the dysfunctional, failing Independent Financial Advisory firm which Henry has kept going through sheer stubborn willpower for almost ten years. Henry still believes, but by no means as confidently as he once did, that he can grow the client list of Stirling Global to the point at which it will become attractive to one of the big corporates who occupy the faceless skyscrapers which every day seem to be edging closer to the scrappy little buildings on Watling Street. He dreams sometimes, occasionally when he has fallen asleep in the office at night after too many bottles, of signing the completion papers in the luxurious boardroom of an American legal firm confirming that he will receive five million pounds, although he understands he may have to accept half of that through an earn-out.

There is nothing global about Stirling Global, the name deriving from Henry's misplaced sense of hubris. It focuses entirely on clients in Britain, prosperous men and women who have worked diligently for most of their lives and like to have someone with a recognised qualification telling them where best to shift their self-administered pension scheme and how to structure that trust fund for the grandchildren. Even now, if Henry were to take part in some contemporary retake of the famous chess games between Kasparov and a computer, and pitched his financial advice against that of a machine operating out of one of those impenetrable glass skycrapers, he would lose every time. This knowledge, which hovers unspoken in the back of his mind, is slowly corrupting the steel core of his self-confidence like rust taking hold of a shipwrecked tanker on a remote beach. Stirling Global, like Henry himself, is an irrelevant error in the sleek functioning of today's London.

Currently, Henry has five people working for him: Evie, Darren Hegarty, Rufus Carter, Jimmy Chatterjee and the lugubrious Jean. Jimmy is a pessimistic thirty-four-year-old Spurs supporter who grew up with two brothers and three sisters in Hounslow. He gets drunk very quickly and giggles when he takes coke. He has been married for two years, has two kids and still lives in Hounslow and he fears that he will never have sex with another woman other than his wife for the rest of his days. He is a diligent worker, bringing in a steady stream of relatively low level business from his group of clients and now that he has passed his IFA exams he can advise on most financial products.

Rufus is the new boy and while he studies for his exams in the evening – that is, when he's not drinking vodka tonics at *The Admiral Codrington* in Chelsea and spending Daddy's money on his dealer – he's on opening, which means getting through to punters like William Cecil and lining them up for a pitch from Evie, Darren or Jimmy. Rufus is twenty-five and the kind of useless, inconsequential piece of privileged trash that this city still harbours all over Kensington and Chelsea. He wears blazers with tasselled loafers and buys his shirts from a bespoke tailor who actually makes them, rather than the Chinese factory ones Henry buys, and he still believes there is a place just waiting for him as a Tory MP. Henry rather likes Rufus because they never had people like him in Yorkshire where he grew up and he is secretly in awe of the ridiculous boy's appalling self-confidence.

We'll come to Darren Hegarty later – he obviously wasn't at the dentist, he was having one more go on the Spanish student he met at a wine bar in Canary Wharf last night – because now Henry is opening the second bottle of Montepulciano in Jamies and it's two-thirty and Evie, who hasn't had any sleep, is telling him about her night.

'Bloody hell, love,' he says, 'you don't think you might be on a hiding to nothing with this girl? If she won't go to a parole meeting unless Auntie Evie makes her, how's she going to learn?'

'It's not about learning, it's about keeping her alive. If she misses another parole they'll put her back in Chelmsford for another two months and she'll just get worse. You don't know what it's like for these girls in those places, Henry. They're like training centres for how to fuck your life up completely. She's this far' – she holds up a thumb and index finger close together – 'from moving from vodka and painkillers onto crack and then it's all over.'

'All right, all right, we'll give her a trial. Jean won't like it though.'

'Jean's got a granddaughter who's not much younger than Jade. She'll be fine.'

'What's she going to do?'

'Oh I don't know. Filing or something.'

'Jean definitely won't like that.'

'All right. Social media. She can set us up a Face-book page.'

'Jesus Christ.'

'I'm covering her wages out of my comms so it's not going to hurt you. Just try and be nice. I'll get her in tomorrow. Has that posh twat got any leads for me?

I've lost two clients this month, I need to replace them. I'm not going to stay long today, I'm going home to bed soon.'

'Want any company?'

'No, Henry.'

'I'll put you down as a maybe.'

Despite his slightly tipsy familiarity, there is an awkwardness between them now, and this is because they haven't slept together since Evie came out of Holloway three years ago. He feels guilty that she did time for a mistake she made while working for him – it offends his archaic patriarchal principles but at the same time he knows she had to take the blame so that Stirling Global wasn't damaged. He justifies this patently egregious formulation by reference to his old sport, rugby: Evie took one for the team. Even so, he feels conflicted and to a large extent humiliated by what happened. The trouble is he broke his own Golden Rule. He'd kept his nose clean in the City by steering clear of all equity plays and then, four years ago, he got persuaded by a man called Felix he met in his City club to take Appointed Representative status to promote the Malawi water refining business. He realises now that before taking the brief on he should have checked the business out more than he did, but the brochures were very professionally produced and they had some good names on their Board: a Liberal Democrat baronet who sat in the House of Lords, that bloke who used to be on Breakfast TV in the eighties. It just seemed like easy money: he got his team to put in extra hours to promote the water business to a list of potential investors he was given by Felix and he shared the excessive commissions with whoever in his team closed a sale. He made sure the core business of Stirling Global carried on at the same time, but in reality, he was utterly thrilled by the sudden flood of cash into the business which the Malawi commissions created. The only problem was his lack of experience in this area led to a lack of oversight and a failure to prevent Evie from making a mistake of language in an email.

Evie blames only herself for her error. She was stupid and she paid for it but ever since doing her time it's all been different. London is different for a start, it feels like an ex, someone she used to know but who now won't take her calls; she feels ghosted by London. "Come home and live with us for a while, love," her dad had said when she came out and sometimes she wishes she had. What is this sense of unfinished business she has, though, with London, with money, with Henry even? Why did she go back to working at Stirling Global when she came out three years ago? Is that really all she can do? Take money off punters in the day, lie awake at night thinking about absolutely nothing and feeling utterly powerless? How did she get to that?

Evie doesn't have much of a friends' network. When

she came out of Holloway that first time, when she was only twenty-one, she took off for Ibiza and stayed out there for five years. That whole period cut a big slice into her life and the people she used to know out there eventually left the island, exhausted like her, and now they're scattered all over the world. Once she'd come back, in the years before the second Holloway stint, she and Henry got together and they were pretty content in their London bubble; they didn't really need anyone else. She's not angry with him at all and she feels sorry for him, because she understands him so well and she knows he feels bad about the Malawi thing and she knows he misses what they had. She does too – they were good together. They used to go to the Royal Opera, take a box at the Albert Hall to see Eric Clapton, eat oysters at China Tang in the Dorchester. Henry made her laugh and despite all his antediluvian attitudes, he had a touching optimism about putting on his best face at the start of the day which she found comforting. They drank champagne and bought piles of coke which the Malawi deal in particular supported before it all went south. They had surprisingly good sex which, as the months went by, kept satisfying her so much that she could put up with his black moods and absurd pretensions. You wouldn't think it either to look at him or to listen to him, but Henry was really very good in bed and she misses that. He used to talk about leaving his wife, he used to take her dad to Twickenham and her mum used to iron his shirts on those very occasional weekends when he'd make excuses to Totnes and Evie would bring him back home for big family lunches, visits to the pub and walks on the beach at Southend. She never used the word "love" with Henry and she's not sure she ever did love him, but she was happy with him and, somehow, she unearthed lots of good things in him.

But all that collapsed when the City of London police knocked on the office door four years ago and now all she can think about is that burning globe on the horizon this morning.

'Come on,' she says, 'let's go and see who the chinless wonder has lined up.'

'Someone called William Cecil,' he says and swigs the last of the wine, which tastes metallic in his mouth now. 'Evie,' he says, and takes her arm.

'Not now, Henry,' she says. 'I'm tired.'

*A*s she reached the end of Watling Street, Lily saw a crowd gathered ahead of her beneath the grand rose window at the eastern end of the cathedral. This was normally where the printers gathered to sell their latest volumes but there seemed more of a commotion than usual. She tried to hurry by to one side but was stopped in her tracks by a fat gentleman being hurled to the ground in front of her, surrounded quickly by a mob of men laughing and shouting.

'Despatch him back to Westminster! Throw him in the Thames, see if he floats! Let's see whether his Roman masters help him now!' came the cries as the crowd gathered around him, kicking him while he feebly protected his head with his hands. His three-cornered hat was knocked off and Lily leaned down to pick it up.

'Don't you favour him, miss,' said a gentleman with the tall hat of the Puritans. He reached out as though to take the hat back, but she whisked it behind her back.

'You treat an old man so? A crowd of you? Does that make you fine men?'

The stranger stood in front of her, smiling, while the others continued to torment the beleaguered older man.

'Do not tell me you favour the religion of our King's

Portuguese wife, my good lady?' he enquired and he continued to smile in a way which infuriated her.

'I favour nothing but the laws of decency,' she replied. 'Let me pass and give this hat back to that poor man.'

'That poor man, madam, has come from Westminster to attempt to stop the publication of my good friend Grimshaw's new pamphlet decrying the Spanish threat. No popery, madam, no popery! Especially not here, in our own City. Let them bask in their sinful ceremonies at St James's, but not here, by God! Here at least we strive to maintain the Lord's word, not that of the Spaniard.'

Lily attempted to run but her weak foot caused her to stumble, and she would have fallen had the man's strong hand not saved her. He leaned closer.

'I have seen you in these parts before, madam,' he said, more quietly now. 'Your foot does cause you trouble, but the Almighty chose to even the scales when he came to design such a face.'

She threw the hat at him as hard as she could and its edge caught his ear, causing him to exclaim. She took the opportunity to move away and managed to get past the crowd of bullies, just hearing as she left the same arrogant voice calling out: 'A fine aim too, madam – I shall look forward to learning more of your accomplishments!'

Chapter Three

Nobody in London had heard of William Cecil before all this. I mean, some people: the doorman at his block, the guy who drove his car, the reception staff at his club. But he wasn't what you'd call a player, he wasn't someone London took account of. He kept a low profile and, after it all happened and people were trying to piece it together, it was as though he had never been there at all. No friends to give statements, no family; no trace of him on any social media; no directorships on Companies House; no images of him if you typed his name into Google Images apart from that strange event in Shoreditch an hour before it all kicked off, when he was photographed blinking into the cameras in front of that poster, a pot of paint in his hand.

Even the extraordinary flat where Evie first met him was owned under a Barbados shell company.

People said later that he hid in plain sight and maybe that was true: William Cecil never seemed to conceal anything and yet now, neither I nor anyone else in London can tell you the first thing about him; he left no trace. There's been hundreds of theories, obviously: he was a secretive multi-millionaire hedge fund guy; he was dying of cancer and only had weeks to live; he was connected with the Russian mafia and used his disciples as mules; he was a perverted sexual voyeur; he was the Messiah. Take your pick. No one really knows, and we'll never know, I don't think. He's just one of those characters in history who, once he gets inside your head, he stays there.

Evie travelled to meet him on the tube the following day, Tuesday. She still hadn't caught up properly on the night's sleep she missed on Sunday night. She'd snatched a few hours at her flat during the afternoon on Monday after calling into the office to take the lead from Rufus, where she phoned the number straight away. She spoke to a very formal male voice who, after a moment's silence, put her through to another man who said:

'William Cecil,' in a quiet voice with just a hint of an unidentified accent. After Evie had begun to speak about Stirling Global's wealth management services, he interrupted and said:

'Miss Sangster, would I be right in assuming you are a saleswoman?'

'Um, well, sort of,' she said, 'although…'.

He interrupted again.

'That is good,' he said. 'I enjoy the company of sales people. I will be happy to see you tomorrow at eleven.'

And with that, he passed the phone back to the original man who gave her details of the address. She was so tired that she didn't register this as being odd: potential clients never agreed to see you without actually listening to the telephone sales pitch. And why did he say that he enjoyed the company of sales people? She went back home to her flat in Wapping High Street, slept for a bit with two fans on to shift the still, hot air and was back on the tube up to Edmonton to see Joy that same evening.

She'd spent a couple of hours with Joy in her front room. She lived in a flat on on the fifth floor of one of a group of council buildings around some communal patches of scorched brown grass a couple of hundred yards off Fore Street. It was now run by the usual outsourced facilities company, so the entrance hall was dirtier than ever. In the lift, which smelled of piss and had brown smudges across the dimpled metal walls, there was a new sign saying "No Spitting" which was translated into several languages underneath with the cheery payoff: "Thanks for working together with Pegasus Facilities Management!" Someone had recently spat on it.

'Sit down, for Christ's sake,' Joy said to her, after Evie had been pacing up and down the carpeted room, opening the door onto the concrete walkway to look down onto the grass for any sign of Jade. 'She'll come back when she's ready. You're making me even hotter just watching you.'

'I want to talk to her,' Evie said, sitting back in the armchair opposite the older woman. 'I want to talk to her about this job.'

'I know you want to talk to her but she's not here, is she? Look darling, you did what you could: you got her to the meeting this morning so we're OK for another week. She'll come back when she's hungry. I'll talk to her.'

'Sorry.'

'Don't be. I'm sorry you didn't get any sodding sleep.'

'I slept this afternoon.'

'You look like you could do with some more. You look shit, love.'

'Thanks.'

'Why did you go and drink wine with that idiot at lunchtime anyway? In the middle of this heat and all. It's Monday, remember? You don't have to drink every day.'

'Now you're sounding like my mother.'

'She and I are going to have a chat this weekend, my girl. Get you back on the straight and narrow.'

'He's not an idiot, anyway.'

'Oh no, sorry, I forgot, he's the brain of bloody Britain and he didn't have anything to do with you ending up somewhere where you bloody shouldn't have been.'

'I met you, didn't I?'

'I was the one who did well out of that, love. You didn't need to meet me. Not there, anyway.'

Joy picked up the pack of cigarettes from the low table between them and lit one. She had dyed black hair which had been treated recently at the hairdressers and was piled up high on her head and with the bright crimson lipstick giving her the look of someone who used to dance to Northern Soul tunes at Dingwalls in the old days. She was ten years' older than Evie and even though this mad summer heat and the cigarettes had dried her skin out, she was a good-looking woman and she knew how to apply black mascara and she had a dirty smile. She was wearing a black and white striped shift she had picked up in the indoor market at the shopping centre and she was resting her bare feet on the coffee table. She tapped some ash into a bowl.

'You can't sort us all out,' she said after a while, gentler now. 'You've got to think what you want too.'

The next morning, on the tube to Baker Street, Evie is thinking about that comment. Joy had made her go home after a while, promising that, when she did finally show up, she'd speak to her daughter about coming to work at Stirling Global. Now as Evie sits on the Circle Line flipping through the free paper without reading any of it she thinks: what do I want? The question had been knocking at her door ever since she came out of Holloway and three years on she still hadn't even been able to address it. She's just been treading water. She looks around the carriage, half-filled now that rush hour is over. A young woman taps on the keyboard of her laptop, next to her an older man stares dully at the moving images on his smart-phone game. A kid further down the carriage, maybe not much more than five or six, stares at her while leaning in to her mother's shoulder. Evie stares back, not even aware of the kid. What do I want?

She comes out of Baker Street station and is hit by a wall of heat. The traffic is noisy and down the road to the left there is a long line of tourists queuing to get into Madame Tussauds. She pauses by a rackety newspaper stand for a moment to adjust herself to the heat again. The sky overhead is a dirty white and the air smells of exhaust fumes. She hears someone shouting and turns to look at a tall skinny guy with his shirt flapping outside his trousers, walking really fast towards her, his eyes bulging and his messy hair all sweaty and a phone clamped to his ear.

'You cunt. You utter and complete fucking cunt,' he shouts into the phone as he passes her and continues on down towards the Tussauds queue, yelling into his phone. Evie feels dizzy for a second and reaches out to hold on to the newspaper stand. She stays there for a while, staring at the skinny man disappearing into the distance, then she turns to leave.

The address she has is for Chiltern Court on the corner of Baker Street and Marylebone Road. Where else would William Cecil live in London? Not in one of those priapic glass monuments that now run all along the south bank of the river, thrusting out decked balconies and architectural reed plantings and owned by gangs of Far Eastern businessmen renting them out to French MBA graduates and American asset strippers. No, he'd have to be somewhere like Chiltern Court: eleven storeys of Portland Stone-clad apartments above Baker Street station, all oiled wood panelling and parquet flooring and fancy architraves, with its lacquered black rococo entrance doors and gold leaf decorations. And a porter who looks up from his small booth inside the entrance hall as Evie steps in, raising his eyebrows.

'I've come to see William Cecil,' she says, taking a tissue from her bag and dabbing at her forehead.

'Mr Cecil is on the ninth floor, madam. Number 110. Take a left as you come out of the lift.'

She rings the buzzer. A small, grave-looking man with dark hair and wearing a white jacket opens the door; he could have been Indian or Chinese, Evie can't tell.

'Mr Cecil will be with you promptly, Miss Sangster,' he murmurs as he leads her across the hall. She recognises his voice as the one she spoke to the day before. The first thing to strike Evie is how humid it is in the flat. London outside is hot enough in this freak July heatwave but in here it seems several degrees warmer and there is a moist perfume in the air, a strong sweet fragrance which makes her think of decay, of decomposition. The hallway is gloomy, an odd hectagonal shape with doors leading off it. One is open to a long corridor from which Evie can hear laughter, several voices sharing some story. As he walks ahead of her, the servant – if that is who he is – makes no noise on the wooden floor. He opens one of the closed doors and stands to the side, his eyes lowered and his arm outstretched, suggesting that she enter.

The room is entirely unexpected. It is huge, for a start: through the subdued light Evie can see heavy embroidered curtains covering the windows which must have been twenty yards away. Unlike the entrance hallway, this room is carpeted and there are heavy blocks of furniture scattered about: a massive leather sofa, some armchairs, a big dining table. As she adjusts her eyes to the semi-darkness, she realises that the cloying sweet smell, even stronger in here, is coming from an incense burner. Next to it is a red candle flickering a weak flame, and behind it sits a life-size statue.

She walks slowly towards the statue. It is a sculpture of a Chinese man sitting cross-legged on a green plinth. He wears a green cloth over one shoulder with a brown drape over the other, which also covers his legs, with ceremonial patterns in green and cream over the brown. His chest is bare and the weak light from the candle plays patterns on the ivory of the stone. The face appears to be both looking at her and ignoring her – the same pale ivory as his naked chest, it is uncannily still in the flickering candle light: his eyes open but not focused on anything, his pale ivory lips closed, his ears hugely exaggerated on either side of his shaved skull.

Evie stands in front of the statue. The plinth on which it sat raised his head above hers, making it seem, now that she is close up, that he is both aware of her presence and entirely dismissive of it. His exaggerated eyebrows are furled in a frown of concentration while his hands are gathered in his lap in calm relaxation; there is something about his whole being which gives the impression of latent energy, of some huge power. She is, for a moment, transfixed and in the silence of this hot, dark, heavily fragrant room she feels both diminished and comforted.

'He is a Luohan. Do you know this word?'

Evie whirls around but cannot immediately see where the voice has come from.

'He is the only one in private ownership. Over one

thousand years old, from the Yixian region of China.'

In the gloom, she now makes out a figure sitting perfectly still in an armchair.

'I apologise if I startled you,' he continues. 'I enjoy seeing my guests encounter him for the first time. You must be Miss Sangster. I am William Cecil. Please forgive me if I do not stand. Do come and join me.'

He makes a welcoming, beckoning motion with his hand as she walks over. He indicates she sit in the armchair opposite him and something about his manner makes her think she should not offer to shake his hand. She sits down.

'Hello, Mr Cecil. I'm Evie Sangster.'

'Yes.'

What to make of that face? As I said, even now there are very few photographs of him, so we just have Evie's impressions. She is struck immediately by the shock of grey, frizzy hair burnishing a strangely enlarged forehead, the pale brown skin stretched over an oddly shaped skull which tapers down so severely into a narrow chin with dark, unsmiling lips. Above them, that mad moustache that everyone talked about afterwards, as though somehow it defined him: thick, bushy, jet black but peppered with grey, ostentatiously curled up into an insouciant lilt at either end. He wore very plain metal-rimmed glasses and behind them, his eyes seem strangely large, the steel grey pupils unmoving in their white canvas, fix upon her.

He is wearing the sort of utilitarian cotton jacket that one might have seen in Singapore or Beijing or Seoul. What is he: fifty, maybe? It is difficult for Evie to tell.

As she sits down opposite him, a door opens and a young woman walks across the room carrying a tray which she sets down on the table between them. Evie said later she looked about twenty-one, and had a classic kind of blonde Californian freshness to her face. She speaks with an American accent.

'Your tea, William,' she smiles and then she kneels down, takes the man's hand which he languidly proffers to her without averting his gaze from Evie, and presses it to her lips, her eyes closed. No one says anything for a second, then the woman stands up, smiles at Evie, and leaves.

William Cecil leans forwards and begins to rearrange the items on the tray. Then he looks up. He is grinning; like a boy, Evie thought later. His face is suddenly transformed, the moustache bouncing and quivering.

'We shall have tea!' he exclaims. 'I think you will like this, it is my favourite.'

He pours from a black china pot into two shallow bowls and pushes one across the table to her.

'You may not have tasted this before,' he says, lifting his own bowl up. 'It is made from tea grown on the island where I was born, Barbados. The smell reminds me of my mother's kitchen.' At this, he laughs, a kind of whinnying, high-pitched laugh.

He sips his tea and she raises her own bowl to her lips. The flavour is delicate, much more delicate than the sweet aroma still coming from the burning incense.

'It smells of flowers,' she says.

'Very good!' he exclaims, nodding his head. 'Bougainvillea. We grow it on the hillsides and the dried petals are mixed in a precise proportion with the tea. It is a recipe so strict that even I do not know it.' And now he chuckles, a deep, musical rumble this time rather than what has come before. He closes his eyes as though to savour a private sensation.

He puts his empty bowl down and once she has finished, the door opens again and the same woman paces silently across the carpet, does the same routine of pressing his hand to her lips with her eyes closed, then removes the tray and its contents. As the door closes with a slight click, Cecil leans back.

'The Luohan, Miss Sangster, was a warrior monk. He and his seventeen fellow Luohans all passed through the Path set out by the Buddha to achieve transcendence but having done so, they remained in place to protect the Sacred One's temple. They combined, the eighteen Luohans, the strength of warfare with the tranquillity of Buddhahood. An interesting mindset, would you not agree?'

'I imagine so,' says Evie.

'You imagine so,' he replies, smiling. It is a strange smile, not one in which Evie recognises any friendliness. 'The eighteen Luohans followed the Buddha's path scrupulously for ten years before they attained the status of Luohan-hood. They cast off all worldly attributes and dependencies and they developed extraordinary levels of martial arts skills as part of their own spiritual development and as a commitment to protect the Buddha for their entire lives. And you imagine that they might have had an interesting mindset?'

Evie shrugs.

'I'm not big on Eastern stuff, I'm afraid.'

He seems to wince slightly at this.

'No, you said on the telephone that you were a saleswoman.'

She recalls now the slightly odd conversation on the phone yesterday.

'You said something about liking the company of sales people,' she says. 'That struck me as a bit strange.'

'Did it? But sales people are such fragile creatures, don't you think? Like the wren: such a tiny, delicate bird yet with such a loud and gregarious song. Are you fragile, Miss Sangster?'

'I don't really see myself like that,' she says.

'Of course you don't. What do you see yourself like?' Again, there is nothing friendly in his enquiry.

'Oh, I'm OK. I get along, like everyone else.

You know.'

He is silent.

'I don't really sell, anyway,' she says, hurriedly. 'I just advise.'

'Really? Do you find success in your efforts as an adviser? It would appear from the brief research which Chan did for me that the company you work for is not particularly successful. Why is that?'

She shrugs again.

'There are worse operations in this town,' she says.

Here he laughs, again that curiously high-pitched giggle.

'If I may say so, Miss Sangster, that does not make for a ringing endorsement. I wonder at the object of your exertions in this field.'

'I'm sorry?'

'This rushing about, coming to see people like me, pretending that you have sufficient knowledge to advise me on how I might arrange my affairs when even a cursory meeting indicates a complete imbalance within you. Your qi, my dear girl, your inner energy: it is flailing about with indiscriminate passions. You are directionless and yet full of motion. You have the look of ceaseless and entirely pointless endeavour. Why do you bother? Look at me: I restrict my own exertions to a morning swim at my club. I find immersion in water to be such a calming experience, don't you? No wonder Christians are so fond of their baptisms.'

Evie sits in the fragrant gloom of this strange room, with the heavy curtains just shifting slightly from the breeze perhaps from an open window and, unusually for her, is at a loss for words.

'I wonder if the temperature is unsettling you,' he says after a while. 'I find the English weather preposterously cold – they call this a heatwave? They should try Calcutta, as I still prefer to call it. My favourite city. Have you been there, Miss Sangster?'

She shakes her head.

'No, I'm from Southend,' she says.

He smiles that enigmatic smile again. 'I know. Chan undertook the usual research for me. The house on the marshes.'

Evie frowns. 'How do you know?'

He waves his hand. 'Oh come, Miss Sangster, the establishment of correct information is the least of the challenges we human beings face. If we are to reach the heights, to taste the sweetness of glory, we must build our cathedral on solid foundations.'

Again, she doesn't know what to say to this. The room is silent. He blinks at her behind his glasses.

'I've never been to India,' she says after a while. 'I haven't done much travelling. Ibiza for a while, you know.'

'Ah. You have me at a disadvantage there. I always meant to visit the shrine to the Phoenician Goddess, Tanit, on that island but I never made it. A much-conquered piece of rock, Ibiza.'

'I spent a few years there working in a couple of clubs,' she says. 'A place called Space.' And she smiles then, remembering Space and how they used to sing 'A Place Called Space' in the early morning. She is aware of how strange it is suddenly to be in this room with this man in the middle of London in this out-landish July heat and talking about the Ibiza days. 'We used to have chill-outs in rooms like this in the early morning. Lots of sofas.'

She laughs at that and then he leans forward slightly. His lavish moustache is so vivid, so bristling, as though it has its own energy. He waves his hand in front of him as though to brush away her comments.

'Tell me, Miss Sangster, what brings you here? Other than your business, of course, which we can always talk about at some point if you insist. There is always time to discuss the trivialities of business. It is a sport which interests me less and less. But unless I am wrong, and I seldom am, I feel you have something you would like to talk to me about. Do feel free. The girl will bring us more tea if we become thirsty.'

Evie sits very still for a little while, looking into those unblinking grey eyes, feeling suddenly quite adrift. Then she gets up abruptly and walks over towards the statue. She stands in front of it, her back to William Cecil, and she begins to speak.

'I find myself thinking about the sun,' she says. 'All

the time. Mainly about it rising, about how it looks when it appears every morning. I think about it all the time and it's driving me mad now, just sitting up there every day beating down on us, turning us into toast. I feel like I'm going crazy.'

Now Evie has taken the plunge and instead of pitching William Cecil the services of Stirling Global in managing his portfolio of investments, she has blurted out something unexpected. Most of us, we don't really think properly. Not really. Every so often, we either say something or we write something in a text or an email which makes it seem as though we have been thinking things through, but in reality, proper thinking is just too tough. We spend our days and nights bouncing around this implacable city just trying to stay alive, the most thinking any of us does really is working out how to get to the supermarket before it closes and wondering whether our kid needs to see the doctor about her cough and imagining what it would be like to kiss that guy sitting opposite you on the Central Line. You're better than me? You think long and hard about your life and your place on this earth and what constitutes your soul? Good for you. You're a better person than me then. Me, I sympathise with Evie and the way she's just announced this fixation with the burning morning sun without knowing she was going to say it.

William Cecil doesn't say anything or move and

Evie carries on, still directing her speech at the statue.

'Yesterday morning, I was up at the top of this tower at five-thirty watching the sun come up in the east. You know how the last dark gets really dark and then you see the light suddenly go grey and then it goes silver and then suddenly this…this sun just appears out of nowhere and it seems to me that it's somehow really monstrous and I can't take my eyes off it.'

She stops, feeling slightly breathless and a little flushed in her cheeks. Behind her, William Cecil is silent and motionless.

'I mean, I always used to like the sunrise when I was in Ibiza. Everyone did. You paced your night right so when the sun came up it was a proper trip. But I don't mean that. That was pleasure. This just seems…I don't know. It just seems like this means something which I don't understand and I'm not sure I really like either.'

'Why should you like it?' he asks quietly and she turns around. She stares at him across the darkened room and for a second their eyes are locked on each other, his clear and calm behind his metal-rimmed glasses, hers feeling strained to her, bulging almost.

'Why should you like it?' he repeats. 'To like something, that seems to me to be a particularly contemporary compulsion. This new world which is coming out of Silicon Valley in America, is it not all based on liking? But to like something, some might say that is the most placid, the most feeble, the most defenceless of all human responses. Whoever built a new world by liking things?'

'But do I want to build a new world?'

He shrugs. 'I have no idea. Although it would appear your current world provides you with little of what you need.'

'What does it mean then, me thinking about the sun all the time?' She walks back over and sits down in the chair again.

'I don't know. What do you think it means?'

'Maybe it means that I want it to burn me up.'

'Ah.'

'Now why do I say that?'

More silence. Evie turns and looks back at the statue of the Luohan standing in front of the flickering candle.

'Are you asking him?' comes his amused voice.

She looks back at him and there is a flash of anger in her voice now.

'I was there yesterday morning with the daughter of a friend of mine I met when I was in prison three years ago,' she says, looking defiantly at him. 'Her name is Jade and she's twenty-four now and I'm worried about her being on the streets and drinking and getting drugged up and her mum isn't strong enough to protect her. I met her mum in Holloway and I was in because they said I did a fraud and she was in because she bloody nicked a stupid piece of jewellery to give Jade on her twenty-first and now I don't know what's going to happen, because Jade keeps being sent in to Chelmsford for resisting arrest when she's out of her head and one of these days she's not going to resist arrest she's going to bloody die from an overdose or from something stupid and I've got to stop it, I've got to make her better.'

Now Evie is actually panting and she can feel her heart racing. After a while, he shrugs a little contemptuously and says, 'She will probably survive. People are stronger than you think. Unless you know how to break them.'

Evie is so flustered she doesn't pick up on what he's just said.

'I am aware of your periods of imprisonment,' he continues. 'Chan informed me.'

'Is there anything about me Chan doesn't bloody know?'

'Nothing of any significance, I would imagine.'

'Oh, fuck's sake,' she says, hanging her head down and looking at the floor.

After another silence, he says, more gently this time, 'Tell me about prison.'

'Holloway? It wasn't so good the second time round. Everything's so ugly, all the strip lights and the lino on the floor and plastic chairs and the crap food and the hour you get to walk around outside on the concrete and all those poor girls going crazy and screaming at each other and screaming at the warders. They make it like that because they know you're just shit, so it doesn't matter how they keep you. I only survived it this time because I met Joy. She's a bit older than me. If she didn't smoke all those fags and dry her skin out, she'd be bloody stunning. She helped me to pass the days inside. It's boring. I sorted out her credit cards, she taught me Northern Soul moves. I was in there because I was a bloody idiot, but it's no place for a nice woman like Joy, what did they go and send her there for?'

'Imprisonment, as I understand it, is designed to serve both as a deterrent and as a punishment. I imagine the judge in her case was thinking of both.'

He looks at her, his face impassive. Evie feels a wave of tiredness come over her and she yawns involuntarily.

'Sorry,' she says. Then, 'Anyway, Christ knows why I'm telling you this. I suppose I've buggered up my pitch to look after your funds, haven't I?'

'It's an unusual approach, I will grant you that,' he replies.

'It's not one I've tried before.'

'No.'

'Shall I just carry on?'

'As you wish. I have all the time in the world. You are, if I may say so, a troubled person, Miss Sangster. I had a feeling that there was something you wished to talk to me about. Perhaps I will be able to help you.'

Evie pauses for a moment. Then,

'That was my second time in prison. I got in trouble when I left school and I was living with my mum and dad in Southend. I got in with some people and I ended up selling forged methadone prescriptions. I'm not proud of it. Particularly now I'm trying to sort Jade out. I don't know why I did it. No reason probably. I just did it, then I got caught and I spent a year in Holloway, then I came out and I went to Ibiza.

'The first time in, you see, I knew I'd done wrong. I mean, at the time: I knew it was wrong selling those prescriptions. So I didn't care about going in. My mum and dad cared about it more and I worried about them, but I thought it was just what happened if you did the kind of things that I did. But I suppose it did what it was supposed to do, because when I came out I told my mum and dad I wasn't going to do anything like that again. And I didn't. I stayed at home a bit with them, because I wanted them to know that I was going to be all right, so I worked in a pub in Southend for a few months. I behaved myself. And it was my dad actually, after a while, he said, "It's all right, you don't have to stay with us forever. I know you're going to be all right. Don't hang around here, not at your age. Go and have some fun."

'So I did, I said goodbye to everyone, I went off to

Ibiza and apart from holidays and Christmas and that, I didn't come back for about five years I suppose. I didn't keep up with anyone from the old days, I just slipped into the Ibiza life: it gets you like that. It's good but you can't do it forever. I mean, it would kill you, if you lived out there all year round like I did. Even outside the summer season, when all the kids have gone back to Manchester, you're still on the island...you know, it sends you a bit crazy in the end.'

She looks hard at him.

'The coke, I mean. And the bennies. And the vodka.'

He blinks.

'I can imagine.'

She laughs.

'Yeah, I'm sure. Anyway, looking back now, it seems like a million years ago. I miss it, I miss my friends. I used to see them sometimes, one of them would pitch up in London and we'd go out but it wasn't the same. There's lots of good things on the island, lots of good things you don't get in London. You know, one minute you're dancing on the Terrace as the 747s blast right over your head, the next you're sitting in an empty lagoon and the water's a perfect blue and the sand is a perfect white and you're thinking that this is how it was when time began, you're thinking that you're part of a new race of people, you're just totally, sublimely happy. But then that's the thing, you can't stay there. No one does. Everyone has to get out at some point.

Turns out that being that happy isn't something you can keep up. There's a sell-by date on it. So I met this man called Henry who was out there on some stag do and he made me laugh. I suppose he reminded me of my dad a bit. Larger than life, always put a brave face on the day. I like that. He told me I could make good money in London working in the finance business. So I came back and started working for him. He'd just started this new company, Stirling Global. And here I am.'

At this, she shakes her head ruefully, and Cecil raises his eyebrows slightly.

'As I said, Chan looked into your company. Its performance does not inspire confidence.'

'Tell me about it,' she says. 'It's just that it's almost ten years ago now. Since I started working for him. Ten bloody years, including the five months in Holloway. I'm thirty-five years old. I've got a flat in Wapping and an Audi A6 and what else have I got?'

Evie looks hard at him.

'I knew what I was doing. I knew he was married but he only saw her at weekends because she didn't like London. I mean, she must have known about him and me, we were together right from the start, from when I met him in Ibiza. There's no way she didn't know he was with someone; I don't think she cared, really. She sounds like that sort of person. She could have got him back if she'd really wanted, couldn't she?

I would have done. If I thought my man was with someone else and I still wanted him, I'd make him come back. Wouldn't you?'

William Cecil sits quietly, blinking behind his spectacles.

'Well, whatever,' she continues. 'I didn't feel bad about it and I still don't, even though it's all over between me and him now. Holloway put a stop to all that. I don't feel bad about the mis-selling thing either. We didn't know it was all fucked up. I thought they were actually cleaning up all that water in Malawi, I didn't know it was all talk. Am I supposed to know everything? That guy, the surgeon, who complained about losing all his money. What did he give it to me for then? I didn't make him. I just told him about how they were refining water in Malawi and how the company which was doing it was going to make loads of money by doing this good thing and he thought that if he bought shares then he'd double his money, treble his money. Am I responsible for him being greedy? Am I responsible for Henry's wife? If she'd wanted the kind of life that Henry and I had, she'd have shared it with him, wouldn't she? I don't think she even likes him, to be honest. She's just one of those women who like having a husband providing for them. She knows she'd keep the house in Devon if he left her, so old Henry's a bit stuck really. If he left her now, he'd end up in that flat in Ealing on his own, doing his Canadian military exercises on the kitchen floor on Saturday mornings and going to Sainsbury's to buy microwave meals for one. I can't help him any more, that's all finished.

'London's like this big wave, you see. It's like those massive waves you see those surfers on, the really huge ones where the surfers are just tiny in comparison. The really good ones, you see them right at the top of that huge curve of water and for ages they're carving this beautiful trail through the water and it looks like it could last forever. London is the biggest wave you can ever get and if you're ready for it, you can surf it for such a long time. But then the wave gets stronger and stronger and eventually it crashes down over the top of you and you're gone. I mean, you're really gone. You're under the water and everything is upside down and inside out and going round and round and sometimes you think you're never going to come up again. And now all I can think of is the sun, right up there, burning day after day, getting bigger and bigger.'

After a moment's silence, he says quietly,

'Fire and water, Miss Sangster. A potent combination.'

'You mean I'm talking rubbish. Bloody surfing, what do I know about surfing?'

'I mean quite the opposite: you have finally said something significant. The burning sun and the towering wave: these are two of the most powerful symbols we humans have. Symbols are not symbols for nothing. They have a meaning.'

'Then why am I going on about them?'

He shrugs.

'Perhaps you are not. Perhaps it is they which are "going on", as you say. Perhaps they are just using you for their expression.'

After a while, she says,

'I don't really get that.'

'You don't really get very much, I'm afraid,' he sighs. 'But I can help you with that. The fire, the bulk of water. They have an existence, an energy, which does not necessarily depend on their consistent man-ifestation. You do not have to feel or see the fire to know that it still exists. You are bound up in your simplistic material worldview, like a child you still believe that the fire or the water somehow depend upon you for their continued existence. They do not. This is a Buddhist notion. The modern way of thinking places us, we human beings, in the centre of existence, makes us believe that the world is a stage for our own performance. This room' – here he waves an arm slowly about him – 'would be construed in this way as being my "character" defined, my soul expressed in interior design. But that is not the case. This room is where you and I are currently talking but it does not really exist beyond an enclosure of air which feeds us. The Luohan there, he sits patiently to remind us of that fact. The world exists but we are an irrelevance.'

'I feel like that sometimes.'

'I am not talking about feelings, Miss Sangster. Feelings, as you call them, are for the most part the habituated repetitions of a persona forged in childhood. They are the first elements to be discarded when one embarks on the path of true understanding. To understand the world as our friend the Luohan understands it, you have to dismantle everything you have ever known and begin painstakingly to rebuild your understanding, pebble by pebble, grain of sand by grain of sand. It is a life's task and even then, only the finest, most disciplined of adherents truly reach their goal. Most do not achieve it by the time their bodies expire, so they return in another form to try again. You are, I am afraid to say, an unlikely candidate for such a serious undertaking. However, were you to accept and understand your failings and submit yourself to the path, you might conceivably make some progress. I could guide you in the right direction.'

At that moment, there is a ping from her mobile phone. The noise breaks into the quiet of the room and, from habit, Evie reaches into her bag and pulls it out.

'Sorry,' she says, and quickly looks at the message. It is from Jade. *I'm at Bank Station. Mum said I should text you when I got here.*

'Oh God, I'm sorry,' she says. 'I've got to go.' She texted, *Wait there – will be with you in 20 minutes.*

'I'm really sorry,' she repeats. 'It's Jade, I've got to go and meet her.'

He springs to his feet, startling her with the suddenness of his movement. He strides across the room, and she notices how athletic his form is. He moves with the ease of a twenty-year-old.

'That is your choice,' he calls over his shoulder. 'You would benefit more from staying here but I will not attempt to persuade you.' He stops beside a table and picks up a sheet of paper from a pile. 'Here,' he commands, holding it out. 'I give the occasional talk in London. Touching on the subjects we have spoken of. I suggest you attend.'

Evie walks over to him, takes the piece of paper and hands him her card in exchange.

'I didn't mean…' she begins, but he waves his hand in front of him again.

'Enough,' he says. He takes the card and examines it. 'I will contact you, although not about business.'

He claps his hand loudly and the door opens. The man who had let her in appears at the entrance.

'Chan will show you out.'

'I'm sorry,' she starts again as she stands up, and Cecil interrupts her once more.

'Sorrow, Miss Sangster, is the sea on which we all sail.'

Lily could not read but her mistress Hannah, always convinced that tradespeople would cheat her father and her at any opportunity, had given her a list of the ingredients for London Treacle and instructed the maid to make sure that Doleberry read out to her the ingredients of his latest batch so that she could be sure there were the correct number.

'And do not think you can fool me, dolt,' her mistress had shouted down at her from upstairs as she left. *'I shall know if the Treacle be tainted and I shall know who to punish.'*

Who else but me, Lily had thought as she had left. *Who else but me is to be punished — it is in my design to receive punishment.*

Doleberry's shop was dark and fuggy with fumes, smoke whirling out of pots hung above fires, and the apothecary himself was irritable.

'I do not have times for these games,' he barked, arranging glass bottles in a case before him on the counter. *'The Treacle is as it always was.'*

Lily coughed but shook her head.

'I am not allowed, Sir, I am not allowed to purchase without knowledge of the ingredients.'

'Bah,' the man snapped, then stole a look at the nervousness in the young woman's eyes and relented. 'Very well, young lady, if it must be your mistress's pleasure.' He pulled over a ledger book and flicked through the pages. 'Here we are, this week's batch: I did mix rosemary, sorrel, peony, basil, angelica, marigold, nutmeg, mace, cloves, powder of deer's horns, opium, honey and a dash of wine. Now, does that satisfy you?'

Lily had counted off the ingredients against her list and they came to the same number, so despite not being able to read she could confirm.

'But the wine, Mister Doleberry, the wine is from Malaga?'

'Yes, it is,' he chuckled. 'Wouldn't be from Kent, now, would it?'

Lily felt uncomfortable as she did not know where wine might come from but her awkwardness was concealed as two men entered the shop. They were dressed as men of commerce do, with long coats, prosperous bellies and florid faces. They ignored the young woman and marched straight to the counter.

'Tobacco, Doleberry, be smart about it. No time for dallying.'

The apothecary stole another quick glance at Lily, who had stepped to the side of the counter.

'Just finish serving this young lady her Treacle, gentlemen, then tobacco you shall have in plenty.'

One of them glanced irritably at her but the other

continued a conversation they must have been having as they approached the shop.

'I tell thee, Baxter, Sir Robert will be at the Dutch before light fails. The conditions are fine. Let him fire their ships and then let him fire more of their damned towns. Let Frisia burn, I say, let it burn their women and their children from their homes, let it cast them out for good.'

'Have a heart, Foster,' the other replied. 'He did destroy a thousand homes just last month at his bonefire at Terschelling. Let him destroy their fleet but let him have a care for the innocent.'

'The innocent?' the first barked back. 'Innocent? Those Hogen Mogens have the blood of just sacrifice running in their veins. Let the Lord our God guide Sir Robert well today, let him make a torch of their ships and then let him destroy their filthy homes for good.'

As the apothecary sealed the glass jar with wax he looked over at the two men.

'I read a pamphlet this morning myself, gentlemen,' he said, 'which said the English fleet was ready to invade our Dutch neighbours this very day.'

'Aye they will, Doleberry,' said the one called Foster. 'And it will be a grim and just reckoning. Our English fire shall cleanse the sins of the Dutchmen and shall as ever bring justice to those lands.'

'Ah well, it is a fierceness,' said his companion, 'but a fierceness which shall bring us some pleasure to our *pocket.' And he patted his bulging coat with a lascivious smile and both men chortled.*

'Your Treacle, child,' the apothecary said gently, handing over the flask to the girl. 'Go in peace,' he added after she had handed over the tokens and hurried from his shop.

Chapter Four

Angel Hernandez drives his ten-year-old silver Nissan down the A10 along the same route that Evie and Jade took on the night bus on Sunday. It's midday on Tuesday now and he will be at his first job, the apartment block in Spitalfields, in twenty minutes. Angel – he pronounces it Ann-Hell, the Spanish way – is a thirty-six-year-old Colombian who got asylum in the UK four years ago after his brother was shot dead in Bogota by a drugs gang. In Bogota, Angel had a good job as an accountant and made enough money to give him, his wife and their two little girls an apartment overlooking the river. Then his brother, who was a policeman, was killed after he unwisely gave an interview on TV about the progress of the War Against Drugs and Angel submitted to the entreaties of his mother and his wife Marta's mother to flee Colombia. Angel had nothing to do with the police or with drugs, but with his brother dead, he risked a similar fate simply because his name was Hernandez. He didn't want to leave and neither did Marta, but they finally agreed when his dead brother's boss at the police station said that they couldn't guarantee the family's safety.

Four years later and Angel is driving his old Nissan past the tree-lined council blocks on Stamford Hill, the windows open because there's no air con. Angel quite likes this unusual heat in London, it reminds him of home. He's ready to start the three cleaning shifts which he does each day from twelve-thirty to eight-thirty: from twelve-thirty to four, he cleans the four storeys of the apartment building next door to the old market in Spitalfields, then from four-thirty to six-thirty he cleans another smaller block round the corner, and then from seven till eight-thirty he cleans the office building in Watling Street where Stirling Global is based. All three jobs came to him from an agency he was introduced to by the Jobseeker people and the hour and a half in Watling Street is a new addition – he only started there a week ago. Angel is a gentle, kind, family man with a round face and a tubby belly. He works as a cleaner because his qualifications do not entitle him to do any kind of accounting work in the UK and, besides, his English is not so great still.

Angel's life is both surprising and disappointing to

him. It didn't occur to him that he would be working as a cleaner; in the rush to leave Bogota they thought only vaguely about how he might be able to use his professional experience in a new country. His daughters like London though and that gives him some comfort. They like visiting Westfield shopping centre on Saturdays, they have friends at their school in Tottenham and the eldest one, who is twelve now, has started to think about make-up. Angel lives for the weekend when the four of them can spend time together – by the time he has driven home in the evening, his children are usually asleep. He'd be home quicker if he went on the tube but the tube is so expensive that he avoids it. He has put on weight since he came to London, because he eats badly during the week – he buys chocolate bars and bags of crisps from the Tesco opposite the apartment block even though he starts most weeks pledging silently to give them up.

Angel doesn't talk to anyone during his working day. Occasionally, he will have to phone in to his supervisor but, other than that, his time is spent with the vacuum cleaner padding up and down the corridors of the blocks which are always empty because the inhabitants, mostly young people in their twenties and thirties renting, are at work. By the time he gets to Henry's office, the Stirling Global people have gone home. He shuts himself off from the daily realisation of how much he dislikes his life by playing music constantly through the flimsy white earpiece of his phone. Angel is a jazz and soul man and he plays vintage seventies bands like the Crusaders which remind him of the all-night clubs in Bogota where he and his wife used to dance before they were married.

Nothing about London makes much sense to Angel. He can't understand how he's ended up cleaning the carpets of people younger than him who would probably have been working for him as trainees back in Bogota. He can't understand how they seem to make so much money that they can buy their shopping in Waitrose when he and Marta bulk buy rice and potatoes from Lidl. He can't understand how he fled his home because of the threat of drug-related violence and now finds himself living in Seven Sisters where kids knife each other every week over some gang dispute. Once a year, he and Marta take the kids back to Colombia for a three-week holiday, which they can only just afford now. Marta's part-time job in the indoor market café has become a zero-hours contract since the Council insisted on human resources changes as part of a deal to delay knocking down the market, and some weeks they don't ask her in at all.

Pretty soon, Angel is going to discover something in Henry's office which will be very significant for this story I'm telling you but, for the moment, we're going to leave him tapping his fingers on the steering wheel at the red light in Curtain Road as the DJ plays Chic on the car radio. Meanwhile, Henry is beginning to perspire slightly on that telltale upper lip of his as he answers the questions of the two children who have been sent to his office by the Swedish financial services firm which has expressed interest in acquiring Stirling Global. There is a dirty grey-white fan whirring behind him on top of a filing cabinet and his hair flutters every time the round cage judders back. His irritation stems from the suspicion that the Swedish group doesn't take him that seriously, otherwise they would have sent more senior people to conduct this footling due-diligence session. The boy is fair-haired, looks about seventeen and wears jeans, loafers and a crisp white shirt with cufflinks, while the girl looks maybe twenty and wears those statement spectacles under her sensibly cropped auburn bob. They're actually older than Henry's furious guesswork, because they inevitably did three years at MBA schools in the US after graduating – he from Stockholm University, her from University of Barcelona – and they've been working their way up the business in London for a couple of years now.

He doesn't know anything about Förster Jennhusen but they seem already to know lots about him. A few months ago, Henry answered an ad on the back pages of the *Sunday Times Business* section, one of those little box ones with a rule around it which says "BUSINESS EXITS – CONTACT US NOW FOR A FREE APPRAISAL ON VALUATION AND EXIT PLANNING" and so far, he's paid some introductions agency almost ten grand to line him up with suitable business partners to begin the process of offloading Stirling Global and its precious client list for the sum he considers both reasonable and respectful. From the way this conversation is going, it looks to him like Förster Jennhusen might not be the saviour he was speculating upon this morning in the flat in Ealing. He'd woken up a little blurry after the session he'd had the previous evening with Darren and Jimmy which followed on from the wine he'd drunk with Evie at lunch, but he'd done his usual exercises on the bathroom floor, his hairy stomach squashing onto the tiles each time he did a press-up and, after a shower, he'd examined his face in the vanity theatre mirror, its bright lightbulbs lighting the words, in Hollywood lettering, "MIAMI" and "VICE".

'Gentlemen,' he said to the mirror, patting his hair and stretching his lips wide to examine his teeth, while his cock dangled in the sink, 'I think you'll agree that the Stirling Global client list has a consistent level of quality which surpasses that of most Chartered Financial Advisors in this country. We're proud of our record in delivering great returns from offering sound advice to solvent people.'

He used that line again in the meeting a few minutes ago but the girl actually interrupted him and asked if he could explain how Stirling Global's CMS – Customer Management System – worked and what steps they had taken to fall in line with the new data regulations.

'I'm sorry to interrupt,' she says, not even looking at him but checking the time on her iPhone, 'but we don't have much time today.'

'Jean,' Henry barks across the office. 'Bring us over one of the client ID files please.'

Jean stands up and reaches to grab one of the lever arch files that fill three long shelves on the wall above her desk. She brings it over and lays it on Henry's desk. The purple covering of the file is frayed at the edges and the whole thing is so full of paper that the cardboard front flops open. Henry grabs it and flicks the metal catch, letting him heave a wedge of paper from one side to the other.

'This will be a typical example,' he says. 'Full records of all the transactions the client has made on our watch, three-monthly assessments of the performance of their portfolios, client financial statements, it's all here.'

'So this is the hard copy version of the database, right?' the girl asks, frowning cautiously at the bulging file like it's something she's never encountered before.

'This is our database, yes,' Henry replies. 'Five hundred and thirty-seven very happy clients, at the last count.'

'No, I mean, what software is this all stored on?' the girl asks, looking directly at him now.

'Jean, what do you use for this stuff?' Henry shouts out again.

'What?'

'Typing up these client reports.'

'Oh. Word. We're all on Word in here, Henry, which you'd know if you ever typed your own letters.'

The two young people exchange a glance then the boy says, running his finger down a column on his iPad,

'OK, let's leave that for a second. Can I just raise something else? There's an FCA Red Flag on the company from four years ago. Something to do with Malawi Water? Can you just run us through that?'

'No problemo,' Henry replies. 'Old news. We were encouraged to look at a business venture by a previous employee called Evie Sangster which initially seemed promising but which we decided not to pursue.'

'So this person doesn't work here anymore?'

'No.'

At that moment, the door opens and Evie walks in with Jade following on behind her.

'Hey Evie, how did you get on with William Cecil?'

This of course is Rufus, so stupid he needs time in the mornings to remind himself which way to tie the knot in his tie. Jimmy stifles a snigger, while Henry glares over at them. Darren, meanwhile, coolly appraises Jade who's looking quite different to when we saw her the previous day in the restaurant. She's put on a lot of make-up which covers up the blotches on her skin and her mohican now looks sharp against the pale blue top her mum made her put on this morning. She's wearing tight white jeans with a heavy belt which looks like it used to belong to Lemmy from Mötorhead. She's got the same high cheekbones as her mum, the same sassy confidence her mum has.

The two young people at Henry's desk exchange another glance then the girl says,

'Look, I think we've probably gone as far as we can today. We'll come back to you if we need any more information.'

They get up and shake hands awkwardly with Henry across the desk. Henry is disgusted by the limp handshake the boy gives him, then they shuffle just as awkwardly past Evie and Jade and are gone.

'You've got a one o'clock down at Jamies with Bernie Richmond,' Jean calls out. 'He's there already.'

'Fuck it,' Henry mutters and wearily stands up and grabs the pin stripe jacket from the back of his chair. 'All right, Evie?' he says, quite resignedly.

'Yeah,' she says. 'Henry, this is Jade. Jade, Henry. Henry is the boss.'

'All right?' Jade asks brightly.

'Not really, no,' Henry replies and walks out, slamming the door behind him.

There is a brief silence, then Darren laughs.

'Don't worry, Jade, that's just Henry on a good day.

I'm Darren. It's a pleasure to have you here.'

Darren has a Northern Irish accent, the warm, earthy and slightly melodic tone of which is part of what makes him a great telephone salesman. He's not that tall, maybe five-ten, he's good enough looking without being a headturner and he has a glint in his blue eyes which women immediately notice. His remarkably consistent strike rate with women is a source of envy and confused admiration with Jimmy but also stands him in good stead with Henry, who considers the ability to pull as being as significant as the ability to drink straight for eight hours. Darren notices things about women and has the knack of making them realise very quickly that he has done so. He would never pull such a clichéd stunt as guessing a woman's perfume or star sign – that kind of stuff is strictly for teenagers and amateurs. No, the secret of Darren's success with women is the same as the reason why he's a good salesman – it's a natural-born instinct which he is far too vain to examine. Darren will spend long minutes in the bathrooms of pubs and clubs gazing at his reflection in the mirror, tucking a black curl into his collar or licking down a stray eyebrow, careless of the ribbing which less successful male friends give him as they splash water down their jeans while scrubbing their hands. Then he'll go back out into the bar and walk straight up to a woman he hasn't spoken to before and tell her something she didn't think anyone knew about her. He's a class act and absolutely heartless.

Darren gets up and walks around the nest of desks where he sits with Jimmy and Rufus and offers his hand to Jade. He's wearing the trousers of a blue Prada suit and his crisply ironed Italian cotton shirt has a very subtle pale blue beading on the edges of the double cuffs. He leaves a slight trail of Gucci Guilty in the air as he passes the boys. Jade shakes his hand and laughs; she's slightly spaced out today from a few Diazepam she took this morning and she doesn't really know what she's doing here other than her mum really wanted her to do it.

'Just try it for a day or so, love,' her mum said last night when she finally got in after Evie had gone home. 'Evie really wants you to and, well, you never know.'

'But what do they do there?' Jade had asked. 'I've never worked in an office, Mum.'

'No idea, love. Something to do with money. Evie will look after you. Just do it for your old mum.'

And now Evie is watching Jade grinning at Darren and he's holding on to her hand slightly too long. Evie manoeuvres the girl towards Jean.

'Jean, this is Jade. She's going to help us do some social media stuff. Rufus, Jimmy – Jade.'

While some awkward introductions are made, Rufus pipes up again about William Cecil.

'Oh, he hasn't got any money,' Evie says, dismissively. 'Timewaster. I need real leads, Rufus.'

Downstairs in Jamies Wine Bar, Henry has bought a bottle of Sauvignon Blanc and is squeezed into a small corner table with Bernie Richmond. Bernie is one of the five hundred and thirty-seven Stirling Global clients and he hasn't placed any business with Henry for five years. He's sixty-seven, a retired accountant and he comes up to London from Sevenoaks whenever he can to meet up with men he refers to as his "old muckers", Henry being one of them. He never buys a round if he can avoid it and he has an unfortunate tendency to bubble saliva on the surface of his fleshy lips, spattering the table and Henry's suit with occasional sprays. Henry is always happy to stump up a bottle or two for Bernie once every few months because it reinforces his self-perception as the head of a successful CFA business guiding its clients to a prosperous retirement. The fact that Bernie is like most Stirling Global clients and scrupulously avoids making any financial commitments advised by the firm is not something Henry dwells upon.

Henry raises a glass.

'Death to the enemies of Yorkshire,' he intones and Bernie smiles wetly and gulps eagerly at the white wine.

'Business good?' he enquires.

'It is what it is,' Henry replies cryptically. 'Nobody in London's doing much business in this heat. Lot of interest in the firm at the moment though, Bernie. Between you and me, I might just accept an offer one of these days. Bunch of Swedes are the latest to be sniffing around. I wouldn't let it go for less than five though.'

Bernie carries on smiling, his eyes glassy. As an ex- accountant, he knows very well that Stirling Global would struggle to raise a valuation of fifty thousand, let alone the five million Henry has talked about for the last few years. But Bernie is a man who considers it polite to sing for his supper so he nods and takes another gulp.

'You know what these guys are like, Bernie,' Henry continues. 'Big players, these days. It's all going multinational. But they need the agility of firms like ours to give them the edge over the competition. We may not have the swanky offices but we've got the client list, the reputation, the track record. One of these days I'll hand over the keys but I'm in no rush. Let me fill your glass.'

While they chat, a man and woman in the distinctive jet black uniforms of the London Fire Brigade emerge from the door to the kitchen with the wine bar owner. These are London firefighters Steve Edwards and Linda Appiah and today they are visiting all the businesses in Watling Street to advise owners and renters on fire safety. They're based at Upper Thames Street fire station and they regularly make visits to as many of the little offices, shops and bars still tucked away in the lanes and alleys of the City as they can. They're not required in the ultra-efficient, soaring new blocks with stupid nicknames like the Cheesegrater and the Gerkin that have sprung up recently but there's still enough of the old City to need regular checks on defunct smoke alarms and out-of-date fire extinguishers. Steve likes these trips because he's middle-aged now and he prefers a slower pace and the chitchat and banter with people in offices. Linda knows it has to be done but it's not really her cup of tea: she's twenty-seven and she only qualified as a firefighter in the Brigade two years ago and, for her, it's action she craves.

They squeeze past Henry and Bernie and thread their way through the nests of tables towards the front door where they shake hands with the owner. People look up at them as they leave; there's something emblematic, something almost mythological about the Brigade in London and those black uniforms seem to suggest both safety and trepidation. Steve, with his too-wide hips and slightly waddling gait, offers reassurance just by turning up but Linda is the real deal and, as she's the final person we need to be aware of in this story I'm trying to tell you about London, we can think about her a little more as the two of them stand outside in the blazing sunshine in Watling Street while Steve looks up the name of the next business they are due to visit.

Linda applied to join the Brigade about three years ago but she's been thinking about fire most of her life, because her mum died in a fire in their house in Edmonton when she was just ten years old. Her dad had taken her out ten-pin bowling as a treat and neither of them carried mobile phones around with them in those days, so they didn't get any warning about the fire while they were out. By the time they got back, the house, stuck in the middle of a terrace the other side of Pymmes Park, was a smoking black shell and there were fire engines slewed across the street and groups of neighbours gathered around, some with blankets over their shoulders. Linda can still remember that scene clearly, as they turned the corner into their street after getting off the bus from Tottenham where the bowling alley was. She's re-enacted it enough times in therapy sessions over the years; in fact, she did so recently when she went for what she calls a top-up session with a counsellor. They find out everything about you at the Brigade when you apply to join because they need to know whether you're the sort of person who's going to be able to deal with the intensity of the job. They had a lot of discussion about Linda before accepting her and it was the consistency of the reports from her counsellors and therapists over the years which swung it in her favour: she really wasn't in any way unbalanced by what happened when she was ten; in fact all the professionals said the opposite, that her stated desire to help stop what happened to her family from happening to others was both true and an accurate description of her core life motivation.

Linda's grandparents on her mother's side came over from Ghana in 1960 and settled in north London where her mum was born. Even though she's had a really good relationship with her dad all her life – he moved recently into that block that rears up from Edmonton Shopping Centre where they give sheltered accommodation to older people – she changed her surname to her mum's, Appiah, when she was eighteen as a tribute to her. Her dad didn't mind, he understood. Linda's mum's family, the Appiahs, were business people and they carried on trading when they emigrated to Britain in 1960 but her dad didn't come to Britain until 1981. He's an intellectual and escaped Jerry Rawlings's thugs during the coup in Ghana that outlawed all political parties including her dad's, the People's Independence Party. He landed in Britain with just a suitcase and came to stay with a cousin in Edmonton where he met Linda's mum who was helping her parents to run a couple of restaurants.

They'd come to family life relatively late, he being forty-five and his wife thirty-six when Linda was born, so when the fire took his wife away from him, he was a fifty-five-year-old man with a grief-stricken little girl to raise on his own. He decided then that he would do whatever he had to do to make sure his daughter built the resilience to overcome their tragedy. As a socialist intellectual, he knew everything about theories and strategies for combatting racism, but now he was responsible for a ten-year-old black girl having to grow up with no mother in a white imperialist city. She wasn't bookish like him, she never enjoyed the work side of school, so it was he who encouraged her to pursue the boxing which is so much a part of her life now, which has shaped that powerful, lithe physique that stands out in the heat of Watling Street among the slowly meandering crowds of office workers. She draws attention, those huge green eyes under the thick wavy dark hair, the sculpted cheeks and full, carefully edged lips; men and women look again as she passes. She moves easily, a panther threat in her walk.

Maybe Evie's mum and dad didn't help her out as much with their liberal, relaxed approach to parenting; could they have prevented Evie from straying into the badlands out there in Southend if they'd taken a different approach? Who knows? It's certainly a thought that Evie's mum dwells upon a lot late at night. But with Linda's dad, his love for his daughter was a fierce, unremitting commitment which was strengthened by his own intellectual discipline – he never allowed either of them to indulge in a moment's self-pity. 'If we cry,' he told Linda on her thirteenth birthday, 'then we cry because we are thinking how beautiful your mother is, and that makes us happy and gives us strength. We don't cry because we are sad.' When she finally worked out at seventeen that she was gay, he was the first person she told. Even though recently she moved to King's Cross to one of those new shared ownership scheme flats near the canal because she felt she needed some physical space from Edmonton, she still speaks to her dad every day and eats with him twice a week.

'Stirling Global,' says Steve, as he marks off Jamies Wine Bar on his list and sees which business is next. He looks up. 'That green door there, I reckon.'

'How can these people sit around in a crappy wine bar drinking on a beautiful day like this?' Linda asks. 'I don't know about checking their fire safety, it's their cholesterol I'd worry about.'

'Don't get started,' Steve says, patting his generous stomach.

She smiles at him and play-punches his shoulder. Although this is routine work, she enjoys Steve's company, there's no side to him. Linda doesn't really have side but she's not necessarily what you'd call easygoing either. Her ingrained habit of speaking completely honestly about everything, learned through the tough teenage years she spent after her mum's death, can unsettle people sometimes, but only those people who have something to hide. They walk across the street towards the green door. Office workers are queuing now in the chain sandwich bars and the street is busy although everyone's walking slowly to try and combat the temperature.

In a few minutes they're up in Henry's office, which now has a crowded feel to it.

'Anyone here called Jean?' Steve asks cheerfully.

'Oh I completely forgot you were coming,' says Jean, opening up the scruffy desk diary. 'Oh God yes, Fire Brigade visit,' she reads. 'Lucky you caught me – I was out for a panini soon.'

'Won't be long, love,' Steve says. Linda wishes he wouldn't use the word "love" to women he doesn't know but it's not something she's going to beat him up over. She smiles at the older woman.

'Smoke detector OK?' She scans the ceiling and spots the white apparatus hanging open with a space where the battery should be. 'Ah.'

'Bloody Henry,' Jean says. 'He said he'd buy batteries at the weekend.'

'Probably used them on something else,' Darren offers helpfully and Jimmy sniggers.

'You don't need me to tell you how important those things are, love,' Steve says to Jean. 'They'll give you those precious minutes you need to get ahead of the flames. Want to show me the fuse boxes?'

Jean leads him over to the other side of the room and Linda walks around looking at the plugs.

'Do you know if these get tested?' she asks Evie.

'Normally they'd have a sticker on with the date of the last inspection.'

Evie raises her eyebrows. 'My guess would be that they've never been tested. Is that bad?'

Linda smiles. 'Well, it's not like an exam. We don't fail you. Although I'd say you're not doing very well.'

Evie smiles back. 'No truer word was spoken,' she says.

For a second, they look at each other. Then Linda looks around the untidy little office.

'What do you all do in here anyway?'

'Financial advice. You know: pensions, savings, investments. All that.'

'Oh. My dad needs some of that. He gets letters in the post which I don't understand any more than he does. SIPPs and ISAs.'

'We do all that,' Evie says.

'He gets confused though. He's seventy-two now. He's clever but he's got some early stage dementia.'

'Oh, I'm sorry.'

Linda shrugs. 'He's OK. It's life.' She's still looking at Evie. 'But maybe you can tell me about all the money stuff?'

'I can talk to you about it, absolutely,' says Evie and she leans down to open a drawer and takes a business card from a box. 'Give me a ring when you're not working and I'll talk you through it.'

Linda takes the card and reads it out loud: '*Evie*

Sangster. Chartered Financial Adviser. Fancy. Thanks.'
She reaches out a hand. 'Linda Appiah. I'll take you
up on that.'

Steve comes back over with Jean and spends a few
minutes giving them all a slightly admonitory summary
of the office's failings and he and Linda are back out
on the street. Steve is chuckling.

'Nice work, girl,' he says. 'Not a second wasted.
Good looker too.'

'Steven Edwards,' she says with an angry frown
and leans towards him threateningly, which makes
him laugh even more.

'It's all right, my lips are sealed. What goes on tour,
stays on tour. Ow!' he squeals as she tweaks his ear
roughly.

Upstairs the office is unusually quiet and then
Darren says,

'Was that fucking gorgeous firefighter coming on
to you, Evie?'

'Don't be a twat, Darren.'

'Oh my God she so was,' says Jade.

'Oh for God's sake,' says Evie and picks up the
phone to make a client call while Darren and Jade
cackle together.

That evening, at eight o'clock after everyone at
Stirling Global has left for the evening, Angel pushes
the vacuum cleaner around the carpet, Bootsy Collins
pulsing through his earpiece. He hasn't met anyone

from Stirling Global in the first week of cleaning there – he lets himself in with a key and each day there's been no-one left at their desks. He pauses by Evie's desk and picks up a flyer which is lying on top of her intray. It has a picture of some kind of Chinese statue, a man sitting cross-legged with a green and brown shawl over his shoulders. His frowning pale head looks down into clasped hands. A headline reads *The Buddhist Path to Happiness in London.* He reads the copy beneath; he doesn't understand some of the words but he sees a name – William Cecil – and a date. He takes his phone out of his pocket and photographs the flyer then he puts it back on Evie's desk and carries on hoovering.

As Lily came out of Doleberry's shop she decided to take the more southerly route back to Pudding Lane. If she dropped down Puddle Dock Hill she could reach Thames Street and walk back along that road to avoid St Paul's. She did not wish any further delays to her errand and if the men were creating disturbance still, she wished to avoid it. Braving the bawdy women and the boatmen on Thames Street was better than being delayed again and being punished back at the bakery. Even oysters for Master Farriner would not assuage his daughter if she were late.

She clutched the clay jar of Treacle under her cloak and crossed over Ludgate Street. She walked as quickly as she could past a couple of young climbing boys who were black with soot from top to bottom of their skinny little frames as they stamped their brushes and cried out at her 'Sweep for the soot Miss? Miss?'

'Madam, may I walk with you a while?'

The voice behind her was familiar and as she turned, she saw the same face, smiling still under his tall dark hat, and rubbing a mark on his forehead ruefully. She flushed.

'I am sorry, sir, to have caused you a mark,' she

said, 'but I am late and I must continue my way.'

'Then I shall take that as consent to accompany you on your way and I shall ensure no-one else impedes your passage this fine morning,' he said, and stepped up his pace to walk alongside her.

Lily was self-conscious of her limp and did not enjoy the company but there was little she could do.

'I am heading for Thames Street, Sir,' she said. 'It is not a street for gentlemen, you may wish to take your leave now.'

He laughed at this.

'I will take my chances, madam. I am no high-born fellow. I am but a servant of God, and a soldier to boot.'

'Why must men glory so in war?' she found herself saying, and then immediately regretted such an impulsive outburst. She crossed over the street and hurried down the slope to Thames Street, where the smell of the filthy water that sits in all the plaster and the rafters of the warehouses along that long thoroughfare seemed to echo her thoughts. The street was busy with the shouts of men unloading goods and the raucous laughter from a group of drunks slouched on the ground. Carriages loaded with cargo picked their way along the cobbles, their wheels clattering noisily, and the street was so narrow in parts that here and there they had to walk one behind the other in order to keep a pace.

'A philosopher too?' the man called out from behind her after her impetuous statement, but his tone was not

unkind. *'You do not approve of our King's determination
to conquer the Dutch?'* he asked, his voice still loud to
combat the noisy street.

She continued walking and after a sedan chair had
squeezed past them he caught up with her again at her
side.

*'I do not know, Sir. I should not have spoken. I know
nothing of such matters. The gentlemen in Mr Doleberry's
shop were speaking of it.'*

'Gentlemen? Hah,' he scoffed. *'I watched them follow
you in. They are no gentlemen, they are men who trade
in lives at the Exchange. Fat men who talk of money.
Usurers, madam. They work in this City of ours by
gambling other men's money on a future they cannot
own. I call that dishonesty, madam.'*

'They talked of a sea fight today,' she said, curious
at his frankness with her. For the first time, she glanced
up at him and saw that he was an older man, though
not so old. He had dark hair nestling under his black
hat and a scar running down his left cheek.

'Yes,' he said. *'It is the King's admiral, Sir Robert
Holmes, who is chasing down the Dutchmen's fleet. I
hear he is outside of Boulogne.'*

'And he means to set fire to them?'

*'As he has done before. That is what your idle gen-
tlemen would have discussed. They will have money in
that game, be sure of that.'*

'How so?'

'*Our King has no money, so he depends on such men to loan him the money to pay for his ships. Each ship that he sends to fight, Mr Doleberry's customers will benefit twice or three times over. It is what happens inside of this City when the gates are opened every day at Ludgate. They stroll in and take their seats at the Exchange and they fill their guts with the blood of the innocent.*'

Lily suddenly thought of her mother, who she would see the following day. She looked up again at the man walking alongside her and saw him frowning into the distance.

'*You may be right, Sir,*' *she said.* '*There are those in this City of ours who even the Lord our God does seem to have forgotten. Come Dutch, come Devil, can life be worse for such as them?*'

He glanced at her.

'*He does not forget them, Madam. Fear not. Our Lord keeps governance over all.*'

There was comfort for Lily in his words and for a while the two walked side by side without speaking.

Chapter Five

That's the other question people asked after it all happened, all those talking heads on TV, the paid pundits, the puffed-up politicians, the pub philosophers: was London crying out for William Cecil or was he just a freak, a phantom, a black swan gliding down the Thames? Was there something about this new London of ours which either encouraged him or even somehow conjured him up, made him necessary? Were we all so bewildered by this new city of ours that we needed him to come and talk to us?

Because it is new. Believe me, I've been here for years, woman and girl. People like me, we're Londoners first, British second; it's what we are, it's our identity. And for those of us who have lived most of our lives here, we can all see it: in the spaces that used to be London, that used to be ours and are now not ours but someone else's. The sleek marble and limestone redevelopments with pointless water fountains and acres of blank white stone where uniformed private security guards come up and ask you what you're doing there, tell you to get off your bicycle, put your cigarette out. You sense it in the exhausted eyes of commuters having to travel longer every morning because they're pushed further and further out to find anywhere they can afford to live. You understand it when even Google Maps gives up on some place you're trying to find because there's already a new block that's sprung up in the way since the last camera van drove by taking photos for Silicon Valley. You see it in the sterile new wide pavements creeping in everywhere, where people don't trundle shopping trolleys on the way to the grocery any more but instead pull clattering suitcases on the way to some sodding Air BnB apartment. In fact the whole town feels like one big airport terminal, the shops in Regent Street an endless snake of Duty Free boutiques selling luxury tat that none of us need. People arrive at Heathrow, bewildered and exhausted, from long haul economy flights with huge suitcases filled with all that's left of their lives somewhere else in the world and they find themselves blinking at a tube map in Terminal Five trying to work out where they're going, while short-hop business class suits slip past them and into cabs to disappear off into glass office blocks where they'll plug themselves back into the mainframe that sustains them.

Who is it that's taken our city away? I don't know, and I don't even want to know really. I just refuse to apologise for being here, I refuse to ask permission to go where I please, I refuse to tell you what my intentions are, I refuse to tell you anything at all about me or to apologise for a single bloody thing. So sod you. Maybe I should have joined up with William Cecil, like those others?

Anyway I didn't but already both Evie and Angel are separately thinking about going to the talk advertised on the flyer. It's not till next week so let's get to the end of this week and go out to Southend with Evie and Jade and Joy. Mikey — the boy that Jade hangs around with in Edmonton — is not a boyfriend, Jade doesn't really do that, but he's the person she spends most time with, sharing her life with the vodka and the opiates and the spells of trouble on the streets and outside the shopping centre in the evenings. Mikey's not with them because Jade is making a real effort this week to try and stay clean while she's doing this weird thing of going into Evie's office and if she met up with Mikey then she'd get out of her head and everything else could go to fuck. Mikey's WhatsApping her now as she sits in the back seat of Evie's Audi, her mum and Evie talking in the front as they nudge through the Friday evening rush hour traffic out east on the A13.

The thing with Jade is she doesn't make very good

choices about what she does in her life, but she's twenty-four now and as time goes on she gets fewer and fewer alternatives presented to her so it's more and more likely that she'll choose to do something which isn't really very good for her. She's bright, she's got her mum's quick wit and humour but she doesn't have much self-control when it comes to expressing things so she can get loud and mouthy very quickly. Maybe in another environment they'd have tagged her much earlier on with one of those modern illnesses like attention deficit disorder or whatever it's called and they'd have dosed her up with drugs but Joy isn't really a fan of all that and she thinks that good old-fashioned family stuff is the way to keep her daughter safe. Joy worries about what would happen if she wasn't there, but having to worry about that is still better than having her daughter drugged out of her mind on some pills prescribed for her by an exhausted GP.

Joy was there earlier this week, luckily, when Jade tried not to go back to Stirling Global after her first day there. Joy found her on Wednesday morning sitting at one of the food benches in the roofed-in open space inside Edmonton Shopping Centre when she was supposed to be on her second day at work. Joy was pulling her shopping trolley behind her with a few bits and pieces from Asda in it and she was heading to the Somali tobacconist in the Centre where they sometimes had cutprice fags that came from God knows where.

Joy hasn't worked since she came out of Holloway which she doesn't mind because it means she can look out for her daughter more. She spotted Jade from a long way off: the red mohican stood out and every now and then she could hear her daughter's raucous laugh. As she came closer, she saw that she was with Mikey.

'I thought you was at work?' Joy asked as she came up. The two kids were sitting at the table with a half-eaten KFC in front of them and they were smoking weed. 'And what are you smoking that here for? They have security here, you know. Do you want to get banged up again?'

Mikey, who was a skinny kid with a mop of black hair which went over his eyes, raised his hands up and shook them like he was pretending to be scared and Jade laughed.

'I'm not talking to you, you little tyke,' Joy said. 'Jade love, you've only tried it for a day. What's the matter?'

'Nothing's the matter, Mum,' Jade said. 'Sit down and have a spliff with me and Mikey. Chill.' And both kids laughed again.

Joy did sit down but only because she'd started crying and she wanted to cover herself up. Joy never cried but somehow this just got to her and she didn't do anything about the shopping which rolled out of the trolley on to the floor. She just sat there with her head in her hands and she cried.

Mikey looked at Jade and rolled his eyes but Jade put a hand over and roughly shook her mum's arm.

'Stop it Mum, what are you doing?'

Joy shook her head but carried on burying her face in her folded arms, her shoulders shaking as she cried silently. The shopping centre echoed with voices and shouts because of the high roof and people wandered past the table heading for the brightly lit shop booths on either side.

'Mum,' Jade said again. 'Stop fucking crying.'

After a while, Joy lifted her head wearily. Her black mascara was smeared under her eyes.

'What you make me do that for, love?' she asked softly, looking at her daughter. 'My bloody make-up's spoiled, I suppose?'

'Yeah,' said Jade.

'I'm off,' said Mikey and he slipped off the bench and started walking away. 'Laters,' he called out.

'Sod it,' Joy said, and pulled a packet of cigarettes out of her pocket and lit one. 'They can bloody arrest me too.'

'Mum, don't be stupid, it's no smoking in here.'

There was a pause and then both of them laughed.

'You look terrible, Mum.'

Joy pulled on her cigarette and looked at Jade.

'I'm sorry, love. That was a bit out of order, wasn't it? Don't know what came over me.'

'You don't cry, Mum.' Jade looked confused.

'I know, love. No time for crying. I just...'

'Is it that job of Evie's?' Jade asked. 'I just thought maybe you wanted me to go in for a day or something. I don't know. It's weird.'

'What's weird?'

'Evie's place. That office. Them all sitting around there. Is that what you want me to do?'

'Oh Jade, you know I just want you to be safe, love. I want you off that stuff.' She pointed at the still-smoking spliff.

'I didn't mind it,' Jade continued, taking another pull. 'I mean, it was all right. It's just weird.'

Jade hasn't ever really worked, not for any length of time. When she left school in Edmonton she'd get jobs in the usual places like the big Asda but she was soon out on her ear after telling customers where to get off. She's been in Chelmsford twice, both times for antisocial behaviour, and the periods when she's in coincide with bouts of self-harming, so she carries on cutting herself and making ligatures out of string for a few weeks after she's come out. Joy's learned, with help from the woman at Social Services, that she shouldn't confront her daughter head-on about these things, but instead try and help Jade to find some space that's less stressful for her. When Evie visited her in Chelmsford last month, one of the warders said she was worried about Jade and wasn't there some way she could be kept busy when she was out? The thing is, Jade is intelligent enough to know that she needs to make a change; a part of her hidden away inside of her knows she doesn't want to end up on the streets properly with Mikey and all the others, sitting up for days in some flat in Edmonton with the curtains shut and people lying on the floor and heating up shit in a teaspoon with a lighter.

'It probably is, love,' said Joy. 'I've never done an office, I don't know.'

'Evie's been texting me,' said Jade, picking up her phone.

'Why don't you tell her you'll go back tomorrow?'

Jade shrugged. 'Could do, I suppose.'

'She's a good one, you know that. Evie.'

'I know, Mum.'

They both sat at the table smoking then Jade saw a security guard heading slowly in their direction from down the other end of the mall. Normally, she'd have waited for an argument, a fight even, but she looked at her mum with her mascara all over her cheeks and she said, 'Come on Mum, I'm taking you back home.' She got up and went round the table to pick up the shopping that had fallen out of Joy's trolley.

'Got to go to the Somalis,' Joy said. 'Fags.'

'All right, we'll go there then home.'

Joy stood up and they both stamped their cigarettes on the concrete floor.

'Got me behaving like a bloody teenager,' Joy grumbled.

Jade took her mum's arm.

'I'll text Evie when we get in, tell her I'll go back tomorrow, shall I?'

'Yes. Tell her that, love.'

So Jade did go back on the Wednesday and sitting in the back of Evie's car now you could see her young skin was already benefitting from the healthy *Pret à Manger* salads Jean had forced on her this week. She let Darren buy her a JD and coke after work on Thursday and that's also quite strange and quite nice, having a good-looking bloke showing her some atten-tion. They only had one drink but he said they should do something next week and she sort of knows what that something is and doesn't mind the idea of it.

Evie lets Joy do most of the talking in the car. She's telling her about how she used to come down to the Isle of Dogs in the '80s with Jade's dad to go dancing in the pubs down near the river where the soul DJs had residencies. They're just driving past Canary Wharf on the raised flyover where, to the right, the thuggish stumps of glass and steel with their HSBC and JP MORGAN logos stare sullenly at you and all those old pubs have gone; nowhere in this bleak, bleached landscape for high waisters and plimsolls and backflips and shimmies. He went back to Ireland, Jade's dad, and Joy says she hopes he still gets his dancing shoes out every now and then but in reality, they both know he's probably just nursing a pint in some chain pub in Donegal.

As Joy tries to remember the names of some of the pubs they used to dance in and Jade sits quietly in the back texting Mikey, Evie starts thinking again about William Cecil. He's phoned her twice this week. The first time she was in the office and he just said:

'Tell me, Miss Sangster, how you felt after our conversation.'

It was a sudden, direct question and all the others were sitting at their desks, Rufus was on the phone to someone and Henry was arguing with Jean.

'Um, it came as a bit of a surprise. I'm sorry if...'

He cut her off. 'Please do not waste my time with courtesies. I am interested to know whether you have potential. I doubt very much whether your firm will be able to assist me in any way, but you strike me as someone who needs, how shall I say it, a re-adjusting.'

'Oh.'

'I sense you are amongst your colleagues. I will telephone your mobile number this evening at eight o'clock.' And with that he put the phone down on her. That evening, after she'd been to Waitrose to buy supper, she kept looking at her phone as it got closer to eight, then she'd shake her head and go and put the TV on and start cutting up tomatoes. At ten past eight, the phone rang.

'Miss Sangster. I apologise for being late.'

'That's all right. I'm not really doing anything.'

'Indeed you are not. You feel humiliated by your inability to escape from the situation in which you find yourself. You are wasting time attempting to sell second-rate financial advice to people who would do better to take it from more authoritative sources. You are wasting your own time and the time of the people with whom you deal. You have regrets about the past and you fear the future. You fantasise about being obliterated by the burning sun because you suspect it offers you the prospect of freedom. But that freedom, Miss Sangster, depends on your ability to survive the fire. Will you survive the fire?'

Evie stood at the kitchen worktop, the phone in one hand and the knife she'd been using on the tomatoes in the other. She was silent for a moment.

'I don't know,' she said softly.

'Good,' he replied and for the first time she heard sympathy in his voice. 'It is best that you start with nothing, it will make it easier for you to prepare yourself. I suggest you come to the talk I mentioned, it is next week. We may have an opportunity to discuss further there.'

And with that he hung up, leaving Evie standing in her kitchen, tomato juice dripping off her knife onto the white tiled kitchen floor.

Now the traffic has loosened up and soon they're skimming past the dusty beeches and oaks that line the road out towards Southend and the three of them are laughing as Jade tries to explain to her mum what Henry is like:

'He's like really bad-tempered, but in a funny way, like he's got an itch on his arse and he can't tell whether he likes it or hates it.'

Evie hasn't heard a better description of Henry before and she can't stop laughing and they're like this now, the three of them, for the next forty minutes until she steers the car right off London Road in Hadleigh and heads towards the old castle ruins which was the first thing she'd see every morning when she woke up as a kid and looked out of the window. She turns left onto an unmade road and the car rumbles over stones and potholes and suddenly over there on the right is the view, the view that is imprinted on her mind, the view that stayed with her all those years in Ibiza. The long, low hill they're on slopes down south towards the estuary and in the shimmering heat haze Two Tree Island breaks the space between the land and the sea and, further away, Canvey Island marks the end, the end of London really because this is where the Thames finishes up, this is the last gasp of this city we're all so churned up about. A big container ship is slowly making its way up the channel towards Tilbury Docks and there's a flock of geese heading the same way against the sun sitting low in the west. This is where you can stop thinking about London, this is where London gets out of your head and you can finally leave it behind.

Up ahead at the end of the lane, sitting in isolation on top of this hill and surrounded by hedges, is her mum and dad's house with the old barn at the side and the mast of her dad's boat which has been sitting there on blocks for the last few years, sticking up above the shrubbery in front of the garden. When Evie turns the engine off there's just that late summer silence. As they get out her mum appears round the side of the house with a yellow gardening apron on, a basket with freshly cut runner beans in one hand and a cigarette in the other.

'Oh thank God for that, another smoker,' says Joy and the two of them start talking as though they've known each other for years, and Evie and Jade carry bags in through the front door straight into the huge kitchen where her dad is stirring something in a big saucepan. He turns around as they come in:

'There she is,' he smiles. He's a big bear of a man, wearing jeans and a faded blue smock and his beard is mostly grey, his hair a tousled affair of greys and browns. He comes over and gives Evie a big hug and when his daughter introduces Jade he smiles and says:

'We've heard all about you, love, I'm glad you've come.'

'Mum and Joy are outside smoking already,' says Evie.

'I've banned her from the house,' he says. 'Put my foot down.'

'I'll bet,' says Evie and at that point the two women come in through the front door, both smoking, and her dad just raises his eyebrows and smiles again. Evie's mum is a handsome blonde woman, small and bird-like with sharp eyes and her skin tanned from a summer's gardening; she and Joy, with all her coiffured jet black hair piled up on her head and her red lipstick and pale indoor complexion, are like opposites. Her mum drops the runner beans on the kitchen worktop and says, 'As requested, sir,' then turns to Jade. 'Now you must be Jade. Come on, I'll show you your room. You're going to be in Barbara's old room.'

Evie has two sisters: Barbara is two years older than her and has a house about thirty miles away on the Sussex border. She's an air hostess for BA and lives on her own in a cottage which she bought with her ex-husband. Rachel is the oldest, just turned 40, and lives in France with a French artist and their two kids. Evie's family is clearly very close, rooted solidly in the hill earth above these estuary marshlands.

Her dad, Andy, is still running his shop-fitting business and over on one side of the big kitchen there's a messy table with a laptop and papers scattered about, two mobile phones sitting on them. He's never had an office, runs the whole thing from his head and a tele-phone. He has teams of blokes out at different locations at all times, and he keeps them all in line while bringing in a constant supply of new work from the property developers he's worked with over the years. Evie's mum, Frances – although everyone calls her Frankie – is retired now from her job in Social Services in Southend. When Evie got into trouble fifteen years ago, Frankie was dealing with cases like hers. She's never really been able to forgive herself that she wasn't able to keep her daughter safe but she and Andy have learned that you can't be responsible for the whole world, the whole time, you can only do what you can do.

Later on, after supper when Jade's already asleep up in Barbara's room and Evie is sitting outside in the garden with her dad sharing a cigar and a glass of rum, Joy helps Frankie with putting dishes away.

'I'm glad Evie's got you,' Frankie says. 'She's so independent. Won't listen to anyone.'

'She fusses over me like I'm an invalid,' Joy says. 'I'm an old fool, I know that, but she needs to have a care of herself every now and then.'

'She's always thought she can do what she likes.'

'Well, she can't, can she? What's she doing in that job of hers? That bloke, the one she works for, I can't say I like the sound of him. I know she used to be with him, but he's an arsehole if you ask me.'

Frankie laughs. 'Henry? I suppose he is a bit of an arse, isn't he? I used to be rather fond of him when they were together.'

'Bloke like that getting her stitched up. And he's got a wife somewhere too, hasn't he? That's not a decent fella.'

'Oh dear, I suppose I did turn a blind eye about the wife. They just seemed to have a nice time together.'

'Until he got her banged up. Nobody put me in Holloway, I did that all on my ownsome. Your Evie didn't ought to have been there. I want a word with him one of these days.'

Suddenly Frankie tears up and she leans both hands on the sink. Joy puts her arm around her.

'It's all right, love,' she says softly. 'We'll both look out for her.'

But Evie that weekend, she mostly wanted to try and talk to Jade, get her to think a bit about her life back in Edmonton, Mikey, the drinking and the gear. She's been a good friend to Jade and to Joy over the last three years, but like Joy, she's really not been able to do more than be around for Jade when she's needed; Jade's mood swings are so ferocious that you soon learn not to try and take them on full tilt. Being out here would give her a chance to talk to her properly, try and work on the progress that this week in the office might have begun.

Andy and Frankie's house is a rambling old place

that they've had almost thirty years now and it sits on the last stretch of grass common before the land slopes down towards the flat levels of the salt marshes. It feels completely isolated although you can walk to old Leigh in about twenty minutes and Southend itself is only fifteen minutes away in the car. There are quiet sunsets from the back of the house where you see swirls of starlings patterning the sky and you hear the snap of marsh waders picking up flies. The garden sits all around the house and Frankie has planted vegetables all over the place and Andy has dilapidated sheds where he keeps knackered old lumps of machinery: lawnmowers, chainsaws, bits of the diesel engine for the boat he's been fixing up for years.

It's so much home to Evie even though like her sisters she spent years away from it; all three of them in their different ways are locked in to this place. So she's got this thought in her head that she wants Jade to think about Edmonton the way she thinks about it: like it's an anchor. Because she stepped off the yellow brick road when she was young like Jade, she ended up in prison like Jade's done. She wants all that to stop and maybe she can get Jade to think about her patch of north London not as somewhere where she gets fucked up but as somewhere where her mum is and where she knows she can always go back and recharge. The indoor mall in Edmonton where the fruit and veg shops have piles of onions and sweet potatoes and chillies and plantain; the old war memorial on the roundabout; the Overground station at Edmonton Green which stinks of weed but lets you watch the sun go down while you wait for your train; the recreation ground the other side of the main road beyond the cemetery where Joy and her dad used to take her to the swings when she was little – they're always going to be there like the hooting owl sweeping over Hadleigh Castle is always going to be here. It all just means the same thing, which is that there is somewhere where you were made and where the someone that is you has a home.

Although Evie doesn't know this yet, this is how Linda feels about Edmonton. She was only able to move down to King's Cross because she knew it wasn't far from her dad's flat and everything she does in her life – her work for the Brigade, her boxing, her nights out with friends in Shoreditch – everything is somehow validated for her by the knowledge that her dad is walking slowly down Fore Street to go and eat some rice and chicken in the same café he's eaten in for years and have a game of chess with one of his old boys there and that there will be fresh flowers on her mum's grave in the cemetery the other side of the shopping centre. For Angel, it's more difficult: he's too far away from Colombia, he can't be sure what's happening there in the forty-nine weeks when he's stuck here in London and he knows his mum doesn't tell him everything when he phones her once a week. More and more he wishes he hadn't left but then he sees his daughters growing up and making plans to see their friends at Nando's in Tottenham on Saturday and he thinks he had no choice. But it doesn't make him feel good and maybe that's what William Cecil picked up on? Maybe that's why I'm so fascinated by him? Because he took one look at us all and realised we were ripe for...what? Picking, I suppose.

On the following day, Saturday, Andy has to go off to visit a job his men are working on in Ipswich so the four women go for a stroll after a late breakfast. They walk down the side of one of the sloping fields, wander around the ruins of Hadleigh Castle (Joy smoking, Jade on her phone as usual, Evie talking to her mum about her dad's weight) then drop down to the path by the water which takes them to Two Tree Island. They cross over the bridge and then leave the road for one of the sandy paths that snake through the island, surrounded by pale, dry grass, low scrubby trees and flowering shrubs. The sun still beats down on them but somehow, out here in the nature reserve by the estuary, its rays feel kinder, less aggressive than they do in town.

'That's Golden Samphire,' says Joy at one point, pointing at some yellow flowers.

Evie laughs.

'How do you know that? Mum, is she making that up?'

'No she's not, you naughty girl. She's quite right.'

'Don't tell me, you know what that is too,' says Evie, pointing at some pinky purple flowers on the other side of the path.

'Sea Lavender,' says Joy, leaning over it and picking a stem. 'Didn't tell you I worked in a flower shop in Camden when I was your age, did I?'

'I've heard it all now,' says Evie. 'She's got green fingers.'

'That's the nicotine,' says Jade and Evie laughs and Joy tuts at her daughter.

Frankie and Joy begin to reminisce about the heatwave of 1976, which the news channels kept going on about because that was the last time there was anything like this heat here. They can both remember it, they were both at school and Evie and Jade listen with amusement as the two older women talk about the boyfriends they'd had back then.

Their conversation comes to a natural end after a while and all you can hear is the sound of their steps on the brittle, dry path and the chirp of crickets in the bushes. The sun is right overhead now, burning down on them from a bleached sky.

Then Jade says:

'I quite fancy that Darren in the office.'

'Oh God, no, Jade. Not Darren,' Evie says.

'What's wrong with Darren?' asks Frankie.

'He's too much of a player,' Evie says.

'What does that mean?' Jade says.

'I mean, he's too promiscuous,' says Evie, and Joy laughs then and says:

'Blimey girl, when did you leave Sunday School?'

'I don't want to marry him, for Christ's sake,' says Jade. 'I just fancy him. I might shag him if he's up for it.'

'Jade Franklin, wash your mouth out!' says Joy but Frankie is laughing now and Evie feels embarrassed.

They walk around the island and end up on the most southern tip where the old road disappears into the water at Hadleigh Ray, separating the island from Canvey. You can see the mouth of the Thames from here and the hot breeze over the surface of the water is whipping up white horsetails over the sea where Viking raiders and Spanish pirates and Jewish cloth workers and Venetian spice dealers and German U-boats and American yachts and Russian merchant ships and Norwegian fishing boats and all the hundreds of thousands of vessels over the centuries made their way up the estuary towards the riches and the defeats and the hopes and despairs of London Town forty miles up river.

In the end, when it was all over, they thought about this weekend and how maybe that was the last time they ever had any peace. But now everyone is relaxed and later on that day they all enjoy the genial ribbing of Andy which takes place while he cooks their Saturday evening meal, and the next day Jade likes seeing her mum chatting endlessly to Frankie over packets of fags while they both prepare the Sunday lunch and she even agrees to try a computer course after Evie talks to her about it. On the Sunday evening, when all three of them are sorry to leave Hadleigh and head back on the A13, Jade says from the back of the car:

'He's proper, your dad. And your mum. They're proper.'

'I know,' says Evie. 'So's this one here, though,' and she slaps Joy's thigh over the gearstick.

'Cheeky mare,' Joy grumbles but she gives Evie a kiss and a hug when they pull into the parking spaces outside her block. And Evie drives back home down to Wapping thinking about William Cecil.

Lily listened while the gentleman continued to speak to her as they hurried along Thames Street. As they dodged carriages and avoided brawling sailors, he seemed keen to tell her of his life, of the years fighting in the war with the Parliamentarians when he was a young man, of his service to Cromwell. He kept referring to some debates at Putney. She had heard of Putney, it was a village to the west of London, but she had never been there. He spoke of it with a kind of reverence.

'We envisaged a fairer world, there, madam,' he said. 'After the fighting was over, after we had restored the Lord's justice and brought to an end the tyranny of King Charles...'

At this she gasped and tried to stride forward, away from him. Even she knew that the rotting heads of the men who had executed the previous King were still decorating the church at Westminster. But he seemed oblivious to the dangers implicit in his words and kept catching up with her to continue speaking.

'We gathered at Putney, all us soldiers, and we spoke of the world we would create from the flames. A world where no man owned another, where all men owned the land together and shared its bounty. A world where you *were as much the baker as your master.'*

She frowned at him and shook her head.

'I have no place in such words,' she said fiercely. 'I have a living to keep and a mother to care for and God only knows both hang by a thread. If I be taken for a heretic such as you, then what good will that do me?'

He lowered his head and spoke more softly this time, despite the uproar of the street.

'I understand, sister,' he said. 'I have no family, I have no-one to care for or to care for me. I forget myself.'

They continued walking and she looked at his serious face once more.

'There be others of your thinking?' she asked, curious.

He nodded. 'I speak seriously,' he said. 'We tried to make that world. A Level World, that is what we called it. We were many, but time and fortune have taken their toll. And now it has come to this.'

He waved his hand angrily.

'A city where Papists once more roam free, a city of usurers, a city where a decent maid such as you can walk in fear of retribution from an unfair master, a city where mammon has triumphed once more. It was twenty years ago, madam, almost to the day, when we triumphed over an unjust king and we spoke of building our new Jerusalem here, and what have we made? A new Gomorrah.'

Lily was silent. She did not understand some of her companion's references and as was her way, she elected

to keep her counsel. Yet despite her fears of his outspo-
kenness, his fervour was exciting to her.

They walked in silence for a couple of minutes and
she felt him looking at her.

'I apologise, madam,' he said. 'I have spoken too
earnestly, too soon.'

She looked up at him.

'No, sir,' she said. 'I am just unused to such talk.
But…it is pleasing to me.'

He nodded gravely, looking ahead again. Then suddenly, he stopped and stood in front of her, causing her
to stop too.

'May I tell you, madam, what I truly believe? It
comes from our days at Putney: "The poorest he that is
in England hath a life to lead as the greatest he." What
think you of that, now?'

'But sir, is that not the stuff of dreams?'

'Yes, perhaps, madam. Perhaps. Yet when we dreamt
it then, twenty years ago, we thought it to be true. And
is not thinking it the greater battle?'

Chapter Six

The talk, like everything else about William Cecil, is at an unorthodox time: 9pm on Tuesday evening. Then again, he was looking for particular types, wasn't he? He wasn't interested in those Londoners who were safely at home at nine in the evening, sat in front of their boxsets trying to put their worries out of their minds for an hour.

Evie bribed Jade into going with her by agreeing to go to the M&M store in Leicester Square after work to buy some personalised M&Ms for Joy's upcoming birthday. Jade is entranced by the idea of buying American chocolates that had her mum's name on them, although they are almost late to the talk because the strict letter count on the sweets meant she could only get Joy Frank or J Frankli and they spend what seems to Evie like an age debating which works best. Finally she drags Jade out of the store clutching several boxes and into a cab and soon they are speeding east on the Embankment. Evie points out the dagger of the Shard shimmering in the evening heatwave haze.

'What is it with you and views of London, anyway?' Jade says, flicking through her photos of the M&M store to find the best one to put on Instagram.

Evie is grateful to have Jade with her, it feels slightly less weird to be going at all having her there, as though somehow Evie can pretend that going to talks in the East End about Buddhism was just something else that Jade needed to know about to get used to office life. She feels utterly confused about why she actually wants to go at all, so it feels much easier making light of it by being with Jade. They are going to get a pizza afterwards in Wapping and Jade is going to spend the night in Evie's spare bedroom.

The talk is held in one of the smaller assembly rooms in Toynbee Hall just off Whitechapel. Maybe he chose that place because it's been a refuge since the late nineteenth century, picking people up when they've stumbled under the weight of London. People pass through it, steady themselves, get some energy back; old people come there in the morning and drink tea and chat about the old days, or play a spot of bingo in the afternoon.

Evie and Jade are already sitting down when Angel arrives. He is the last one in as he's had to walk over from Watling Street. He'd told Marta he was going to an English language lesson because he too felt embarrassed about his curiosity about the flyer he'd found on Evie's desk. Angel is a rational man, a numbers man and it already disturbs him that his state of mind in this foreign city is so confused that he even thinks of coming to a talk like this.

Apart from Angel, who sits at the back, there's about thirty other people in the room. Chan is sitting in the front row, completely still and looking straight ahead at the wall behind the speaker dais. There's an older Chinese-looking man sitting in the second row but everyone else is youngish, twenties or early thirties: it's a mix of nationalities, two serious-looking German girls in the front row with notepads ready, a guy with dreads at the back trying to look nonchalant, a Japanese couple whispering nervously. Evie is trying not to look over at Chan, then she recognises the young blonde woman sitting in the front row near to Chan, the one who served the tea in Cecil's flat. She's smiling broadly and holding hands with a guy next to her. Then Evie sees that quite a few people in the room are holding hands and they've all got that same expectant, excited smile on their faces, as though they know what's coming and they just can't wait.

Angel is probably one of the older ones and that makes him feel awkward again. Unlike Evie, he doesn't notice that half the audience are holding hands. He's all over the place really but he doesn't have long because a couple of minutes after he's sat down, William Cecil appears from a side door and walks straight up to the dais.

He's light-footed and walks swiftly. The dais is only a step up off the floor but as he's a tall man he appears to tower over this scattered little audience. There is silence for a moment as he gazes calmly at them, his eyes behind his metal glasses passing from one to another, the bright light from the fluorescent tubes on the ceiling glinting on that huge dark forehead, the grey frizzy globe of hair illuminated with an almost fluorescent haze, the thick black moustache quite theatrical now. He is wearing the same cream-coloured cotton jacket he had on when Evie met him last week, and his long, wrinkled fingers grip the edges of the rostrum, the flesh under his nails startlingly pink.

'Welcome,' he says and his deep voice fills the small room like honey.

'Like you, I have lived in this city, this London, for some time. Perhaps some of you are natives and have spent your whole lives here, perhaps others are like me and have arrived relatively recently. It is all the same. I suspect whatever our individual stories, we share a common desire, for why else would we all have gathered here this evening, if not to explore new possibilities? We are, I feel, all open to the manifestations of what the Buddha called vinnana or sometimes prana, that is, the force and substance of the living world. Let us investigate together this evening, let us open our minds.

'What is our purpose in being here: in this excellent hall, in this city, in this country, on this planet which we call Earth? Do you define your purpose? You, madam' – he said, pointing at a woman in her late twenties with long black hair – 'when you wake in the morning, do you remind yourself of your purpose? Perhaps you remind yourself of your responsibilities to come that day in your working life: you have a meeting you must attend, a document you must write, some telephone calls you must make. Or you are aware on wakening of the tasks which face you with regard to your family, how you must ensure your children are dressed, fed and readied for school. It is a very human characteristic, to feel an attachment to a set of responsibilities, to feel that we must pay attention to and answer those responsibilities.

'But sometimes, even when we welcome the responsibilities we identify – the need to protect a child, the desire to succeed at the workplace – sometimes there are still additional burdens placed upon us not of our own making: the stresses of commuting, the unfair allocation of resources, the pressure caused by low pay. Are these burdens shared out amongst us equally? No! Some of us, it seems, are destined to receive more than their fair share and that, my friends, can make this London of ours a difficult city to love sometimes.

Am I right?'

There are one or two nods in the audience, Angel included.

'Yes. These extra encumbrances can occasionally make living in London seem difficult. It can seem, I suggest, that all our efforts somehow are directed towards surviving in London, rather than living. And yet we do live, we do all live, like the birds which sing to us every morning. How then are we to learn how to survive and having done so, to flourish? That is what I would like to talk about and why I believe you have joined me here this evening: to think about how that great spirit, the Buddha himself, might approach the challenge of living in London today.

'Some of you may already be familiar with his teachings; others, I suspect, may be coming to him for the first time. I myself originally encountered him in my home land of Barbados many years ago, the veil drawn aside for me by a wise gentleman who earned his living by cleaning the house in which my father, my mother and I lived. There was much poverty in Barbados at that time, and this esteemed person was paid very little by my parents for his long and onerous tasks. But even to my youthful eyes, it was clear that he manifested a tranquillity which went far, far beyond the ideas of happiness which my father, for example, expounded over his evening cocktails. If I have achieved anything in my own long life, I hope it may be that I have learned a speck, an atom, of that gentleman's wisdom which, I discovered one day, derived from his own readings of the teachings of the Buddha.

'At the heart of those teachings lies the knowledge that our lives, the lives of all living creatures, are composed of suffering, from the moment when we first appear in the world to the second we depart it. To live is to suffer. The word the Buddha himself used was Dukkha, and in literal translation that means "that which is difficult to bear". Let us reflect on that for a moment, let us share that thought here in our temporary refuge from the clamour of the city. To live is to suffer. Do you not feel a momentary sense of relief when I say that? Is there not calm to be found in the expression of that eternal truth? For what the Buddha offers you by his profound observation is the knowledge that whatever pain or unhappiness you experience in your life, this is merely the natural rhythm of being, its familiar expression. Suffering is the air we take in through our first breath.

'Am I right? Do we suffer, we friends gathered here this evening?'

Again, some more nods and Angel is staring hard at William Cecil now. Evie glances at Jade and is surprised to see she's actually listening for a change.

'Why do I suggest that this insight might afford us a sense of relief? I can see already from some faces here tonight that I may be correct, but why is that? I say it is because the recognition of the confluence of life with suffering has the effect of linking us, of binding us to one another through the sense of shared experience. If I know that you suffer as I do, then the burden of my own predicament is somehow shared.

'But no, I hear some others of you say. That cannot be so. The rich man in his luxury mansion, he does not suffer like I do. He has people to run after him, to fetch him things, to drive his children to their expensive school. The successful young couple in their luxury flat, both advancing rapidly in their careers, shopping at the finest shops, eating at the tastiest restaurants: they do not share the challenges which are inflicted upon me every day. Their suffering, if they have any at all, is not akin to my own.

'So perhaps the distribution of suffering is unfair? The Buddha understood that, because he too was originally a rich man. His father was one of the richest men in the land and wished for his son to inherit his wealth and to enjoy a life of indolence. But the Buddha rejected his father's plans and set out on his own to find out the truth about life on this earth. He travelled far and wide and saw how for too many people, the reality of life is that so many of us face almost insuperable challenges merely to survive. In his day as in ours, the spread of fortune was unfair.

'Would he come to the same conclusion if he were

to visit this city of ours today? I think so, don't you? I think he would look at all these luxury apartments, these lavish restaurants, these monstrous skyscrapers and he would say: who profits from these? How do they contribute to the happiness of all? How do they bring solace to the many? This is a cruel city, he would say. Don't you agree?'

More nodding and in the short silence, Angel says out loud: 'Yes!' At this, several of the audience who are holding hands look at him, smiling, and several of them then call out too: 'Yes!'

William Cecil gazes at Angel for a second.

'There,' he says, quietly. 'There, our friend confirms it. Yes sir, the Buddha would say this is a cruel city.'

He keeps his eyes fixed on Angel for several seconds, then he resumes.

'In my long life I have travelled to over one hundred countries and have spoken with men and women of every colour, race and religion, and never once have I encountered a rich man whose wealth had delivered him of his birthright of suffering. If anything, he exacerbates his troubles by the accumulation of problems, stress and antagonism. Yes, he may enjoy the view of Monaco from his yacht but inside his soul yearns for freedom with just the same plaintive call as your own.

'And yet it does not feel that way, does it? When we struggle to find the means with which to keep on going, this city, this new London, seems designed to trip us up at every corner. I say to you now, I believe even the Buddha himself would be shocked by some of the things I have seen here. Shocked, I say. For although he was a man of immense compassion, he was also a strong man, an angry man even, a man who could not tolerate the arbitrary allocation of woes.

'If the Buddha were to come amongst us, he would demand action. That, I know.'

He thumps the top of the rostrum with both fists. 'Action!'

He lets the word hang in the air and looks once more at Angel who is now gripping the edges of the plastic seat. The room stays quiet and William Cecil takes a few seconds before he continues.

'But let us go back first to how the Buddha developed his thinking. As I said, he left his father's care and took it upon himself to explore the realities of life on earth. He found misfortune wherever he went and as a man of almost infinite compassion, this distressed him. And so he meditated, famously under a tree which is still celebrated as the location where his most profound thoughts emerged. He asked himself: if man is born to suffer, how might it be possible for every one of us – not just a select few but every single one of us – to throw off the burden of suffering?

'The solution he discovered was in the rejection of attachment. Only by releasing himself from the ties that bind him can man truly begin to deliver himself of the yoke of suffering. Attachment to what, you ask? To sensuality, to opinions, to unkind thoughts, to any sense of self or what the psychologists would call ego, to practices and habits which keep him tied to a certain way of life. Surely there is a limit, you ask? Surely some attachments are necessary: the ties of duty, of family, of love? But why? Why should there be limits? Because by learning first that our lives are dominated by suffering and then that this suffering can be released by the slow, steady and methodical abandonment of all attachments, every man can set out on the path towards an ultimate freedom whose name he gave nirvana.

'Yes, I see you recognise this word. You all know it: nirvana. There was even a popular music group who took it as their name. The word expresses an idea of perfection which is attractive, is it not? If I were to say to you now, nirvana is a place we can find together, would that not be something worth fighting for?'

Evie looks at the hand-holding members of the audience, and they're all nodding wildly, grinning at each other, clutching each other's hands.

'But let us explore it more deeply. The actual word is nibbanah, which in the original Pāli Canon of the Buddha's period means an unbinding. An unbinding from what? An unbinding from the attachments which are the root cause of our suffering. He who has achieved this state of bliss, this nibbanah, is one who has cut himself free of all the ties which previously he believed to be so important to him: ties of friendship, ties of anger, ties of lust, ties of family, ties of nationality. Set yourself free from them!

'But how can I abandon my family, you ask? You do not, my friends. That is the joy of the Buddha's teaching. By releasing yourself from the grip of your family, you become a free person and in your freedom will find yourself so much better equipped to ensure that those around you are protected. Is that not the most beautiful of logical contradictions? In order to protect those you love, withdraw yourself from their claims and see how they will flourish.

'Now how does this wisdom apply to our particular situation, to our need for help in surviving life in London today? Let me tell you a further story of the Buddha's teachings.

'The Buddha defined the tragedy of man's imprisoning attachments as being like a fire. For what is fire but a combustion of elements, a raging fury which depends upon the ingredients which cause it to spark, to crackle, to burst into flame, to roar into terrible, fearful and neverending inferno? And those ingredients, he realised, were the attachments of every man's life which continually fed the flames of his torment. So this is what the Buddha taught: that the purity of the flame can be released from the fuel of attachments which cause it to rage. Liberated from this fuel, the flame becomes a thing of beauty, like fire unbound.

'Who amongst you feels the heat of this fire in London?' And at this point he looks straight at Evie. 'Who amongst you dreams that one day, the fire might roar but leave you untouched, safe, sacred? Hmm?'

Evie feels she must be blushing and looks away for a moment. William Cecil turns his attention back to the audience.

'London is an inferno of suffering created by attachments which do not serve us well. Can you not feel it now, the heat of suffering, thundering down upon you day after day? Do you not long to escape it? Of course you do. And you should. You must! But how can you? You, you gentle, weak creatures, faced with the crushing weight of this city – how can you fight it alone?

'The answer is, you can't. But join with me and I will help you to release that Samma-Vayama, that strength and virility which lies hidden inside of you. Join with me and we will unbind ourselves from the flames of suffering. That is the message I bring you from the Buddha: you have it within yourself to become great, to become a warrior, to become invincible. Let London burn with all the savagery it deserves and let your minds become like a fire which is unbound.'

By this point, William Cecil is gripping the rostrum so hard it seems to be shaking and his forehead is sweating. He stares wildly around the room then his gaze settles once more on Angel.

'Join with me and I will show you a majesty beyond your wildest imagination.'

The whole speech was probably much longer than that, but that's the core of it as I remember. It was a pretty impressive performance, I think you can tell. He was like one of those old time preachers in many ways. He was transformed: he was a shaman, he was a prophet.

Throughout the show, Chan stays looking perfectly ahead but once the proceedings are drawn to a close, he goes up and confers briefly with Cecil, then turns and walks through the lines of chairs to Angel, who is just standing up and getting ready to leave. Chan goes up to him, speaks briefly to him and then gives him an envelope. Angel's face is unforgettable then: his eyes are wide and fierce as he looks back towards William Cecil for one last time before he turns and rushes out of the hall, the envelope in his hand.

And Evie? She feels confused. She waits in her seat while Jade says she wants to go and find the toilet. Had he meant to talk about fire because she was there, or was that just something he did? She didn't really relate to much he'd talked about but even so, that was odd. The two German girls are speaking with him, then as they turn to leave she stands up and walks over to him.

'Mr Cecil? Evie Sangster.'

He looks at her without smiling. His face is shiny with sweat.

'Yes?' he says.

'I thought your talk was...interesting.'

He looks at her but does not reply.

'I didn't know about all that,' she continues, feeling she has to fill the silence.

'No, of course you didn't,' he says.

'I'm sorry, I didn't mean...'

He waves his hand dismissively.

'You understand little. You are like a helpless infant placed in the dark forest, alone and defenceless.'

'Well, actually...'

He interrupts her.

'You know, Miss Sangster, that I could help you. You know that I could teach you how to stop being so helpless, I could show you how to become the person you could be. I could teach you the path of the Luohan. Without my teaching, you will perish. I think you know that.'

'I...'

Again he interrupts her.

'If you resist, there is nothing I can do for you.'

And with that he turns and leaves the room by the same door he had entered, followed by Chan who glances impassively at her for a brief moment. As the door closes behind them, Evie looks around her and sees that the rest of the audience has now filed out of the exit. She stands alone at the front of the room, the bright fluorescent lights shining over her. She feels drained, and puts her hand out to the podium to steady herself. Her head drops and she closes her eyes. All she can feel is the heat from the light bulbs above her, as though they are now all directed at her, weighing her down with their energy. Was he right? Was she really so helpless? Was it so obvious that she lacked the strength to make changes in her life?

She shakes her head, opens her eyes, looks out at the empty room.

'Fuck,' she says and her voice echoes back at her. 'Fuck, fuck, fuck.'

At that point, the door the two men had used opens once more and Jade comes back into the room. Evie is so thrown that she doesn't notice how quiet Jade is, she doesn't notice the corner of the envelope peeking out from the pocket of her jacket. She is pleased when, a little later, Jade doesn't seem to want to discuss the talk over their pizza in Wapping High Street.

That's what we do, don't we? We're like Evie, I think, we just keep on trying to hold everything together.

*A*s they neared the junction with Fish Street Hill, which was where she would bear left towards Pudding Lane, Lily found herself telling this strange man about her mother and how she feared for her, living ill and alone in Spital Fields. He listened gravely as they stood at the lane's corner.

'Your father?' he asked.

'Long gone,' she said. 'He was sent to Newgate when my mother was still carrying me. There did he die, even before my birth.'

'On what charge was he committed to that foul place?'

She shrugged. 'He caused the death of a gentleman who did try to tarry with my mother. They hanged him.'

The man's face hardened and he looked past her, into the distance.

'I could tell an injustice in you,' he said. This time he spoke softly. 'Not just today, when you were so brave as to challenge our mob, but before, when I have seen you about these parts. You do carry yourself with a dignity which speaks to me of the same injustice against which we fought all those years ago.'

'I must go,' she said.

'Let me try and help your mother, at least,' he said,

turning to look at her. *'I know something of the old medicines from soldiers with whom I fought in the war. One in particular, a rare man, named Culpeper. He saved my arm at Newbury, just by the application of certain choice leaves. He is no longer with us, but his medicines live on. If you permitted, I could bring some to your mother.'*

'I know not,' she said, *feeling uncomfortable and trying to head to the bakery.*

'Think on it,' he said. *'I shall take my supper this evening at The Sun here in Fish Street – if you think of joining me to continue our conversation, you shall be most welcome indeed.'*

'My master waits,' she said, and began walking away. When she got to the low door of the bakery with the sign hanging above it, she turned and suddenly called out,

'What time do you take your supper, sir?'

'Nine of the hour, madam,' he called back.

She nodded and reached for the handle of the door.

'My name is Joseph,' he cried. *'Joseph Fairtree.'*

She opened the front door and was gone.

Chapter Seven

Instead of taking the Central line back out to Ealing on Wednesday evening, Henry takes the City line from Bank to Waterloo and joins the early evening commuters staring passively up at the black departures board on the concourse. He sees there's a train to Wandsworth Town in five minutes and he queues patiently to get through the ticket barrier and on to the platform. Normally he would be getting enraged by now; there's nothing worse for him than being caught up in rush hour commuter land in this unremitting summer heat: the unpleasant press of soft human bodies, the inane chatter into mobile phones, the sour smell of sweat. But tonight he's got a first session with a therapist – or the head doctor, as he had described her to Evie – and he's determined to remain calm and relaxed so he doesn't start sweating into the armpits of his sand-coloured linen suit. He likes to make a good impression on arrival, wherever he is.

Evie was surprised when Henry had told her last week that he'd booked this session, but she was encouraging and let him talk about it.

'I just find it harder for that happy face I put on in the morning to last me the day like it used to,' he said to her at Jamies, before the wine had made him sentimental. 'You know, smile and the world smiles with you. All that.'

'I know,' she said. 'You were always great at that, Henry.'

'It was just a trick though. Even back then, it was just a trick. I didn't like people then any more or any less than I do now – present company excepted – it's just that I took a practical approach: if I'm surrounded by the bastards, I might as well make the best of them. And it used to work, really: put on that smile in the morning, and the day turns out all right. It's just that it doesn't work any more. I'm not having another go at you, love. It's me. I'm getting old and bitter. All I can think about is selling this sodding business and going to live in some place in the sunshine, Spain or something. I'll play tennis two or three times a week with some fellows at the local club and at the end of the game I'll nod and say thank you and take my leave and I'll have some lunch in a bar and watch the sport and in the evening, I'll read Dickens and watch the sport channel and that's how I'll live. I don't want to spend time with human beings any more, I'm not going to end up living in bloody Totnes with that woman for the rest of my life. I just want to be left alone, play a bit of tennis, sit in the sun. And I thought about it last week, I thought: if that's my idea of what I want, what seems like a good life to me, then that's pretty fucked up, isn't? So that's why I'm going to see the head doctor.'

At Wandsworth Town he turns right and heads over towards the south bank of the river between Wandsworth Bridge and Battersea Bridge. The therapist he'd found online had given him one of those new London addresses: an apartment in somewhere called Cobalt House which is part of the improbably named Bowline Quay Development. He's given himself plenty of time so he doesn't arrive ruffled but he's starting to get concerned that all these glassy blocks look the same. Cobalt House is supposed to be off Horizon Road and he's just passed a sign saying that's the road he's in but it feels like he's stepped through a mirror into an estate agent's brochure: it's all low-level limestone and concrete boxes with ash-coloured trees and plastic-looking shrubs, the apartment blocks loom over him with their tinted balconies, here and there young people with clean skin and optimistic faces walk purposefully to and fro. Inevitably, the layout of the blocks has created competing wind tunnels and the sudden gusts of summer breeze make Henry fretful; the unexpected presence of wind in the city often leaves him feeling vulnerable, reminded somehow that there are forces he can't control. A marble channel between two of the buildings is filled with fast-flowing water and he follows its path. The water is clear and the marble is a shiny cream colour. There must be a motor in it somewhere to keep circulating the water and to enable it to make the gurgling stream sound which the architects thought would add authenticity. Henry is flagging and he considers sitting down on the stone beside the pretend river but then he looks up and sees a sign saying Cobalt House and across the white flag-stones there's another block with two young people in running gear walking out through the glass doors.

Upstairs on the fourteenth floor, the door to the apartment is opened by a woman with short blonde hair and glasses. She smiles.

'Henry,' she says, and steps back to let him in. 'Nice to meet you.'

She walks back into the apartment and he follows.

'Have a seat,' she says, 'I'm just going to get my notepad.'

Once she has left the room, he walks across to the floor-to-ceiling window and looks out over the Thames. One of the passenger ferries is speeding up river and coming the other way is one of those party boats with tiny figures up on the top deck dancing. He watches them for a moment, then turns away irritably. He looks around the flat – steel-framed chairs and sofa, a dark wood bookcase filled with neatly stacked books, a round glass dining table in the corner.

The woman reappears, carrying a tray with a jug of water and two glasses. Henry notices also the box of tissues, which makes him wince.

'Nice place you've got here, um, doctor,' he says.

'Thank you, Henry,' she says, passing him a glass of water. 'Just call me Alice, it's easier.' She sits down in one of the chairs and he takes another, the other side of the glass coffee table.

'Cheers,' he says. 'Death to the enemies of Yorkshire.'

She smiles thinly.

'I'm a Dorset girl,' she says. 'But I don't think we've got any feud with Yorkshire.' She opens the pad on her lap. 'Take your jacket off if you're warm,' she says. 'This heatwave is just never going to end.'

He stands up again, takes the linen jacket off and drapes it over the back of one of the dining table chairs. As he sits back down, self-consciously holding his stomach in, he takes a glimpse at the therapist while she writes something in the pad and then underlines it. Probably mid forties, he thinks. Quite trim.

'I've never lived in one of these new places,' he says. 'How long you been here?'

'Oh, a while.'

She looks at him calmly but doesn't say anything.

'Must be an interesting job,' he says.

'What would you like to talk about, Henry? I would have you down as a City man.'

'Guilty as charged. Oiling the wheels of industry.'

'And do you like the oiling?'

He shrugs.

'We all do what we can I suppose.'

'Maybe,' she says. 'Is that what you do, what you can?'

'Well, we all turn out to be something, I suppose.'

'And how did you turn out, Henry?'

He looks away for a moment, back out through the huge glass windows to London spread out below them.

'Disappointed, if I'm honest,' he says after a while.

There's another pause, then she says, 'What was it you were hoping for?'

'Oh I don't know. I suppose over the years that changes, doesn't it? When I was a lad in Yorkshire, I wanted to play for Leeds. I wasn't particularly disappointed when that didn't happen, they weren't as glamorous as those bastards in Manchester. Then you get into minor and major targets, don't you? Getting off with the best-looking girl in school, not getting off with her but making her laugh, getting your first pay packet, scoring the winning try for the rugby. When you're young, unless you're bloody Bill Gates, you don't have much of a life plan, I don't think. You get a job, you play rugby, you get married, you find out your wife can't have children and you don't really mind that because that's another expense shelved, then you start thinking those holidays in the Caribbean in the back of the *Sunday Times* look tasty so you work out how to get the money in to pay for that, then you want to go for three weeks, not two, then after a few flights out there you land one time and you think, "Is this all there is?" You know, like the song. So you set up a business and you spend more time away from home and you meet someone you click with, I mean, really click with and then you fuck up again and you start wondering how many times you can go through all this. What was I hoping for? Absolutely no idea. I just know I didn't get it.'

Henry's upper lip is damp with perspiration again and his fists are clenched. Alice doesn't say anything.

'I mean, obviously that's just pathetic,' he continues. 'I mean, I'm not trying to complain, I'm not that stupid. I know I live a privileged life, I could be trying to fight my way onto a fucking rubber inflatable in the dark in Calais harbour. I know that. I suppose it's just that, I'd like to know now, if this is it, in which case I'll just get used to it, or if there's some way I can, I don't know...'

'Make it better?' she asks.

He nods. 'Yes, I guess so.'

'And how do you think you might make it better?'

'Money used to do the trick. You get money, you can buy an Aston Martin, you can drive to the south of France, you can drink good wine, you can score decent coke.'

'Why not do that, then? Is money an issue?'

'Well, it's not quite as visible as it used to be. But I'm not sure it is the answer. Evie – she's the one I clicked with, by the way, before I fucked it all up – she went to see some bloody Buddhist yesterday evening, that's her answer. I can't be doing with that, it's bad enough my bloody wife and all her mates in Totnes clanging their wretched yoga gongs. But Evie seems to think there's something wrong with her life, with living here in London, with working for me, with… well, I don't think that.'

'You don't think what?'

'I don't think there's anything wrong with her and me.'

'But she does?'

'Yes.'

'What do you think, Henry?'

'That I miss her.'

'Ah. So it's Evie who could make it better. Are you sure it's as simple as that?'

'Is that wrong?'

Alice shrugs her shoulders. 'No idea,' she says. 'It

just seems quite a responsibility this Evie has got, to ease your disappointment.'

Henry bristles. 'Well, it's not like that, is it? It's not about me wanting her to sort me out. It's about me wanting us both to get what we want. What used to make us happy.'

'But doesn't Evie have a say in that?'

'Of course she has a bloody say in it!' he exclaims. 'I'm just saying, if I could work out a way to enable the both of us to get back the good stuff, the good life we had together, then that's got to be the right thing for both of us, hasn't it?'

'I don't know, Henry,' Alice said, calmly. 'Let's try and unpick that without making you too upset.'

'I'm not upset!' Henry shouts, and he stands up and walks over to the window.

'I prefer my consultations to remain seated if you don't mind, Henry,' Alice says.

He stands with his back to her for a moment, looking out over the river, almost quivering with anger. Then he flinches his shoulders, turns round and heads back to his chair.

'Sorry,' he says, more quietly this time.

'There's no need to apologise, Henry,' she says. 'We're working together, we're doing the work. This is how it goes sometimes. But let's try and keep some calm here. All I was trying to ask you was whether you had considered that Evie's solution might not be the same as yours and if that is the case – I'm not saying it is – but if it is the case, then perhaps it would be good to consider strategies for combating your disappointment which don't rely on her.'

'What, like I try learning a foreign language or I start volunteering at the local hospice? Maybe I could join the fucking Ramblers?'

'I don't know, Henry. Those all seem quite solution-focused ideas. I was thinking more about taking some time to analyse your feelings of disappointment.'

'Oh, give it a break,' he mutters. His head drops. Alice sits quietly opposite him. Neither of them says anything for a while. Then he looks up. His upper lip glistens angrily.

'No, actually I don't want to take some time to do that,' he snarls. 'In fact, I think that's bullshit. I think what I need to do is get hold of some money and rent an Aston and take Evie to Nice or Paris or Madrid and stay in a bloody good hotel and lock ourselves in for the weekend with some champagne, some good coke and bloody excellent room service.' He stands up, grabs his jacket from the chair. 'Sorry to have wasted your time.'

And he leaves.

Across town, over in Shoreditch, Linda Appiah punches the bag in the gym. She's wearing blue Nike shorts and training top and her white boxing shoes

come half way up her shins. She wears a blue headband
to catch some of the sweat, and the red cushioned
head armour she put on for the session she'd just had
with one of the girls in the ring. She ducks and feints
in front of the bag, throws two swift left jabs then
smashes into it with her right. Her feet pad steadily,
none of the pathetic dancing some of the City boys
do to pretend they're pros. She joined this gym when
she moved to Kings Cross last year. It's OK; just off
Brick Lane, it's an old traditional gym but there's more
self-conscious types in it than she's used to. Feet on
the ground, back on her heels as she drops her right
shoulder, forward as she lands a right hook into the
bag, bends her knees, jabs. Her gym in Edmonton
where she learned to box was a community place and
she misses it. Her dad first took her there when she
was twelve – they were offering Tai Kwundo classes
and he wanted her to learn self-protection. But it was
the guys in the ring who caught her attention: close
up, their boxing was like a slow, violent dance and
the sound of their rapid exhalations and explosions of
self-protective breath entranced the little girl. She
sways in front of the bag, left to right, then leans in
and pushes it, steps aside to allow it swing by her, then
next time lets off a volley of left and right jabs that
leave her whistling the breath out of her lungs. She
spent her teenage years in that sweaty, stripped-down
place but even though she misses it, she's getting used

to living in town. It's convenient: she ended her shift at Upper Thames Street at three today and the gym's only a ten-minute cycle from there.

She moves away from the punchbag, wraps a towel around her neck and takes off the headgear then wipes the sweat from her face. She slowly undoes the laces on her gloves then the protective bandages on each hand, watching the two Greek guys helping each other to lift weights. One of them, the one whose black hair is lacquered back over his head even more ostentatiously than the other's, looks over at her and nods. She nods back.

'Nice work, Theo,' she says. 'Tell me when you need a hand with those heavy weights.'

He smiles and she picks up a skipping rope. While she's skipping, which is her last routine today, she thinks about her dad. She's going to meet that financial consultant in an hour to talk about his money but the other thing she's got on her mind is his book. He's been writing a political history of Ghana but he's been writing it for ten years now and she wants him to get it published. She's proud of her dad's intelligence and academic credentials but she's always been the practical one; he's lived inside ideas and theories but sometimes you just have to act. Linda is strong on affirmative action. She's going to find him a publisher.

Half an hour later Linda is wheeling her bike up a one-way street. Shoreditch is like a cartoon version of everything that's happening to London: boys with beards and plaid shirts setting up coffee shops and internet businesses, girls with firm tanned sexless bodies talking to each other about rental yields and natural antihistamine lotions. I could go on forever about how ridiculous Shoreditch is but everyone else does too so it's not very interesting and anyway Linda doesn't think like that, she's a live-and-let-live person; if I'm honest, I'd prefer to have her approach to life than mine but we are what we are, as Henry might say.

At the end of the street she pedals away and her dark hair flows over the white shirt she's got tucked into her jeans. She rounds the City Road roundabout and heads back towards St Paul's; it's ten to six and she's due to meet Evie at Jamie's Wine Bar at six. There's plenty of time, she doesn't want to push the bike in this heat, especially after she's spent twenty minutes cooling down in a cold shower in the gym. She wants to get her dad's money sorted out – he refuses to talk about it, says he won't entertain bourgeois conventions about accumulated capital – but she knows across the various accounts, he has a couple of hundred thousand, mainly going back to insurance policies from the time of her mother's death. She needs to get him sorted out in case he will have to pay for care. Practical again.

And then there's this woman, Evie. There is

something about her, that brief conversation in that scruffy little office when she was doing the rounds with Steve. A bit older than Linda, something cool about her, something which sets her apart from all the other office workers. She isn't gay, that is obvious – or at least, Evie doesn't think she's gay. Linda's gaydar is pretty accurate these days and she can tell that Evie thinks of herself as straight. She isn't a classic beauty but there is something very attractive about her and something also in those brown eyes that is interesting. She is handsome, not beautiful. Linda likes handsome women.

Evie is already sitting at a table inside Jamies when Linda walks in. She's looking at her phone, glass of wine in front of her, and Linda walks up:

'Hi, Linda Appiah.'

Evie looks up.

'Oh, hi Linda, sorry' – putting the phone down – 'Evie Sangster. What can I get you?'

Linda sits down, smiling.

'I'll have what you're having. And some tap water please, just come from the gym.'

'Oh God, don't make me feel bad. Don't tell me, you're really disciplined and you go three times a week.'

'Four actually,' and they both laugh. Evie gets up and walks to the bar to order the wine and Linda watches her. As she walks back through the tables, Evie remembers what Darren said in the office and how he and Jade were laughing about it and it suddenly makes her feel self-conscious. She sits back down.

'On its way. So, your dad?'

'Straight to business!'

'Sorry.'

'That's OK. I'm not a small talk person either really.'

Linda tells her about her dad, about how he's showing some early signs of dementia, about how she's trying to get him to a memory clinic and she's worried about his future if it gets worse. She tells Evie what money she thinks her dad has and where it's kept and she explains that most of it came from when her mum died. Evie looks up from her pad where she's been writing notes:

'Oh my God, I'm so sorry. In a fire? How old were you?'

Linda shrugs. 'Ten.'

'Oh no. What happened?'

Linda tells her the story of how she and her dad came back from ten pin bowling to find their house in flames.

'And yet you...'

'Work for the Brigade? I know. Everyone seems to think that's weird. Everyone apart from me.'

'I'm sorry, I didn't mean...'

'It's OK. I know. It seems strange to people. But when it's happened to you, it's different. Fight fire with fire, that's me.'

This image is suddenly so overwhelming for Evie that she can't think what to say and instead she takes a gulp of wine. She has this image of a burning house in her mind and this woman opposite her just a little girl, standing holding her dad's hand, watching the flames. And then she thinks about William Cecil and how she told him that she feared she wanted the sun to burn her up.

'Obviously we don't fight fire with fire, we fight it with fire retardant foam usually but you know what I mean. Are you all right?'

Linda leans forward and puts her hand on Evie's hand. Evie looks down at it, then leans over into her bag to rummage for a tissue, dabs her eye.

'Sorry. I've just been a bit...I don't know, a bit different recently,' she says. Oh God, she thinks, here I go again. 'It's something to do with fire, I can't really explain it.'

Linda sits back and picks up her own glass. 'Tell me if you want.'

'Oh God, this is the second time in a week I've done this,' Evie says and laughs nervously.

'Done what?'

'Turned a business meeting into a counselling session.'

'You can't have had more counselling than me. I must have the world record. Tell me about it if you want.'

'The thing is, I don't know what *it* is,' Evie says. 'It's just sometimes, I just don't know why I'm doing anything. I mean, I'm good at what I do. I can help you and your dad, that's not the problem. But I feel like I'm sleepwalking, I feel like I don't really know what the point of it is anymore.'

'That doesn't sound so good.'

'No. I was talking to this client last week, I was supposed to be talking about his investments and I ended up telling him I thought about the sun burning me up. He's a very strange guy.'

'There's a few of them in this town.'

'He's some kind of Buddhist. I went to a talk he did actually. Last night. There's something creepy about him, something not right about his set-up. He was quite aggressive to me at the end. Anyway, I thought maybe it was him that made me blurt all that stuff out when I first went to see him, but now here I am again, going off on one, boring you. I'm really sorry.'

'You don't have to be sorry and you're not boring me. It's OK, I don't think you're not capable of helping my dad out.'

Evie takes another sip of wine then looks at Linda.

'Do you ever feel like that? Like everything's going to end? I bet you don't.'

Linda laughs.

'Why? Do I look like Superwoman?'

'Now you mention it, you do slightly.'

There's a slight silence then as they both lift glasses to lips, looking at each other over the rims.

'I was lucky,' Linda says. 'That's one of the things I learned in therapy. When something terrible happens to you, if you're helped like I was to think about it then you learn a lot about yourself. One of my counsellors said that tragedy can deliver happiness in a way that normal life sometimes can't. I mean, it depends, we're all different. But maybe if my mum hadn't died, I'd be someone now that couldn't be here talking to you like this.'

'I can't imagine that. I can't imagine how I'd feel if my mum and dad weren't around.'

'Well, they obviously are and yet you're wanting the sun to burn you up. How does that work?'

'I don't know.'

'Sorry, I'm being a bit crude.'

'No, I like it,' says Evie. She looks at her. 'I'm just not used to not feeling in control. Do you know what I mean?'

'If that's how you feel. I'm not big on control. I'm more reactive. My dad says I'm obsessively practical.'

Evie laughs. 'He sounds all right, your dad. Mine is too. He thinks I should leave my job.'

'Why?'

'Oh, it's a long story.'

'I can get us more wine.'

So Evie tells Linda the story about Stirling Global, about her and Henry, about Malawi water processing and the five months in Holloway. Linda listens and doesn't interrupt her until eventually Evie stops.

'So there we are. I've bored you too now,' says Evie.

'You need to stop all this running yourself down,' says Linda. 'It's not cool.'

'Oh.'

'I'm guessing you don't normally go around dissing yourself?'

'No, I don't. That's what I don't get: I don't know what's the matter with me.'

'What did your Buddhist tell you?'

'William Cecil? I don't know. Nothing really. Not much. Some stuff, but he's...there's something odd about him. That talk he did, it was strange. He wants me to go and see him again but, I don't know...I don't think I want to. There's something not right about him.'

'So what do you think?'

'About what?'

'About you. Why do you think you want the sun to burn you up?'

'Oh I don't know. Maybe I just need to make some changes.'

'From the sound of that arsehole you work for, you could start there.'

Evie raises her eyebrows. 'That's what my friend Joy says.'

'Well, she's right, isn't she?'

'I don't know. I can't just blame him. He didn't do anything wrong.'

This time it's Linda who raises her eyebrows.

'Now you're all disapproving,' Evie says. 'Honestly, the Malawi thing wasn't his fault. It wasn't as simple as that.'

'I like keeping things simple,' Linda says. 'It's easier.'

'My life used to be simple. In Ibiza it was simple. Even with Henry in the early days it was simple. We just used to…I don't know. We just used to enjoy ourselves. It was uncomplicated. He's funny and he's kind and deep down he's not the complete prick that he pretends to be. My mum liked him. He just can't help himself, sometimes. But it wasn't his fault, it was my fault I ended up in prison again. They were all my decisions, my mistakes. Only now I feel like I've lost my bearings.'

'So you're all at sea and you've lost your bearings, maybe that's why you keep looking at the sun. Isn't that what sailors do when their compass breaks?'

'Yeah, and eventually they throw themselves overboard.'

'Well that's not going to happen, Evie Sangster,' Linda says and she reaches out again and puts her hand on Evie's and Evie looks down at it and likes it there. Then she feels her eyes welling up and she tries to stop it but can't.

'Oh God.' She pulls her hand away and dives into her handbag for a tissue, wipes her eyes.

'You're a good person, Evie,' Linda says. 'You're just not very smart at looking after yourself.'

'Thanks,' Evie sniffs. 'For being nice.'

'I'm not being nice. Nice isn't my thing. I'm just telling you.'

It's quite a revelation for Evie having someone being so direct with her. Even her mum and dad tiptoe around her a bit and even though Joy tells her what she thinks, gives her a bit of her mind, this is different: Linda just says stuff straight, as though it's obvious.

While they talk, Angel is upstairs in the Stirling Global office and his phone is going. It's William Cecil again. He switches off the hoover and swipes the phone.

'Hello?' His voice is nervous.

'Well? Did you tell your wife?'

William Cecil's voice is calm, authoritative and implacable. Angel is agitated.

'Yes, Mr Cecil, but she is confused about...'

'I am not interested in her state of mind, Angel,' Cecil interrupts him coldly. 'Did you tell her what I told you to tell her?'

That morning, after the girls had gone to school and Marta had left to do a day's shift at the café in the indoor market at Seven Sisters, Angel had received several phone calls from William Cecil as he was getting ready to set out for work. Cecil had insisted that he call in to Marta's work on the way and tell her that their lives were going to change, they were going to change for the good, he had found a protector for them who was going to help them get the money to escape London and start a new life, somewhere where neither of them would have to work their fingers to the bone for pennies, somewhere where the girls could grow up in safety.

In all honesty, Angel hadn't made such a great job of it. Ever since he attended the talk last week, Cecil has been in constant communication with him and Angel's all over the place now – all he knows is that he has to do what Cecil tells him. Otherwise Cecil gets angry and that scares Angel. So he'd parked the Nissan in a side street by Seven Sisters tube this morning and he'd rushed in to the market, squeezed his way through the narrow aisles bedecked with international phone cards and lycra leggings outfits and had surprised Marta, who was behind the counter of the café, serving plates of rice to three Colombian men. He'd beckoned her over, wide-eyed and nervous and had gabbled to her about William Cecil and how he was going to help them change their lives and things were all going to get better for them.

'But Angel, I don't understand,' Marta had whispered, looking around her to check that her boss wasn't watching.

'You don't need to understand! You just trust me. Everything is going to be OK.'

Now his hand is shaking as he listens to William Cecil on the phone in Henry's office.

'You are a Luohan, Angel,' Cecil is saying, much more calmly now. 'You have been chosen. I have chosen you. You are one of the eighteen Luohans, the special ones, the perfect ones. Do you understand how privileged you are? How remarkable you are? Great things are going to happen to you. Great things. You are a warrior, Angel. You are strong. You are powerful. You will perform your task with grace and with authority and, in return, you will be rewarded beyond your dreams. When the time is right – soon, Angel, very soon – you will be given your task and your new life will begin, a new life for you, for your wife, for your children. You are special, Angel. You have been chosen. Do you understand?'

'Yes, Mr Cecil,' Angel says. He's still now and calm again – Cecil has this effect on him when he speaks to him like this.

'That is good Angel. I am pleased. Now, tomorrow Chan will come and see you when you are working and he will deliver more instructions to you. I will telephone you to make sure you have received them and you understand them. Good night.'

With that the phone line goes dead and for a moment

Angel stands in silence in the middle of Henry's office, the hoover handle still in one hand and the phone in the other. He is very scared.

Jade isn't scared. She's across town in Darren's flat in Clerkenwell, naked and on all fours on his kitchen floor. It turns out Darren is a bit of an S and M specialist and while Jade hasn't done any of that before, she's quite up for it. When they'd shut his front door behind them, he'd just said 'Strip' and he'd watched while she took all her clothes off, looking straight back at him as she did so.

'Get on your hands and knees,' he'd said and she did. 'You can choose your name. You can be either Pig or Dog.'

'Pig,' she said, and giggled.

'Don't laugh,' he said, 'it stops it working.'

He put a dog chain around her slim neck and walked her around the flat and now they're in the kitchen and he's doing a line of coke off the top of the fridge while she gives him a blow job.

'Good Pig,' he says and sniffs. Then he lays a line down on the kitchen floor and hands her the rolled-up twenty pound note and she hoovers it up.

He stands back and admires her.

'You know, Pig, you've got an ass to drive a man mad.' Then he leans over her. 'What are those marks on your leg?'

She turns around so the scars from her last cutting

are not on view to him and says,

'Nothing.'

'Nothing Master,' he says, and she laughs and so does he.

It was eleven-thirty when Lily entered Farriner's Bakery on Pudding Hill once more. The smell of freshly cooked ship's biscuits filled the shop and Hannah, her master's daughter, was piling them up on the counter. She looked up angrily as Lily stepped in.

'Had I not had a care, these biscuits would have burned. What keeps you on such a simple task, dolt?'

'There were affrays up by St Paul's, ma'am, and Doleberry's was filled with grand men demanding tobacco.'

Hannah looked over at her father, whose large frame was squeezed into an armchair in the corner.

'She is an idle huss, Father,' she snarled. 'Why we have a cripple for our maid I do not countenance.'

'What affrays, girl?' he demanded.

Lily laid the flask of treacle down on the counter.

'There was a gentleman being beaten by some of the black hats and there was talk of fighting out in the Channel.'

'Why do you think we make such a stock of biscuits, oaf?' Hannah yelled. 'The King's ships be returning tomorrow from their victory and they will surely need stock.'

'*Why was the gentleman being beaten?*' continued *Farriner.*

'*There was talk of papery, sir,*' said *Lily uncertainly.*

'*She spends the morning talking while I, your daughter, do the work for which she's paid,*' *Hannah said, pointing viciously at Lily with the oven slice.*

'*Pour me some Treacle, child,*' said *Farriner and Lily walked across the shop and through a door into the kitchen to fetch a glass. As she came back in, the baker waved his hand at her impatiently and she limped back over to the counter to the flask.*

'*These be upraising times,*' *he said after he had swallowed the black liquid with a grimace. 'Papists, Hogens, the Spaniard, the Frenchman – there are dangers afoot. It makes my gripe the worse.*'

'*The port you drink from Mister Berry does the greater part of that,*' *his daughter sniffed and as Lily came around the counter to attend to the empty baking trays, she grabbed her ear and twisted it.*

'*Your days be numbered,*' *she hissed and Lily's eyes watered with the pain. 'I will see you out on the street before this month is gone. Then shall you find your true employment, with Mother Midnight in her bawdy house. A pox on you.*'

'*Ah, leave the simpleton be,*' *the old man sighed.*

Lily carried the trays into the kitchen and set them in the large enamel sink then went to fill the firepot with water. She thought about the earnest stranger with the dark hat and the serious, respectful countenance as her mistress continued to shout at her father in the gloomy shop.

Chapter Eight

An hour after the end of his not very successful therapy session, Henry walks out of Ealing Common tube, his nose twitching at the sweetly decayed smell of weed coming off the two kids ahead of him. They soon peel off into Ealing Common to spend the evening getting wasted on a park bench but Henry plods on down the Uxbridge Road towards the flat he bought thirty years ago as an optimistic single Northern accountant relishing life in the big city.

His disappointment burns inside him, he can't tell any more whether that sour twist in his guts is a semi-permanent indigestion arising from all the cheap bottles in Jamies or if his blood just runs hot with frustration at his own failings. Angrily, he kicks an empty coke can, says 'Fuck' to no one in particular. Why can't he fix things? That bloody therapist with her so-intelligent glasses, what the hell did she know about life, about scrabbling around in the dirt like him and so many others, turning up every day just to try and keep everything going, keeping those bloody plates spinning? How could you possibly tell anyone anything useful by just sitting so primly in that perfect glass box in that ridiculous private estate with your expensive glasses and your Moleskine notebook? He's furious with himself for going to see her, he wishes he'd just dobbed the hundred and fifty quid to the Big Issue bloke he buys from every week. Sometimes he can feel the pressure in his veins so strongly, his head is throbbing in this awful heat. Why won't it bloody rain?

It seems obvious to him that the glories of his relationship with Evie – the sex, the communication, the understanding, the sheer pride he felt in having this tremendous woman with him in so many different London scenarios – were all facilitated by one thing: financial success. When they first got it together, Stirling Global was actually making decent money, with clients like Bernie Richmond entrusting their savings to him because in those days Bernie and others hadn't fully grasped how incompetent Henry actually was as a financial adviser. Then the Malawi opportunity came up and the cash just poured in for a bit, enabling him and Evie to really live it up – he did hire an Aston more than once, they did drive down to the south of France.

So the only mistake he made was to let Evie write an email which went beyond what, in the eyes of the Financial Conduct Authority, it was acceptable to say to a retired surgeon like Mr Abbas about an ostensibly excellent, ethical and commercially sound plan to refine unclean water in Malawi. That was it! He's worked in the City all his life, all these big firms with their big lawyers and their PR agencies, they're all just selling Malawi water refining schemes really. What was the DotCom bubble all about, then? What about all those companies which the big glass-clad corporations persuade pension funds to invest in which go bust? It's all a lottery, that's the reality, he thinks. There wasn't anything wrong with the Malawi thing, it just didn't happen to work. So one small slip and this fantastic relationship which both he and Evie had, the good times they shared, went up the swanny. He suddenly feels a surge of excitement that he has found the key to unlock the crisis in his relationship with Evie. Why didn't he think of it before? All he needs to do is find a new scheme that will bring in the money and this time he'll make sure he's all over it like a rash, he'll get everyone proper training.

He stops to let two women dressed in black burkas and pushing prams pass him on the pavement – he looks back at them for a moment, looks around the tired landscape of Uxbridge Road with its limp trees, old cars parked on both sides, dirty grey houses all cut up into cramped apartments and he thinks that maybe they could escape, maybe he and Evie could finally escape.

There he goes again, Henry, with his relentless hope. He doesn't get it that hope is a broken currency in London these days. Hope was what filled all those hearts manning boats entering the Thames estuary down by Two Tree Island over the centuries, hope is what drove the Dutch Jewish cigar makers who left their homes for the Spitalfields streets in the second half of the nineteenth century, hope built that loopy Skylon tower on the South Bank in 1951 for the Festival of Britain. Hope is innocent but London is rinsing its streets of it now and Henry, because he's not a very analytical man, just can't identify the antiseptic stink washing the pale limestone piazzas of his adopted city.

Which is why the next day he's sitting in his favourite City club, the Exchange, in one of the lanes off King William Street. The Exchange has a fading grandeur with a wood-panelled lounge bar decorated with gaudy oil paintings of unattractive City types from the fifties. The bar is managed by an Estonian blonde who wears pencil skirts and black heels and the restaurant upstairs serves fatty rare beef with Yorkshire pudding and chemically-enhanced gravy. The membership has been declining rapidly in the face of competition from priapic money altars like the Ned Club over on Poultry and the Malaysian company which bought the

Exchange a few years ago are paying a lobbyist to convince the City of London Corporation to let them knock it down and build a new glass office block.

Henry obviously likes the Exchange because it's one of a number of totemic places that encourage him to believe that he has a useful function. Now it's twelve-thirty and he's sitting on the shiny brown button leather sofa and his pin-striped trousers have ridden up just enough to reveal pale white shins above short grey socks and he's talking to Darren Hegarty and a wiry little man with an alert, rat-like expression, thinning dark hair and a well-fitting blue suit with a silk cloth tucked into the breast pocket.

'The bond market's over-exposed,' the man is saying. 'There's going to be a big failure next year and that will set off all the others. Too many of them aren't delivering the revenues to cover the coupons, everyone knows that and as soon as one goes...'

'Bang,' says Henry. 'Classic domino.'

'Exactly. Property's fucked short term, the Chinese have locked in London rental yields for the next five years and tech stocks are all moving to France. There's no money here, Henry, you know that, you're on the ground. You know the way things are going.'

Henry nods thoughtfully.

'You're right,' he says. 'The glory days are over.'

'For the moment,' the man says. 'They'll be back. They always come back. Fortune favours the brave and it favours the tough fuckers who can hold their cards.'

Henry nods again, pleased with his companion's implied praise.

'So what's next?' asks Darren.

The man turns to look at him.

'Good question, Darren.'

The man's name is Felix Berrenger and he is like one of those gaudy, dazzling dragonflies that hover over a filthy pool of water in a municipal park, their bold and assured colours reflected in the oily surface of the stinking puddle. Men like Felix – they're almost always men, although I think with what I know now from putting this story down I could give him a run for his money – have a lightness of presence which renders them almost unreachable: they never have offices, their business cards are bland and uncertain and they always refer to "my team" and "my guys" and "we" when in fact there is only ever one of them, operating out of some obscure rented flat in Wimbledon when they're not sipping rum and cokes in the Clipper Bar in Puerto Banús.

It was Felix, of course, who introduced Henry to the Malawi deal a few years ago and Henry considers himself lucky – no, he actually is convinced it's a portent – that last night when he rang Felix's number from his flat, Felix answered and told him yes, he was in town and although he and his team were very busy on a major deal, he would find time to meet up with Henry at the Exchange.

'What's next depends on you guys,' Felix continues. 'Your appetite. Are you hungry enough?'

'I wouldn't worry about our appetite, Felix,' says Henry, patting his stomach. 'We know how to look after ourselves.'

'I know that. That's the only reason I took the time out of my crazy schedule to come and see you today. Stirling World is a class act, everyone knows that.'

'Stirling Global,' says Darren.

'Yeah,' says Felix.

'Look,' says Henry, 'I'm up for a bigger play, I've got my reasons and I'm ready to go larger but I can't have any mistakes like last time.'

'That was unfortunate,' says Felix. 'That girl of yours, what was she called?'

'Evie,' Henry replies.

'Evie. Good operator. Unfortunate, what happened. That publicity killed the water business, it was going gangbusters till then.'

'I thought that business was all a bit fucked up?' Darren queries.

'Fucked up? Fucked up? You think changing the lives of millions of Africans is fucked up?' asks Felix, wide-eyed in astonishment. 'They were on course to get that refining plant operational, could have transformed the entire continent, Darren. No more drought, no more News At Ten stories about villagers walking for hundreds of miles to find water, no more photographs of African kids with their ribs sticking out.' He shakes his head. 'The FCA thing with your girl, that just put the kybosh on it, they had no alternative but to stop operations. Damn shame. Me and my wife, we were going to adopt this Malawi kid too.'

'Didn't know you were married, Felix,' Henry says.

'Hmm,' Felix says. 'Anyway, look, I've got to get back over to Canary Wharf, we're closing the deal on the American partnership – got a signing session at JP Morgan, fucking paperwork, Jesus.'

'JP Morgan,' Henry repeats. 'Impressive.'

'That's what I mean Henry: everything's a lot bigger now. Look, we haven't signed the UK licence yet, I can hold the guys off for a few days but you're going to have to be quick. This will all be tied up as sweet as a baby by the weekend – Philip Green will take it but I've got history with you guys, I'm going to tell the team they have to wait to see your offer first.'

Henry shakes his head.

'Philip Green's a good operator,' he says. 'But he's been out in Monaco too long, he doesn't have his ear to the ground here like we have.'

'Exactly,' says Felix.

'So what is it?' asks Darren.

Felix turns and looks directly at the younger man. 'What is it?' He turns to look at Henry. 'You didn't tell him, Henry?'

'Well,' Henry says. 'I wasn't sure...'

'I'll tell you, Darren,' Felix interrupts. 'And in doing so, I make you an insider. I wouldn't do that with any other team. I'm offering Stirling World the UK licence for the fastest-growing franchise in the whole of Western Europe.' He pauses for a moment, looks from Darren to Henry and back to Darren. 'Gener8,' he says finally, lowering his voice with an almost reverential air. 'G-E-N-E-R-and the number 8. The only baby's milk formula with 8 proprietary ingredients which boost kids' intelligence by 25%. It's a spin-off from the NASA space programme in Florida.'

'Unbelievable,' says Henry, nodding and smiling. He pokes Darren in the ribs. 'What did I tell you? Welcome to the future.'

Meanwhile, back at the office there's just Evie and Jean. Rufus and Jimmy have gone out to get a sandwich with Jade. Jean is nibbling at a Croque Monsieur she heated up in the kitchen and reading the online version of Hello magazine at her PC. Evie is trying to draft an email to Linda about her dad's finances but she hasn't got much further than a convoluted apology for talking too much about herself in Jamies last night. Finally she gives up and sits back in her chair.

'What am I doing here, Jean?' she asks.

'Paying the rent, love, like all of us,' says Jean without

looking up.

'I haven't got any rent. I own my flat.'

'Lucky you.'

'I mean, what am I doing here?'

Jean looks up and takes another bite of her Croque Monsieur.

'Come on Jean,' Evie continues, 'you know as well as I do that this place can't last long. Look at it.'

She sweeps her arm around her.

'It's a bloody dump.'

'What's with you?' Jean asks. 'Do you want me to change the cleaner? We only started with a new one a couple of weeks ago. I can get the agency to change him.'

'I don't mean that. You know what I mean. The company, it's on its last legs. You know that.'

'Well, it's seen better days,' Jean admits. 'But Henry's a survivor, he'll think of something.'

'Oh God,' says Evie, shutting her eyes.

Jean watches her, chewing her sandwich.

'It's not this place, love,' she says. 'This place has always been the same, you know that. Up and down.'

'What is it, then?' asks Evie, her eyes still closed.

Jean doesn't say anything, takes another bite of her food. After a while, she says,

'You know what I think? I think you need a holiday. It's not like you, being all ratty. You've been ratty for weeks.'

'Have I? Sorry.'

'Don't have to be sorry. We all get like it every now and then.'

Another pause while Jean continues to eat, then Evie opens her eyes.

'I think I might quit, Jean,' she says. 'I might tell Henry I'm leaving.'

'You can't do that love,' Jean says, looking concerned for the first time. 'What would Henry think? He'd be devastated.'

'Oh for God's sake, Jean, I'm not responsible for Henry!'

'I know, I know, sorry, I didn't mean it that way. But still...what do you want to leave for? It's not that bad, is it?'

'What's not that bad?'

'Working here. I know you two aren't, you know...'

'No we're not, Jean.'

'But it's still not bad, is it? Being here I mean? It's a job, isn't it?'

'I'm thirty-five years old, Jean. It's all right for you, you've got Barry and the family, the grandkids. What have I got to show for it? A bloody flat in Wapping.'

Jean looks at her.

'Henry would have you back in a second,' she says. 'You know that.'

'I don't bloody want Henry back!' Evie shouts.

'All right, all right,' Jean says. 'I'm just saying.'

'Well don't, Jean. Please, don't.'

At that moment the door opens and Jade, Rufus and Jimmy shuffle into the office. Jade is smiling about something the three of them must have been talking about and Evie watches her as they all settle back into their desks. Jade's hair, the red mohican and the shaved back and sides, makes her stand out in this shabby little office like some kind of caged bird but she's still looking well-turned-out: she's wearing a thin summer dress with Doc Martens which somehow looks really good. Jade looks at Evie.

'You look cheerful,' she says.

Evie smiles wearily.

'You look nice,' she says and Jade looks embarrassed. 'Did you get on to that course?' Evie continues.

'Yeah, they can start me next week,' Jade replies.

Jade so far has set up a Stirling Global Facebook page, she's got them on Twitter and she's been teaching herself how to use LinkedIn because she read that's what business people should be using. She's even got as far as booking a photographer so that she can have professional photos taken of all the team so she can do them all LinkedIn profiles. Henry complained of course but he has submitted and Jade is writing his CV this afternoon so she can put up his profile. After that weekend at Leigh, she has applied for a government-funded course in word processing and IT which she can do in the afternoons at a day college in London Wall.

Jade is pretty doubtful about this whole thing of coming into Sterling Global, but it's the first time anyone has asked her to use her brain in years so she's giving it a go. She was so busy being bolshy, being smart, in Edmonton that once she left school at sixteen she almost deliberately avoided anything which required effort. It wasn't cool to make an effort. But now she's eight years older and even her best friend, Mikey, even he sometimes seems, well, just stupid. He's been taunting her about working in an office which does make her uncomfortable but she's sticking with it. In fact this week, her second in the office, Jade hasn't had any Diazepam or Xanax. When she came back from the weekend at Evie's parents, she woke up on the Monday morning feeling OK. She didn't have that rage of impulses surging in her which would normally have her reaching straight for those white pill packets. She even did an evening at home with her mum drinking tea and watching TV and of course Joy didn't comment on it, pretended that this was just what they normally did.

The door opens again and this time it's Henry and Darren. Darren winks at Jade as he walks round to his desk. It was good, their evening last night. Different. Darren made her laugh, and all that S&M stuff was just funny; she could already tell that Darren underneath it all is a softy. And she's never been taken in by softies, so she's not really particularly interested in him. His coke was good though, so she'll probably go out with him again. She's more intrigued about the meeting she's got coming up with William Cecil on Saturday morning. As if her life couldn't get any weirder at the moment, he phoned her while she was out with Rufus and Jimmy and was all polite, even charming, and invited her to come out for a boat ride on the Thames at the weekend.

'Although we hardly spoke at the talk,' Cecil had said, 'I was struck by your intelligence and attitude. Quite an unusual combination. I imagine you do not receive many invitations to come aboard a private cruiser on the Thames. It would be my privilege if that is the case to issue your first.'

Jade snaps out of it, realising Henry has started to talk to them all.

'Listen up, people,' Henry says, standing in the middle of the room. Henry is a devotee of the American cop show Hill Street Blues from the '80s. He pulls out a white cellophane package from his jacket pocket.

'Would anyone like to guess what this is?' he says, holding the packet up. 'Darren already knows.'

'Soup?' Jean asks.

'It's not soup, Jean,' says Henry. He's beside himself with excitement. 'Any other offers?'

'It's not...'

'No, Rufus, you muppet, it's not,' Henry says.

'Friends, Romans, Countrymen, let me introduce you to Gener8. Developed by the NASA Space Team at Cape Canaveral, this is one of only five samples of the Gener8 baby milk formula in this country. The other four are under lock and key in a safe at JP Morgan. This formula has been proven to boost the intelligence of newborn babies by 25%. It is' – and here his top lip starts quivering again – 'the most revolutionary food product to come on the market in a hundred years.'

'Wow,' says Jimmy, the only one in the room with young kids.

'And how have I come to possess this sample?' Henry asks, looking around the team and then finally settling on Evie. 'Because Stirling Global have just bought the licence to market Gener8 in the UK on an exclusive basis for the next five years. We're going to recruit a nationwide team of resellers who will get this remarkable product out into the market and make it the Number One baby food product in every shop in the country.'

'Oh God,' Evie murmurs and crosses her arms on the top of her desk and drops her head into it. 'Oh God.'

Do you know about Spanish Prisoner? It's an old story about money. The story, the way I tell it anyway, is set in the kind of heat that London was experiencing that summer but it's actually from Spain, medieval

Spain or something. It's all about some stupid, idealistic knight finding out that the most beautiful woman in the Kingdom is being held prisoner in a castle, and there's one old fellow who can steal the key for him to let him release her, but first the old fellow wants a few ducats before he'll go off and find the key. So the knight gives him a few coins, never sees the old fellow again, doesn't get the girl. And the moral of the story is, that the old fellow lives off the ducats he earns by tricking dupes into thinking he will find this non-existent key for this non-existent beautiful Princess. The knight is prepared to spend a few coins because the temptation of the glories and prizes awaiting him if he is the one to release the beautiful Princess makes the money seem irrelevant.

Evie knows the Spanish Prisoner story because an old con in Holloway told it to her one night. Spanish Prisoner is the oldest, most effective con in the world. You persuade someone to give you what seems like a little bit of money because they believe by doing so they are going to get a lot of money. They don't believe they're being conned because the person asking for it would surely be asking for much more money from them if they were conning them. The prospect of untold riches blinds them to the obvious truth that the operator is making a living by doing this to different people every day, taking a little bit of money every day from dorks like you.

Felix Berrenger, by selling Henry the UK rights to
Gener8 for £10,000, is doing the same thing. Henry
thinks that the big players – the ones who have those
boardroom tables the size of US aircraft carriers in
those glass skyscrapers – don't even recognise £10,000
as a real sum of money; they wouldn't even bother to
think about it. Which is why he signed the badly
printed A4 contract which Felix carelessly passed over
to him in the Exchange Club; if Felix was out to rob
him, he'd have asked him for £100,000. Evie knows
he's been kippered, Darren suspects the same but is
almost entirely focused on Jade's ass at the moment
and can think of little else.

Spanish Prisoner. Don't think you're above it, either.
We're all giving our ducats to the beggar hoping that
the fat bastard is going to get us out of our own individual hell hole.

Saturday afternoon at the bakery was always a favoured time for Lily, as her master's daughter Hannah would use that time to take in entertainment with her friends. Today, after Lily had served them both a stout lunch of mutton, Mistress Hannah stood in front of a looking glass smearing ceruse into the indentations in her cheeks which remained from her smallpox a few years before; Lily had prepared it for her in the kitchen using egg white mixed in with the ceruse paste. Her hair was piled up into a nest and dark ringlets fell around her fat ears. Now Hannah leaned closer to the gloomy mirror and attached a patch in the shape of a flying bird to her greasy forehead.

'What more inventions can there be for the female face?' grumbled her father from his armchair.

His daughter smirked and turned her head to admire the finished effect.

'The gentlemen of Drury Lane find your daughter most becoming,' she tittered in a slightly grotesque way.

'Bah,' he replied. 'These new playhouses are a plague on our city. 'Twas more decent in the days of the Protector.'

'Decent is what dullards do, oh my Father. Would you have me stuck in here for the rest of my life with

this wretch gawping at me?' She poked Lily in the chest. 'Would you have your daughter not make a fine marriage?'

'Ah,' he seemed to relent. 'Go take your merriment. I shall mind the shop.'

Seconds after Mistress Hannah pushed her way out of the front door, her father fell soundly asleep in his armchair, hands folded over his portly stomach. Lily stood behind the counter of the shop and looked at him. She had worked for Thomas Farriner for three years, ever since her mother had lost her work as a seamstress and they had been evicted from their two-room dwelling in St Giles-in-the-Fields. Farriner was a cousin to her mother and took pity, although he said he could only take the 15-year-old; her mother found a room at Spital Field where she lay now.

Her master was not a bad man but he was lazy and too fond of his drink, a habit he had passed to his daughter, despite all the latter's remonstrances about him; Lily enjoyed the peace of her Saturday afternoon but dreaded her mistress's return in the evening, filled with gin and bile. Yet although she had no money of her own, as she received no pay beyond her board and lodging, she had learned many tools of survival dodging the blows of Mistress Hannah and the relentless tasks of the house and she was certain that her life would not always be described by these flimsy walls.

'The poorest he that is in England hath a life to lead

as the greatest he,' she whispered and felt emboldened
by the words which were so new to her and yet, in a
way, so familiar.

At one point, as she took tokens from an elderly woman
who lived further up Pudding Lane who had brought
her pie in to be baked in the Farriners' oven, she checked
that her master was still asleep then asked:

'Mistress Dyer, what do you know of the debates they
held in Putney many moons ago? After the
Parliamentarians' fight?'

'Putney? Ah child, that is all long history and not
for you to raise its head once more. What brings you to
such thoughts? The King is back in all his glory these
six long years, what have you of such prattle?'

'But you know of it, you know of these talks at
Putney?'

'Leave such talk to the black hats,' the old woman
replied, grabbing Lily's hand. 'There lies trouble, hear
me well.' And with that, she gathered her skirts and left
the shop.

The slam of the door woke her master.

'You have packed all the biscuits, child?' he rasped.
'Not yet, sir. I have been...'

'I care not what you have been doing if you have not
packed the biscuits. They will sell tomorrow when the
King's men return but not if they are untidy. Get to
packing them before your mistress returns with her temper.'

Chapter Nine

Another week comes to an end on Friday evening and still the heatwave hasn't broken. Henry has told his wife that he's staying up in London for the weekend because he has to work on the Gener8 deal, which is partially true, although really he couldn't face the 4.15pm train from Paddington to Totnes, not in this heat. So he's footloose and fancy-free, as he likes to call it, on Friday evening and has persuaded most of the office to go drinking with him, apart from Evie, who's headed back to her parents for a quiet weekend, and Jean who's babysitting for one of her daughters tonight.

They're standing outside the Monument pub, which is about ten minutes' walk from the office. It's half past six and there's probably sixty people standing in shirtsleeves on the pavement outside the pub, sipping pints and shouting and laughing. Henry, Darren,

Jimmy, Jade and Rufus are in a little informal circle of their own, and Henry is telling one of his stories. He's about three pints in and there's a quivering smear of the head from his bitter on his upper lip.

I love this city, even if I go on all the time about all the things that are wrong with it. I've been here forever. I love it, despite what they're doing to it. I love the fact that at the end of August in a heatwave, we're all still here and standing outside pubs and telling tall stories and making ourselves feel that there's some point to it all. I identify with the Londoners who think it's their home; we've never had the money to have a little place in the country to disappear off to, like half the swine in the tall glass buildings. Henry's an honorary Londoner this weekend, he's doing what he likes most, living it up like he was still a single accountant fresh to the city, his gimlet little eyes always on the lookout for a woman who might mistakenly smile at him.

Now he's explaining to Jade and the group that the Monument they're standing next to, which the pub is named after, commemorates the Great Fire of 1666, which began on the night of Saturday 1st September in Pudding Lane. He's a bit of an amateur historian, Henry, and he's been reading about the Fire recently.

'Very interesting fact, this,' he's saying, taking another slurp of the Timothy Taylors, his favourite Yorkshire bitter which for some reason the Monument pub stocks, hence his habit of coercing his staff to walk the ten minutes here. 'Five days of fire, 70,000 people made homeless, 13,000 homes burned down, and yet only three people were recorded as dying. One of them was the poor lass who worked in the bakery where it started, over there. She was the servant girl and no-one even knows her name. When the baker and his family all managed to get out of their house through one of the upstairs windows, she got stuck inside and burned to death.'

'Thanks for that, Henry,' says Jimmy, and giggles because he's just done a line of coke in the toilets.

'I just care about your education, lad,' Henry says.

'Typical,' Jade says. 'That would be me. Stuck inside a burning building while everyone else got out.' She's drinking Mexican lager out of a bottle and she and Darren are planning to sneak off at some point. She's told her mum she's staying with one of her new work friends and Joy realises it's probably the bloke her daughter said that she was going to shag, but she'd rather she was doing that than hanging out with that Mikey in Edmonton.

'We had a fire at our house when I was young,' says Rufus. 'All the horses bolted.'

Everyone laughs at this and Rufus too, although he's not quite sure why they're laughing.

'And another thing,' Henry says, passing his pint to Darren who takes it. 'Once the fire took hold, really took hold on the Sunday morning, the heat from all the burning buildings began to heat the stone streets so it became almost impossible for people to walk on it. Imagine that, lads' – and here he does an unusual dance out into the road, his curiously small feet still clad in his co-respondent shoes, his arms waving out at the sides as though to balance himself on his toes – 'so bloody hot you can't touch the ground.'

And he comes back accepting what he considers to be the admiring laughter of his staff, takes his pint back from Darren, necks it and passes the empty glass to Jimmy.

'Your round, Jimmy,' says Henry, wiping the froth from his lips. 'I'm going to see a man about a dog.' And he heads inside to find the gents, threading through the noisy crowd and making mental notes about which women look like they might be receptive to one of his legendary opening lines. Couple more pints and he'll start moving in.

The next morning, Jade gets up quietly in Darren's Farringdon apartment while he's still asleep, gets her things together and slips quietly out of the front door at nine-thirty. It's yet another sultry day and the streets are quiet as she walks to the tube station. She's still got on what she was wearing yesterday: combat trousers, Vans, and a pink T-shirt that says What Are You Looking At? on the front. She's wearing imitation RayBans she picked up for a fiver in the indoor market and she's put on a fresh layer of make-up in Darren's bathroom. Her red mohican is still in good shape. She swipes through the barrier at Farringdon station and skips down the stairs to the platform, ignores the nervous smile from a skater boy holding his board, waits for the Circle line train for Tower Hill.

William Cecil had told her on the phone on Thursday that his man Chan would be waiting for her on the north side of Tower Bridge at ten-thirty. She gets a bit lost coming out of the wrong exit from the Tube but she can see the bridge, so runs over the dual carriageway, the hot sun dazzling her eyes even with the cheap shades. A car beeps its horn at her as it brakes to avoid her and she waves a finger at it.

'Miss Franklin?' Chan bows his head slightly as Jade approaches the first of the bridge's huge cast iron supports. He's wearing that utility jacket again and immediately turns to lead Jade down the steps onto the path. She doesn't have time to say anything so just follows him as he walks quickly through the underpass and then turns right into St Katherine's Dock. The usual theme restaurants around the water are all busy with summer weekend brunchers sitting outside at tables: tourists and wealthy locals mostly, the Dock being another of those lovely-looking theme parks where us Londoners obediently sit around acting out the planners' vision of urban contentment. Chan swipes them both through the locked gate onto the pontoons and then Jade can see the improbable sight of William Cecil wearing a blue blazer and sitting on the white leather at the back of an open-topped small motor cruiser. As Jade approaches, she sees he is wearing a white shirt with a paisley cravat knotted around his neck. His shock of frizzy grey hair and remarkable moustache set off the most idiosyncratic get-up on a boat in St Katherine's Dock for quite a while.

He stands up and holds out a hand to help Jade board the boat.

'My dear girl,' he beams. 'What a day of it we shall have. Chan is going to take us on a little cruise. We shall have the luxury of sitting back here and admiring the view.'

Chan unhooks the mooring ropes, jumps neatly into the driving seat in front and the boat chugs slowly out into the central water of the Dock. All eyes on the dockside tables are on them, this unlikely pair – the red mohican, the grey frizzy bush – as they sit back in comfort on the leather seats. Jade is laughing, Cecil is smiling broadly while Chan as usual stares steadily ahead, guiding the boat out through the open lock into the river. The morning sun is now high up in the sky, which retains its heatwave off-white pallor, and the river sparkles with its reflections.

'I will confess, my dear child, that this is not all entirely for your benefit. I wish to carry out a little confirmatory examination of the shape of the City and the most advantageous place for that is the water. However, I am delighted to have the opportunity to share the day with you.'

Jade is still laughing. 'Couldn't make this up!' she says.

'Really?' he queries, raising an eyebrow. 'I might have thought one could.'

Chan opens the throttle a little once the boat is away from the dock and they head west underneath Tower Bridge. On their left, the Shard rises up brilliantly in the morning sun.

'Oh, that's the building Evie was going on about when we came to see you,' Jade says, pointing.

'Ah yes, I have had the pleasure of meeting your friend,' he says. 'Do you admire the building?'

'What, that? I don't think anything about it. What's it got to do with me?'

'Excellently put,' he says, nodding his head in appreciation. Then he takes out an old Leica camera in a brown leather case. 'Forgive me for a moment while I take some pictures.'

Cecil points the camera over to the right towards the north bank of the river and takes a succession of photographs as Chan keeps a slow, steady pace up the centre of the Thames. He keeps clicking the shutter until they reach Blackfriars Bridge, then he puts the camera back in its case.

'All right, Chan,' he calls out. 'Now take us for a

little ride to see the sights.'

Chan eases the throttle open a little more and they head further west towards Westminster. Cecil waves a hand at the sights on either side: the stark white boxes of the South Bank complex on the left, the nineteenth century Civil Service buildings running along the Embankment on the right.

'And all these emblems of your proud city, Miss Franklin, they do not, I presume, impact upon you significantly?'

Jade has never been called Miss Franklin before in her life. It rather tickles her.

'If you mean do I hang around here, then no, never. Not ever. I live in Edmonton.'

'Ah yes, with your mother, I believe.'

'How'd you know that?'

'Your friend, Miss Sangster, the one with so many burdens upon her shoulders. She mentioned to me.'

'Evie? Oh yeah, that's how we came to your talk thing, wasn't it?'

'Precisely. However, I suspect your friend's mind is closed to the true adventures of the soul. Unlike yours, my dear. Tell me, were you at home with your mother last night?'

She looks at him and grins.

'No, of course not. That's why you asked me, isn't it, cos you knew I wasn't.'

He shrugs and smiles broadly.

'I was with this bloke from Evie's office, Darren,' she says.

'And what did you do with this bloke from Evie's office?' Cecil enquires, looking coolly at her.

'Oh, well I ended up handcuffing him to one of the radiators in his flat and then I smacked him on his arse with a table tennis bat.'

William Cecil roars with laughter, slaps his thighs and calls out:

'Did you hear that, Chan? She smacked him on his arse with a table tennis bat!'

Chan doesn't respond, keeps chugging the boat upstream. The Houses of Parliament are coming up on the right.

Cecil takes off his glasses and dabs his eyes with the white handkerchief that was sticking out of the breast pocket of his blazer.

'Oh that is really too fine,' he says, still chuckling. He puts the glasses back on. 'And is this fellow still handcuffed to his radiator?'

Jade grins. 'No, I undid him eventually. But I made him sleep in a dog basket. Well, actually he sort of begged me to tell him to sleep in it, so it wasn't difficult. He's got this massive bed with proper sheets and everything, so I slept like a baby. It's weird, isn't it, what some people like?'

'You are of course quite right,' Cecil replies, more seriously now. 'I tried to explain this to your friend but she has what I would call a closed outlook. But you understood my talk, didn't you? Human beings attach themselves to things – habits, relationships, thoughts, radiators even – and in doing so make slaves of themselves. This fellow last night was asking you to act out the timid drama of his life and you choreographed that for him splendidly. I must say my dear, I am profoundly impressed by the rapidity of your mind.'

Jade feels calm in the company of William Cecil. She thinks nothing of sitting in the back of a boat that probably cost a couple of hundred thousand pounds and taking a day trip up the Thames on a hot Saturday morning in late August.

Cecil leans forwards.

'Chan, I think you can drop Miss Franklin and I off here at Westminster Pier. You take the boat back to St Katherine's and meet us back at the flat. She and I will take a taxi there.'

He turns to smile at her.

'Now you'll have a chance to meet the others,' he says.

Mistress Hannah stumbled back through the door of the shop at eight o'clock. The red that she had crayoned onto her lips before leaving six hours before was now smudged crudely and was mirrored by a flush on her cheeks. The patch in the shape of a bird was no longer on her forehead and her dark hair was lank with sweat. She was accompanied by another woman, equally under the influence of Drury Lane gin, and they were laughing loudly.

Lily continued to serve her master the rabbit pie which she had made that afternoon. He sat at the table in the kitchen, slurping from his mug of ale and called out:

'What riots take place out there in my shop?' He chuckled as he heard the two women shriek with laughter again.

Lily turned to busy herself at the sink as Mistress Hannah entered the kitchen, tugging her equally stout friend behind her by the hand.

'And what have we here?' she exclaimed, sweeping her hand in what she appeared to think was a dramatic gesture straight from the stage. 'My goodly father taking his meal' — she leaned down and gave him a slobbery kiss on his cheek at which he roared good-humoured

201

dissent — 'and' — and at this she straightened up and sneered at Lily's back — 'his good-for-nothing idle servant.'

Amidst much laughter and shouts, the two women sat down at the table.

'Bring another plate, child,' Farriner called out.

Lily brought over another setting which she put in front of the other woman whose hair was coloured a dark blue. She began to serve out the rabbit pie which still sat in its earthenware pot in the middle of the table, pushing back the pastry covering and doling out the hot meat and sauce onto both plates.

'More, more, you slattern!' Hannah cried. 'All of it, all of it!'

Lily was due to have her own portion of the pie for her supper but she silently spooned all that remained in the pan onto both women's plates.

'And did you meet Sir Lancelot in Drury Lane?' her father asked with a bleary twinkle in his eye. 'Or possibly the Earl of Rochester?' This set the other woman off into peals of laughter while her daughter attempted to look affronted.

'We did not, Father, although some gentlemen did certainly take an interest and supported that interest by most kindly provision of refreshment following the show.'

More giggles from her friend as both plunged their spoons into the food.

'Ah,' her father continued, winking at the friend, 'but I fear even our success with ships' biscuits will not

provide me with the funds for a dowry to suit such highborn fellows.'

'I shall have no need of a dowry when I wed, Father,' Hannah exclaimed, some rabbit juice running down her chin. 'The gentleman I choose shall accept me for my charm and grace alone.'

'Tell your father who we saw, Hannah,' the other woman said.

'On the stage? Ah yes! Oh Father, it was no other than Nell Gwynn and oh how we laughed as she fooled her paramour into thinking she loved him — while all the time she wooed his father! What a prize example she is to all us ladies of today!'

'If she be an example, may the Lord take care of us and gather us into his bosom sooner rather than later,' her father replied.

'Fear not, Father,' Hannah said, her voice still a little slurred as she leaned conspiratorially towards him over the table, 'your future son-in-law will have met his match in me.'

Then she reared back and shouted at Lily:

'Why no ale for our guest? Quick about it, goblets you wretch, goblets for the table.'

Lily silently brought two goblets over, poured ale into them from the jug, then felt the sharp pain of the pinch of her mistress's fingers on her arm.

'Will you never learn the manners of fine people at table, dolt? Next time bring goblets straight away.'

The two women continued to slurp their food as Farriner told them how hard he had worked during the afternoon and Lily stood at the sink with her back to them and her fingers gripping the edge so hard her knuckles whitened. Noiselessly she mouthed words at the wall and glared so fiercely at it, as though she were committing a prayer, or perhaps a promise.

Chapter Ten

Angel exits Baker Street Station. It's a quarter to eight on Tuesday evening and he's sweating from the airless heat of the Bakerloo line. His life is all swung around now and the last two nights Marta has just been crying because she can't understand what's happening to her husband and he can't seem to explain anything in a way that makes sense. He's been summoned to William Cecil's place for a meeting and so he's going to have to go back to Stirling Global and clean it late tonight and then get home late again. Why can't Marta understand that Mr Cecil is going to help them? Why won't she trust him to do what's right for the family? Mr Cecil said he should be firmer with her and maybe that's right, he's the head of the family and she should respect him better.

Angel has never been here before and he feels intimidated by the plush wood and gold leaf of the entrance hall of Chiltern Court. The concierge looks up and down briefly at the overweight, sweating Colombian man then directs him up to the ninth floor. All the way up in the lift, Angel nervously mutters to himself: 'Nirvana...fire...attachment,' trying to remember all the things that Mr Cecil has told him.

Chan nods silently at him as he lets him pass through into the hallway. Angel can hear William Cecil's voice coming from another room and he stands still for a moment in the dull light of this strangely shaped hall and the thick smell of incense excites him and makes him feel brave. Chan motions to him again and he walks towards a half-open door and into the long, low, darkened room where he sees a number of people standing in a group. They are standing in front of a large statue of what looks like a monk and flickering candles at the base of the statue illuminate the spiralling wisps of incense.

'You are late, Angel. Join the others.'

William Cecil's voice is peremptory, coming from somewhere deep in the gloomy room. Angel walks over to the group of what looks to him like maybe twelve or fifteen people but, as you guessed, as the latecomer to the meeting he makes the eighteenth person. Everyone is looking towards the statue and he obediently turns his head towards it. As he's not very tall and is at the back of the group, he can only really see the Luohan's head with its heavily lidded eyes and exaggerated ears.

'Stand still and close your eyes,' Cecil says. There is silence now in the room and Angel closes his eyes and can sense the breathing of the others around him. The sweet incense makes him feel a little giddy but he keeps his eyes shut and he listens to Cecil's booming voice from the other side of the room.

'Think of the fire which burns inside your mind. Think of all I have told you about this fire, about how its flames are fuelled by all those desires, those attachments, which keep you chained to the life which you know you do not want. Focus on the pain as the flames burn your skin, think how much you suffer.

'You have all told me, all of you, how you suffer and I suffer with you, with each and every one of you in your suffering. I suffer with you in order that I may help you to escape your pain, escape it for good. You are no longer alone. You will never be alone again, you will never need to struggle against misfortune in that brave, solitary and lonely way in which you have lived your life.

'I have taken on your suffering. That is what the Buddha asked me to do. You all came to me with your troubles, your pains, your sorrows and I took them all and I carry them now for you. So that you do not have to. Is that not right?'

They all nod vigorously, but no-one speaks and they all keep their eyes closed. Cecil has stood up now and is wandering amongst them.

'And having taken your suffering, do I not give you the freedom that only the Luohan can know – the freedom to become reborn? To become so much greater than anyone else in this city could dream of becoming? Do I not let you share in the beauty of each other's bodies, do I not hold inside of me the awful burden of each of your lives, so that each of you may be free to blossom, to flower?'

More nods.

'I have chosen you. Remember that: there is something special about each and every one of you. You are not ordinary. You are all changed now, you are becoming Luohans.'

In the heat of this darkened room with its sweet fragrance and the proximity of these other bodies all standing silently next to him, Angel feels a flash of joy as he absorbs the deep voice of William Cecil. This is what certainty is like, he thinks: this is the only thing which makes absolute sense. He feels himself swaying now, with his eyes closed tight, and every so often he feels himself brush against another standing body but they all remain absolutely silent.

'The Buddha came to me in a dream,' Cecil continues. 'I have told you all about that dream. "Gather today eighteen Luohans," he told me. "Go out and find them and gather them about you and prepare for the great day." So I did. I went out into this city called

London and I searched for you and, one by one, I found you. You brought me your pains, your fears, your worries and I received them all gratefully, I absorbed them all so that you should not feel the burden on your own. Now you and I are one, in the service of the great Buddha who now desires us to unleash the power within. There is nothing that separates us, we are a unified thought, we are one beautiful energy. Are you ready, my Luohans, are you ready to unleash that energy?'

Angel nods with his eyes still closed and says 'Yes' but no-one else speaks. He feels William Cecil come close to him.

'Do not fear, Angel,' says Cecil, stroking his hair. 'You are our newest, our final joyous companion. You will learn how we are here. While I teach, you keep your eyes and your mouth closed, your nose and your ears open. Your heart will guide you. You will learn the beautiful truth which we all here already know. You will taste the exquisite delights of the body, the perfect gift of the Buddha to his most favoured servants.'

Cecil keeps walking around the group.

'Yes, my Luohans, you are ready. You are ready to serve Him. By serving me, you serve Him. He watches over you now in this room, He gives you His blessing, He promises through me to give you the strength to overcome your enemies. You are invincible. Keep your eyes closed,' he says as he circles them. 'Keep your eyes closed and focus on that fire. You are the master of your fire, the fire which burns everything and everyone apart from you. Understand that: the fire obeys your command.'

He stands now beside the stone statue and looks at the eighteen people standing in front of him, all with their eyes closed. The room is completely silent. He looks over his shoulder to his right, towards the gloom of the interior of the room, and he nods. From a darkened corner, a slight figure gets up from a chair and walks towards him. The figure is distinguished by the tall Mohican which moves rythmically as she approaches the dais.

Cecil holds out his hand and Jade takes it, smiling, as she steps up to stand beside him on the dais. She is wearing a silk dressing gown. For a moment, the two of them stand still there, the incense curling up around them, the eighteen Luohans all in front of them with their eyes closed, swaying slightly in the sweet heat. Jade is clear-eyed as she looks down upon the group, the smile on her face as she stands there next to Cecil in his familiar cotton jacket is confident, amused, powerful even. This is a different Jade, a very different Jade. Cecil reaches down and pulls the cord holding her gown and it falls open revealing Jade's naked body. He tenderly pushes the cloth of the gown off her shoulders so that it falls to the floor and she stands there naked, her head high, her smile strong.

'Not long now.' Cecil's voice has dropped so that it is little more than a whisper. 'Just four more days, my brave Luohans. Just four more days.'

He begins to stroke his hand over Jade's naked body.

'Yes,' he continues. 'You, my Luohans, you are about to unleash the sacred energy. Feel it within you, feel it at the base of your spine, let it begin to flow up the seven sacred chakras.' He drops his hand down below Jade's belly. 'The Muladhara. The Svadhisthana. The Manipura. The Anahata. The Vishuddha. The Ajna. The Sahasrara.' As he intones each chakra, his hand moves up Jade's body and now she is tilting her head back with her eyes closed. He moves slightly to stand behind her, clasps her now with both hands. 'Keep your eyes closed, my Luohans,' he commands in his deep rumbling voice. 'Summon up your energies, let them flow within you, up through the crown chakra, up, up, up.' Jade's head is resting on his shoulder now and she is still smiling as she leans into him.

'What glories will await you,' he murmurs. 'You Luohans. You who will be spoken of in years to come, who will be praised, who will be lauded, who will be respected, who will be loved. What glories, my precious ones.'

He touches his index finger gently on Jade's lips. In the group, Angel feels an electricity pass through him, he senses the bodies around him, he feels their heat and he smells the sweet sweat on their skin.

'By this time next week, the world will know of your bravery, your fierce wisdom, your true devotion,' Cecil continues. 'The world will bow down before you.'

These words are now so delicate in the still heat of this darkened room that Angel feels they are directed entirely to him.

'All of you,' Cecil continues, 'all of you have shared your deepest thoughts with me, you have now left the cruel cage of the unthinking world. We are one. We conduct the fire, we walk through the fire unscathed, we bathe in its light. We are, my Luohans, unbound from the fire. Listen.'

He reaches down to take Jade's hand and very slowly the two of them descend from the dais and begin to walk amongst the standing group side by side, brushing gently against each one as they thread their way amongst them. Angel strains to feel the proximity of Cecil's body, keeps his eyes clenched tight shut as Jade's breath plays upon his face as she passes him.

'Listen. The fire is raging now, its flames are raging through you, up and up and up. But it makes no noise, does it? It is absolutely silent because it is now unbound from the attachments which before tormented it. Listen to the silent symphony we create and glory in it,' Cecil whispers. 'Listen to it.'

While William Cecil and Jade pad softly on the thick carpet in and around his disciples, Evie sits opposite Henry across town in Jamies, a second bottle of Côtes du Rhône in front of them.

'It's not bloody Spanish Prisoner,' Henry is saying.

'I'm telling you, Henry,' Evie says.

'No. No, love, it's not. You're wrong. I've checked it out. Everything Felix told me is on the money: there's this guy in Florida who was part of the NASA set up, he's some kind of mad scientist, but he developed this formula to keep the astronauts alert on their missions and they did a load of tests on it and found that with young minds, it has this additional effect of stimulating brain growth.'

'Oh Henry.'

'There's no Oh Henry about it, Evie. It's real. Listen, Felix is playing with the big boys. They don't come bigger than JP Morgan.'

'How do you know he's even been in their office?' She takes another swig of the wine.

'Whose office?'

'JP bloody Morgan.'

'Of course he's been in their office. Canary Wharf. I've seen it.'

'What have you seen?'

'I've seen their bloody office. You can't miss it.'

'You mean you've talked to them about this Gener8 thing?'

'No, I mean I've seen their office. I went with Darren to the Boisdale down there last month and you can't miss it, huge great glass place.'

'You went just to look at the JP Morgan office?'

'I didn't go to Canary Wharf specifically to look at their office, I went with Darren to get a bloody drink, but while I was there I took a look at it.'

'I bet Felix hasn't seen it.'

'What is it with you?' Henry's lip is quivering again. 'You never used to be like this, Evie. Where's Fortune Favours The Brave gone?'

'That was your phrase, not mine. I don't think Fortune favours anyone.'

'Listen.' He changes his tone, more pleading now. 'Listen: this is our chance. I'm serious. Come with me on this thing. It's you I'm doing it for, don't you see? Don't you remember what it was like, before, before I let it all go wrong? Evie?'

She looks down at her glass, lets her hair fall over her eyes. She shakes her head slowly.

'You didn't let it all go wrong, Henry,' she says quietly. Jamies is still quite busy so her voice is hard for him to hear clearly and he leans in. 'It just happened, it wasn't your fault. And of course I remember what it was like, you idiot. Of course I do.'

He reaches over and grabs her hand.

'Then let me make it happen again,' he says.

She shakes her head.

'I can do it,' he persists. 'In six months, between us we'll have recruited resellers around the country and they'll be reselling to their teams. It's a licence to print money, every one of them will be paying us on every packet of the bloody stuff they sell. It's going to be back like it was, I know it. You and me, we can be back like we were. You know we can.'

'And what if it's not, Henry? What if I'm right, what if Felix has sold you a pup and that formula is just custard powder? Are you saying that then we're not together? So we can only work if bloody Gener8 works? Where do you think that leaves me?'

'I don't know what you're on about.'

'For God's sake, can't you hear how stupid you're sounding? Can't you?' She grabs at her glass and knocks back the wine. She puts it back empty on the table and looks at him. 'I'm quitting, Henry,' she says.

'What?'

'I said, I'm quitting. I'm leaving Stirling Global. I'm not doing it any more.'

They stare at each other for a moment and the conversation of the other customers carries on, someone's laughing loudly on the other side of the room. His mouth twitches then he looks away.

'I mean it,' she says. 'I'm sorry, Henry.'

He looks back at her.

'It's that bloke, isn't it? The one you've been going on about. The fucking Buddhist. What are you going to do, join a bloody ashram?'

'I don't know what I'm going to do, Henry. But

what I'm not going to do is waste any more time. You know it's Spanish Prisoner. You know it is. And you know what, Henry? You should quit too. Just pack it in. Go back to Totnes. Sell your flat in Ealing. You don't need to be doing this anymore, you really don't.'

'That's what your Buddhist says, does he? Has he got any more brilliant advice for me?'

'It's nothing to do with him. I only met him once.'

'Oh yeah?'

'What does that mean?'

'You know.'

Evie laughs, a brittle, unhappy laugh.

'I don't believe it. You think I'm shagging William Cecil!'

'Well, are you?'

'Henry, for Christ's sake, he's about a hundred and two, he's a weird old man and I met him for half an hour two weeks ago and for some reason I told him a load of stuff I don't tell anyone. I don't know why I did and I don't even like the guy very much or even trust him. But even so, he's not the reason I'm leaving. I'm leaving because I've had enough and you must have had enough too. Why can't you see it? This city, Henry, it hates you and it hates me and if you carry on here it will grind you down and you'll end up in St Thomas's with a bloody heart attack and where's the sense in that?'

'I never had you down as a quitter.'

'I don't care anymore, Henry,' she says, standing up from her chair. She's a little unsteady, they've pretty much finished that second bottle. 'I don't care what you say. I don't want you to be unhappy, I don't want you to get taken for a ride, but I can't help you. That's all. You're on your own.'

'Ah give it a break,' he mutters. Then, as she picks up her bag and turns to leave, he calls out, 'I'm not giving up on us, Evie.'

She walks out of the wine bar, crosses over the street and lets herself in to the building where the office is. She has shopping she bought at lunchtime to take home. When she's inside the empty office, she sits at her desk and looks around. She knows she is leaving now – she just had to say it to him and now it's said, everything can change. There's no rush, she can work things out for the next month or so, make sure that Jade is getting on OK before she actually goes.

Evie has sat in this office for years. She looks at the cheap mdf desks, the messy computer cables on the carpet, Jean's hopeful green plant on her desk, Henry's ghastly briefcase collapsed against the wall. Suddenly it's all meaningless to her. There's no rush of adrenalin, no feeling of release even – just nothing. She leans her chin on her hands as she notices the effect of the wine. Joy would tell her off if she knew she'd been at it again, drinking on a Tuesday evening. She closes her eyes. Just before she drifts off to sleep she remembers a time when she and Henry stayed at Claridges one night after going to a concert in Hyde Park and she remembers how sweet he was to her up in that plush bedroom, how he made her laugh, and the memory fills her with sadness.

A little later she's woken with a start when the office door opens and Angel enters. He's much later on his shift because of the meeting at William Cecil's flat and he's as surprised as her to find someone in.

'Oh, sorry,' he says and stands looking at her.

'No, no,' she says, flustered but trying to make it seem as though she wasn't asleep. 'I just came in to pick up some things.' She leans down and picks up the Tesco carrier bag from the floor by her desk.

He wanders over to the cupboard and starts getting the hoover out. Evie looks at him as she gathers her things together on the desk.

'My name's Evie,' she says. 'You've just started here, haven't you? Jean told me.'

He turns.

'Sorry?'

She notices how strong his accent is and something about him seems familiar.

'Cleaning the office,' she says. 'You're new, aren't you?'

'New, yes. Three weeks,' he says.

'I'm leaving,' she says. 'I mean, I'm handing my notice in. I'm going.'

'Sorry?'

'It doesn't matter.' She looks at him. 'Haven't I seen you somewhere before?'

He shrugs. 'I don't think so.' He starts to unwind the cable from the hoover. He wants to think more about what happened at William Cecil's place, he doesn't want to talk to this woman.

But Evie is good at faces and she keeps looking at him.

'Yes I have,' she says. 'You were at that talk, weren't you, the talk by William Cecil?'

He starts, drops the hoover cable.

'Mr Cecil?' he says, his eyes wide. 'You know Mr Cecil?'

'Yes,' she says. 'Well, I don't really know him, but I've spoken to him. How about you?'

'What do you mean?'

'Why did you go to his talk?'

He stares at her. Suddenly he remembers how he first saw the flyer on Evie's desk and now he wants to tell her, maybe she will understand, not like Marta.

He points at her desk, his face a little rueful. 'Poster,' he says. 'I see poster on your desk.'

She looks at her intray and remembers taking the A5 flyer from William Cecil when she met him.

'Oh. That's a weird coincidence. What did you make of it anyway, his talk? I was a bit confused by it all.'

'Mr Cecil is great man,' he says after a moment.

His eyes are shining bright, she remembers that later when she thinks about their conversation.

'Really? What makes you say that?'

'I say that because it is true,' he says, almost contemptuously. 'Mr Cecil is great man,' he repeats.

'So you say,' she says.

'He speak to me,' he continues and he beats his fist on his chest. 'Many things. Mr Cecil help me and my family. Not long now. Just four days.'

'What's in four days?'

Angel looks worried.

'I no say.' Then a moment of pride: 'He choose me. Mr Cecil. Me and the other…Luohans.' He has difficult pronouncing the word but Evie remembers it from her visit to Chiltern Court.

'Did you say Luohan?' she asks.

'Yes.' Angel is flipping between arrogance and fear. He would like to tell this woman more, about how Mr Cecil has told him that great things are going to come to him but he is nervous too, because he has also been told that he must not talk about anything.

'Isn't that the statue in his flat?' she persists.

He shakes his head. 'I no say.' He bends down to pick up the hoover cable.

'What's your name?' she asks.

'Angel,' he replies dully, without looking back at her.

'Angel,' she repeats, pronouncing it as he does. 'Oh

I see, Angel like in angel. That's a nice name.'

He looks at her, the plug in his hand. 'I live here four years,' he says. 'Four years. No money. I no stupid.' There is a flash of anger on his face now as he jabs his head to make his point.

'I'm not saying...'

'In Colombia, I have apartment, business, friends. Here, nothing. Nothing, nothing.'

'I'm sorry,' she says.

He exhales contemptuously.

'You sorry. For what? You sorry for me?' He shakes his head. 'Mr Cecil, he understand. You, no.'

And with that he turns on the hoover and plugs the white earphone back in his ear.

Evie suddenly feels exhausted, exhausted by everything and everyone. She looks blankly at him for a moment, then she gathers her bags and walks out of the office.

Angel is relieved she has gone. He shouldn't have spoken to her about Mr Cecil but it was such a surprise to hear her mention his name. He didn't see her at the talk and he had left as soon as Chan gave him the envelope. That was ten days ago now. He remembers tearing the envelope open in his car, seeing the handwritten note from Mr Cecil and the telephone number.

When he had phoned the following day it was as though Mr Cecil knew him inside out, knew all his frustrations and his fears. He'd spoken to him for an hour and then every day since, at least two or three times. Sometimes Mr Cecil was kind, sometimes he was strict, even angry. Angel had to learn to respond quickly because Mr Cecil didn't like him to hesitate. When he hesitated, Mr Cecil shouted at him and that scared him. He had to please Mr Cecil, he was one of his Luohans now, he had to behave like one.

It would be fine. In four days' time they all would undergo their ceremony, that's what he said this evening. All eighteen of them. It would be like nothing they had ever known, he had said. And once they had undergone the ceremony, they would be changed for ever. The others tonight, when Mr Cecil's talk was over and they opened their eyes, they were so nice to him. They hugged him, the men and the women, and some of them kissed him on the lips.

Angel had had enough of being treated like a fool, of being treated as though he were simple. Like that stupid woman. What did she know?

He was a Luohan.

In all the press coverage after – and you can imagine, the coverage went on for ever, is still going on: the newspapers, TV, books, films, it's still a massive chunk of media activity – quite a lot was found out about the other seventeen Luohans and how William Cecil lured them in. He recruited the first ones a few months before and began to encourage them to spend nights at his huge apartment in Chiltern Court. He encouraged them to sleep with each other and he got them used to attending daily talks standing, eyes closed, in front of the stone Luohan. Angel was the last piece of the jigsaw. He got to Angel quite late, because he only really got his claws into him a week before it happened and a lot of people think that was the only real mistake he made: he didn't give himself enough time to really get Angel completely under his control but he had this self-imposed deadline so he just went with it.

He found his people through a variety of ways, you can read about it because there are several books now just focusing on William Cecil's Luohans. Some he picked up, like Angel, from his talks. He gave these talks all over London and a pattern can be pieced together from eyewitnesses who agreed that he seemed to focus especially on one or two individuals who he could see were responding very strongly to his speech: either they identified with what he was saying about how tough London was and how something needed to be done to make it fairer, more bearable; or they somehow responded at a deeper level to his hypnotic presence and delivery. Maybe Angel fell more into the first category but he was certainly also responsive to Cecil's influence, as they all were.

Those who were recruited at talks were all at some point given an envelope by Chan at the end of the talk and after that Cecil would bear in on them using the telephone as a weapon. Even the great Darren Hegarty could have learned a lot from William Cecil's telephone sales technique. Some he just met randomly: in the park, on the street, in coffee shops, even at a dinner party in one case. People said he seemed to have an uncanny ability to identify weakness, to pinpoint with absolute precision the emotional uncertainty in a person which could make them vulnerable to him. It wasn't enough, though, just to find uncertainty; in Evie's case, his diagnosis of her state of mind was shockingly accurate, enough to really destabilise her, but she still retained this strong inner core which would make it impossible for him to make use of her temporary bewilderment. She was probably in line as a potential recruit by coming to that talk but she would never have succumbed – not Evie.

No, the people who became his Luohans had a fatal combination of unhappiness and defencelessness: they lacked the emotional ability to resist him. In some cases they probably never had it, in others they'd had it ground out of them by London's remorseless pressure, or by dysfunctional parents, or both.

They were, beyond the inherent weakness which bound them together, a pretty disparate bunch. Several like Angel had menial jobs in the City doing either cleaning or security work. Falusa was originally from Algeria and she was a single mother with two kids at school in Tooting and had a zero-hours contract cleaning offices on London Wall. She and her husband had managed to get visas because he was classed as a political refugee but he'd returned to Algeria two years ago with another woman and she'd lost touch with him. She was nursing a quiet and growing anger about her life which Cecil surgically dissected after she attended one of his talks at a community centre near her two-bedroom flat where she lived with her daughters.

Richie was a 34-year-old boiler room telephone sales guy who'd spent the last ten years selling phoney stocks to gullible retired people. He was the son of an Edinburgh GP and Cecil – who struck up a conversation with him in a coffee bar at Liverpool Street station – swiftly discovered that the combination of guilt and ten years of cocaine had turned what had once been a shy, polite grammar school boy into an explosion waiting to happen. Then there was Annabel, the daughter of an Earl who was interning at a City law firm. Cecil sat next to her at a dinner party in one of the flats in Chiltern Court after he'd got chatty with the hostess on occasional meetings in the lift. Annabel came back to his flat after the dinner and sat drinking Chan's tea in the dark, hot lounge and told Cecil how she harboured desires to sleep with her mother and kill her father.

Rosalda was an Italian translator who spent her days translating commercial contracts for a property firm based in Holborn and her nights alone in a studio flat in Camden writing erotic romances that no-one would publish. Bernard was a middle-aged ex-member of the Revolutionary Communist Party who had finally run out of ultra-left breakaway factions and had dived headlong into a self-curated miasma of mystic spiritual beliefs. Tullah was a security guard whose parents had run a Christian church in Nigeria and who held apocalyptic views based on his persistent reading of the Book of Revelations night after night in the empty lobby of an office block in the City. Poppy was a Californian hippy who had plenty of inherited money and an entirely undisciplined mind which was filled with self-help books and watered down doses of Buddhist philosophy.

After they were all rounded up in the days and weeks which followed, most of the eighteen suffered severe breakdowns of one kind or another which they largely endured in secure units after they were sentenced. They all told the same story: he was a great leader, he was a Messiah, he was Buddha reincarnated; whatever he was, he was going to save them, he was going to lead them to a new life where their suffering would end.

Those months they all spent hanging out in Cecil's apartment – not one of them looked back on them with anything other than joy. That's the thing. Even now, sitting in their cells, they're all looking forward to being reunited with him.

They believe that Cecil is a direct descendant of the Buddha and they believe that they are his Luohans, that they will live lives of glory forever more. That's not such a bad thing, is it? Obviously, it turned out bad but to believe so strongly in something, maybe that's pretty comforting. Sometimes I'd like to believe so strongly in something that it opens me up to the core. I don't imagine I ever will. But for Angel, even though it created torments for him when Marta failed to understand, his faith in William Cecil gave him release from four years of growing incomprehension, frustration and unhappiness. It made him feel like he used to when he was a kid growing up in Bogota, when the world seemed full of light.

And Jade? Ah, well Jade was different. She wasn't one of the eighteen. You know what I think? I think she was just as much the woman William Cecil had always wanted to find as he was an ideal partner to her. I think they were a rare and strange combustion all of their own and I hope she's with him somewhere now, somewhere in the world, and they're making each other laugh and they're drinking that tea of his and maybe they're already thinking about the next event. I don't know, though. I hope so. I hope so.

*L*ily finished washing the plates in the sink as behind her Farriner, his daughter and her friend continued to expound their witticisms more and more loudly. It was almost nine o'clock and Lily knew from experience that it was getting close to the time when her mistress's temper would suddenly flare in drink and she would lash out. She was tired, she was very hungry and she wanted no more of this. She walked over to the table and addressed the baker.

'Sir, I have finished the cleaning and all is tidy in the shop and ready for tomorrow when I am to visit my mother. I would like to go and pray for her now before I sleep – may I take my leave?'

'Yes, yes, child,' he waved his hand, irritated at the interruption to the story being related to him. 'To bed with you, to bed.'

Hannah scowled at her as she passed but she moved quickly enough to avoid any contact. She passed through the shop and looked in at the mouth of the oven where glowing embers still remained. She thought to go back and ask her master whether she should clean them out into the metal pail but thought better of it – she wanted no opportunity for them to keep her behind in the kitchen.

Anyway, Mistress Hannah always prided herself on being the last person to check on the oven.

Lily took care to make sure that the heavy pattens on the soles of her shoes sounded loudly on the stairs as she climbed up. She passed the privy and her master's room, climbed noisily to the second floor where Hannah's room was and stamped up the narrow stairs to the door which opened onto her tiny attic room.

Inside the tiny room, which had hardly any space beyond the hard cot bed in one corner, she took off her heavy shoes and moved quickly. She pulled out a hemp bag from under the bed and began rolling up the few flimsy clothes which lay in a corner on the floor. Her mother's bible, which she had never known how to read, she placed on top, tied a knot in the bag, picked up her shoes and tiptoed back out. She closed the door silently and waited at the top of the stairs, her breath sounding awfully noisy to her, her heart beating so loud it seemed to her the whole city would hear it. The noise of the three of them in the kitchen continued unabated and she stepped down carefully and silently.

When she was almost back in the shop, Lily hesitated once more and listened. Mistress Hannah was shouting now, a sure sign that her temper was about to boil over with the drink. While the voices were raised, she tiptoed to the front door and very slowly eased back the wooden bolt. She pushed down on the door lever, slipped out into the lane then quietly pushed the door back into its place.

Her mistress was too far gone in drink now to remember whether or not she had bolted the door when she came in.

In the three years she had lived at the Farriners, this was the first time she had ever left the house without permission. Pudding Lane seemed quite different to her: the light was low and one or two candles glowed outside of the cramped houses, illuminating the signs hanging down above the doors. There was a wind now, much stronger than this morning when she had been out, and the signs creaked as they swung on their iron hooks. The lane was not busy and she bent down to fasten her shoes back on.

As Lily straightened up again, she looked up one last time to the roof of the house where she had slept without any window for so long. Two dogs barked further down the hill and this hustling wind sent a brief chill through her. She stepped out and began to walk up the sloping lane; after fifty yards or so, she turned left towards Fish Street.

Inside the baker's house, Mistress Hannah hauled herself out of her chair as her father and her friend joshed each other. She needed to visit the privy. A little unsteady on her feet, she tottered through the shop to the stairs, climbed up and made her way to the little room next door to her father's bedroom. Her face was quite flushed now and her brow sweaty. She muttered angrily to herself as she adjusted her skirts once more then instead of heading back down, she continued up to her floor. She stood at the foot of the narrow staircase which led to the attic room and listened. A grim smile played on her face.

'Pray away, dolt, pray away,' she whispered to herself, then pulled herself up the stairs to the attic door. She banged on the door, not so loud that her father would hear downstairs, but enough to be heard inside. Then she put her head to the wood and rasped:

'I told you, slattern, you would be punished for your idleness today. You will not leave this house tomorrow. Let your filthy mother rot away without you.'

And with that, she drew the wooden bolt on the outside of the door so that it could not be opened from the inside. She laughed, then headed back down to join the others.

Chapter Eleven

On Wednesday evening, Linda was cooking her dad
supper in his flat after her shift. His flat is high up in
the block by the shopping centre and it looks out east
towards the big reservoirs over by the River Lea. Linda
is standing at the cooker, occasionally stirring some
home-made chips she is shallow-frying in a pan and
watching the reflections of the sun create orange and
gold patterns on the surface of the lakes. Her dad used
to take her canoeing on the river when she was young
and once she'd started boxing she could outstrip him
easily and used to have to wait for him to catch up,
his long thin arms holding the paddle making him
look ungainly and slightly ridiculous.

'Don't burn those chips,' he calls out from the front
room and she smiles and gives the pan another stir.

'They're OK,' she calls back.

'I don't like them burned,' he replies.

'I know. They won't be.'

It had been a quiet day at work today, no call-outs during the whole shift. Yesterday had been much busier, they'd been called to a factory in Whitechapel where a fire had broken out in a cramped clothing manufacturers. Everyone had got out OK but there hadn't been any fire extinguishers anywhere, so the fire, started by a frayed cable on an industrial iron, had quickly made progress through the stacks of dry shirts and dresses heaped up against the walls. Linda led the attack, climbing up the ladder on their engine and breaking several glass windows in order to shove the hose into the building. It took half an hour for them – there were several engines needed – to quell the flames. When she and her colleagues got inside wearing their breathing apparatus, the place looked like something out of a Victorian drawing: rows and rows of desks huddled close together with sewing machines sitting on top, the thick smoke everywhere, giving it an eerie gloom as they raced up and down the aisles making sure there were no people left inside.

'You're burning them,' her dad calls out.

'I'm not. Mind your own business.'

Even now, the day after, she can still feel the last traces of adrenalin which had flooded through her body. Most days when she's on her shift it's pretty quiet, with training exercises and routine maintenance of kit, some online coursework on pyrotechnics or resuscitation. Then the call goes up and they're scrambling for their kit, strapping up as they clamber into the cab, the radio suddenly alive with crackle and fast-talking instructions. As they lurch through the streets, siren wailing, the heavy engine picking up sudden momentum, they calmly battle-plan, looking at photos of the building on their phones, discussing entry routes. Yesterday, when they got to the factory, there were police already there cordoning off space on the street, moving spectators back. They decided in the cab that she would go up first. When she climbed the ladder to reach the first floor windows black smoke was funnelling out. She could still hear the smash of glass as she rammed the first hose in, could still feel the wall of heat on her face.

She turns off the gas cooker and spoons the chips into a bowl to let the fat soak into kitchen paper. She takes sausages out of the oven and shares them out onto two plates, pours baked beans from a saucepan and then shakes the chips equally onto the plates.

'See?' she says, setting his plate down in front of him on the table in living room. 'Not burned.'

'What?' he says.

'Nothing. Enjoy your food.'

He starts eating straight away. Dennis Mensah, now seventy-two, has always been a skinny man. When he was young and active in Ghana's various political oppositions, his colleagues had called him Sugar because they said he was as thin as a cane of sugar. Now his dark brown skin is stretched tightly over his prominent cheekbones and his shirt hangs loosely over his narrow shoulders. He wears a cloth skull cap because he always complains of the cold and he wears brown tortoiseshell glasses which Linda had picked out for him at the opticians.

The room in which they are eating is lined with books along one wall, above a desk which has a laptop open on it and piles of paper stacked up on either side. Linda had taught her dad the basics of computing over the last few years and now he is able to communicate with old colleagues in Ghana. There are various typed instructions on the wall by the desk which she has stuck up for him to remind him of various things: when to take various pills during the day, what to do if the email doesn't work, phone numbers of various friends in Edmonton. Dennis's dementia is still very early stage but it is significant enough to need such prompts, as she knows it frustrates him to have to phone her up and ask for help.

They eat in silence, which is their habit, and every so often she looks at him and yet again feels the unfairness that her dad's cleverness is being eroded at such a comparatively young age. She, as someone who has never taken to the world of books and learning, is proud of her father's intellectual abilities, just as he is proud of her strength and independence and the way in which she has forged her own life. She is determined to see him finish his political history of his homeland; it was she who found him a part-time typist who is currently turning the hundreds of pages of handwritten text into typescript.

When they finish their supper, he wipes his lips with a napkin and looks at her.

'Good food, Dottie,' he says. Dottie is his name for her, his slang corruption of Daughter which he's used since she was a baby. His late wife never called Linda that and Linda has a special place in her heart for the feeling she gets still whenever he calls her by that name. Unless of course they're having one of their arguments, which are fairly regular, but they always blow over as quickly as they arise.

'How's Sandra getting on with the typing?' she asks.

'She's doing a good job. She's getting better at reading my handwriting and she's working at the Ghanaian words. For an Irish lady she's doing good.' He smiles and when he smiles his face, which for such a skinny man is quite wide, creates folds of skin which make way for his stretching, upturned lips. Linda loves to see him smile.

'She told me she's enjoying it. Where's she got to?'

'2001. John Kufuor became President.'

'I know.'

'You remember Kufuor?'

'I remember you talking about him.'

'Ah.'

'You used to make me recite the names of famous Ghanaians and what they'd done.'

'I did that? I'm sorry Dottie.'

'Don't be. I liked it. Although I wasn't very good at it. I think I told you Muhammed Ali was President once.'

He chuckles.

'He would have been our finest President if he had been.'

'They'll have to add your name to the list when the book's published next year.'

'Ah Dottie, you know it's just a tiny radical press. They'll probably only print about ten copies. And my friends will praise it and my enemies will denounce it and that will be that.'

'You know it won't be like that.'

He shrugs and turns his head aside slightly.

'It doesn't matter,' he says, looking out of the window.

She picks up the plates and takes them out into the kitchen and lays them in the washing up bowl. The sun is still flashing evening shapes of ochre colour on the surface of the reservoirs below. As she begins to wash up and stack the dishes on the draining board, he comes in and picks up a tea towel and begins to dry them.

'I wouldn't have done it without you,' he says after a while.

'What?'

'The book. I'd never have got myself organised. I'm grateful.' And he runs a finger through her thick, black hair.

'Do you know the title yet?'

'Oh, something jazzy, something like Themes of Inequality in Post-Colonial Ghana. What's that book programme you told me about?'

'Richard and Judy.'

'Richard and Judy. Yes.' And he stands back and makes a stance with his hands placed in front of him, then says in a mock TV voice: 'And we now welcome Dennis 'Sugar' Mensah who is going to tell us all about his exciting new book, Themes of Inequality in Post-Colonial Ghana.'

She laughs. 'You're ridiculous.'

He laughs too, a slow high-pitched song of a laugh.

Then he carries on drying dishes. After a while, he says:

'Anyway, you did me good.'

She stacks the last plate on the draining board and pulls the plug.

'I've found out a bit about better things we can do to look after your money,' she says.

'Ah, you don't need to do that, Dottie. Money looks after itself. I don't spend much.'

'I know. But I'm just being careful.'

'You never used to be careful. I had to hold on to

you sometimes, in case the wind took you.'

'You know what I mean.'

'Don't bother me with it.' A pause as she puts the kettle on. Then: 'Sorry. I know you always do the right thing. Whatever you think is best, Dottie.'

'OK. I won't bore you with the details.'

'That's good. My memory's not so good these days anyway, I'll just forget it.'

'You know I'm taking you to the memory clinic next week?'

'Hmm.'

He walks back into the living room and sits at his desk. When she comes in with two cups of coffee, he looks up at her and his eyes are moist:

'I just want you to have a good life, Dottie,' he says. He waves his arm over the piles of paper on the desk. 'This book, my money, my unfaithful mind: it doesn't matter. I just want you to be happy.'

She sets the cups down on the desk and leans in to kiss his forehead.

'I am happy. I'm always happy, dumbo.'

He grabs her wrist.

'I mean it.'

'So do I.' She puts her arm around his shoulder. 'You'll still be saying this to me in twenty years' time,' she whispers in his ear.

Quarter of a mile away, Evie sits at Joy's table drinking from a mug of tea. They'd been out to an

Indian restaurant on Fore Street to celebrate Evie's decision to quit Stirling Global. Over supper they'd talked about what she might do next. Joy thought she should go abroad again, find a sales job in Spain or somewhere. Evie was in two minds about it and kept coming back to the things in London she felt tied to, Jade in particular. But Joy kept telling her what a change she'd seen in her daughter over the last two or three weeks, how she thought she might have turned a corner. Jade hasn't told anyone about William Cecil and she's told her mum that the last few nights, since she spent the night with Darren on Friday last week, she's been staying at his place. The reality is, she hasn't seen Darren outside of the office since then, despite him almost begging her to go for a drink with him, because she's been staying at William Cecil's apartment.

'You've done enough for her, love,' Joy had said at supper. 'I can watch over her. You go and get some sun.'

Now Joy is smoking as they finish their tea and Evie is getting ready to go. Then Joy says:

'Oh God, I didn't tell you. That boy she's seeing.'

'Darren?'

'Darren, yeah. She told me all about it. You'll never guess.'

'Oh God, what?'

'No, it's funny. Bloody weird, if you ask me. But

she told me. They do this…what did she call it? M and S, or something.'

'Marks and Spencers?'

'No you silly cow. S and M, that's it. Sadism, or something. At first, he made her be his slave and she had to do what he said.'

'Oh I don't believe this. Just wait till I get my hands on that little bastard.'

'No, shut up girl, let me speak. She said she quite liked it. Weird, if you ask me. Never occurred to me when I was with her dad. But anyway, this is the thing: now they both have a go at it and when he's her slave, she makes him wear a dress!'

At this she bursts into a deep-throated laugh which turns into a spluttering coughing fit. Evie stares at her.

'Jade makes Darren wear a dress?'

Joy can't speak still but nods her head vigorously. Evie continues to stare at her wide-eyed but slowly she too starts to grin.

'Oh for God's sake, I've heard it all now,' she says.

Joy finally stops coughing and takes another pull on her cigarette.

'Don't you tell her I told you,' she says.

'I'm not sure I'd know how to bring it up,' Evie replies.

She is still wondering about this news twenty minutes later as she sits on a bench at Edmonton Green station waiting for the tube. She never disliked Darren, in fact he and she had always got on fine. He was lazy but when he worked he was very good and she'd been able on occasion to talk to him over a glass of wine about the failings of Stirling Global and what could be done about them. He had never made a move on her, obviously aware of her history with Henry, and she had no interest in him that way. But she realises now that as soon as she had been aware of something going on between him and Jade, she had felt uncontrollably hostile towards him.

This revelation of Joy's though, seems to put it all in a new light. The whole S and M thing is a complete mystery to her, but the way that Joy described it somehow makes Darren seem vulnerable; or at least, it seems to show that Jade and he have some kind of meeting of minds or at least treat each other with a sense of equality. It suddenly makes her feel old. All this worrying and nagging and protecting Jade; maybe this is just something she needs to do, rather than what Jade needs? Is she just some interfering old maid?

'You look thoughtful.'

She looks up and for a moment her view is blocked by the slanting gold rays of the setting sun which sit on the horizon above the low brick wall of the outdoor platform: all she can see is a shape standing over her. The shape moves and comes towards her.

'Oh, it's you,' Evie says as Linda sits down beside her. 'I couldn't see a thing with all that sun. Hello.'

'Hi,' Linda says. 'You're a surprise. What's a nice girl like you doing in a place like this?'

'Do you know anything about S and M?'

Linda laughs.

'You have this habit of blurting things out, don't you? It's quite sweet. I'm not really an expert, if that answers the question.'

'Sorry. It's just I found out this evening that my friend Joy's daughter Jade and this guy in my office are, you know, kind of doing that stuff. It's shocked me, I suppose.'

'Well, each to their own. Does she seem OK?'

'She seems happier than I've ever known her, now you ask. In fact, now I think about it, she seems incredibly happy. Oh I don't know, I think I'm just too old for this stuff.'

'What did I tell you in that horrible wine bar? Stop putting yourself down.'

Evie looks straight at her and smiles.

'You're right. It's nice to see you. What are you doing up here?'

'Making sausages and chips for my dad.'

'Oh God, that sounds nice. Our Indian was a bit rubbish.'

'Chips are my speciality,' Linda says. 'I'll make you some one day.'

'I'd like that.'

'What are you doing here, anyway?'

'Been celebrating with my friend Joy. I think I told you about her.'

'Celebrating what?'

'Retirement,' says Evie, and laughs. 'I chucked my job in.'

'Hey, that's fast work,' says Linda. 'You serious? You really resigned?'

Evie nods and Linda leans over and kisses her on the cheek.

'That's for being brave,' she says.

The evening is still hot up in north London but Evie feels herself blush. For a second, while Linda looks at her, she doesn't know what to say.

'Me and my big fireman's boots,' Linda grins. Evie laughs then and suddenly feels a sense of relief.

'Oh, well maybe I have been brave, finally,' she says. 'It's taken me long enough. I feel like I've been treading water for years. How did that happen?'

'I bet it feels good, doesn't it?'

Evie thinks for a moment, squints her eyes into the dazzling rays of the setting sun.

'Actually, it does,' she says.

The familiar metallic rings from the track herald the oncoming train and they both stand up and begin to walk to the edge of the platform. As they wait for the train to come to a stop, Linda says more loudly to be heard above the noise of the train:

'You should let me buy you a drink to celebrate.'

The doors open and they get in. The carriage is empty and they sit down.

'I'd buy you one now but I'm a bit pooped. Did my second nightshift last night but now I've got three days off. Friday? We could go somewhere nice in Shoreditch.'

'I'd love to.'

The warning beeps ring out and the doors shudder to a close and the train lurches off heading back into town.

Down in Farringdon, Darren is lying on his bed. The Mad Professor's playing dub on his very expensive hifi and the huge open-plan apartment is scented by the grass he's smoking – it's good stuff which he buys direct from an old hippy who grows it organically in Wales, not the forced-grown weed that the kids puff on outside on the street. The flat is stylish in an understated way, on the third floor of a warehouse conversion off Turnmill Street: the subtle lighting picks out just a few pieces of good furniture, like the classic Eames chair, the low-backed right angle sofa from Milan, some interesting big prints on the walls, Edward Hopper and Grant Wood, which reflect Darren's instinct to move to America one day.

He's smart, all right. The last three years, most of his substantial income has derived from the telephone sales work he does for a friend of his when he's out of Henry's hearing. He's such a good closer, Darren, he can spend three hours in his friend's office in

Throgmorton Street on a weekday evening selling equities to retired people and he can make ten grand a night sometimes. He did a couple of hours this evening which is why he's back home chilling now. He's quietly filleted Henry's customer base and in fact last month he got Bernie Richmond to drop thirty thousand into a new internet start-up. It doesn't feel like disloyalty to Darren: he likes Henry, which is why he stays there, but it's not his responsibility to educate him on how to make money. It's dog-eat-dog. Darren also retains his day job with Henry because it provides him with a useful cover of respectability for some of the more hair-raising transactions he conducts in the evening at his mate's office.

Darren's dad back in Belfast was an old school bully, used to beat his mum as well as him and his two brothers. He hasn't spoken to his dad for five years and he still has bad dreams where his dad is climbing the stairs of their council house, pulling off his belt as his heavy steps echo through the flimsy walls. Sometimes he thinks about going to rescue his mum, bring her to London, set her up in a flat in Kilburn or something, but he knows that's just stupid. His two brothers are still in Belfast with their own families and the old man is ill now, so they all play out the Happy Families farce and Darren is the black sheep.

Is his instinct to head off to America one day right? I don't know. America may still be OK for someone like Darren. It may not be too late. They worship money over there, they're not hypocritical about it: everyone should try and make money and if you make it, you're good, and if you don't, well you're probably not going to survive. It seems ruthless to our fastidious taste, obviously, but at least it's honest. We use our glorious history to cloak our own hypocrisies; it's made us hesitant, weak, submissive. There are so many centuries of dashed aspiration, exploitation and sheer rapacity buried in the thick London clay beneath us. Deep under Tower Hill there are the skulls of those sacrificed by the Druids even before the Romans came along with their murderous obsessive-compulsive organisation and even that's almost two thousand years ago. When she was only sixteen, that bitch Mistress Hannah made Lily watch a heretic having his guts cut open on the hill above the Tower – he was of course still alive, as the hangman had cut him down before asphyxiation. Get down on your knees in the low tide mud at Wapping and dig down and eventually, if you keep going, you'll find the handle of a knife someone used to kill his neighbour, the pottery bottle that once held the wine that was used to toast a ruthless eviction, the threads of a baby's smock that died of plague. London is built on earth which is bloated with the sins of our past and now it feels to me like it's starting to ooze out of the ventilation shafts of those cold, glittering new buildings all along the river. We've pretended for all these centuries that we're above it all and now we're craven in our obsequious acceptance of twenty-first century money; every gangster around the world knows it, we're the neoliberal capitalist's privy.

Darren is thinking about Jade, wondering why she wouldn't come back and spend another night here with him. It's not that rejection cuts that deep with him – he's trained himself not to get worked up about it. It's more a surprising jolt to his vanity, he thought she was cool and he thought she liked him. Ah well. He closed someone this evening on a twenty thousand investment, and his twenty-five per cent of that will net him five grand. Not bad.

And over in Marylebone, as the sun finally begins to fade on another exhaustingly hot day in London, Jade lies in bed with William Cecil.

Lily stood outside the Sun tavern in Fish Street. She was scared; if Joseph Fairtree was not inside or if he was but was displeased to see her, she could be in danger, as a young woman on her own on a Saturday evening would attract the wrong attention. But she was exhilarated too by her impetuous flight from the bakery and the flimsy canvas bag on her shoulder reminded her that, whatever happened next, she would not be returning to Pudding Lane. The whorled glass of the windows was steamed up from the inside and she could not make out any faces in the candlelit interior, but the noise of laughter, shouts, the clink of tankards and glasses all combined to intimidate her.

From behind her, the voice of an older woman interrupted her thoughts:

'You be looking for a place to stay, lovely?'

She turned and stared at the old hag who smiled lasciviously at her underneath her filthy bonnet. The woman reached out a bony finger to flick the curls of Lily's hair.

'Such beauty, needs someone to care for it.' The woman reached for Lily's hand but she was too quick, and reached out for the door. As she pushed it open, she heard

251

the old woman cackle behind her.

Now she was inside and the tavern was packed. There were gentlemen in frock coats standing with flushed faces and tankards in hand, ladies in handsome dresses seated beside them, their faces painted, their lips crayoned like Mistress Hannah's had been earlier. The room was hot and smelled of roasted meat and the noise was deafening to her ears – she had never stepped foot in a tavern before. As eyes turned to her, her instinct told her to keep moving and she began to push through the crowd, looking right and left for Joseph Fairtree, trying as best she could to disguise her limp and to look as though she were used to such places. A hand squeezed her thigh as she passed a table of gentlemen and she heard laughter.

She kept moving, her heart now beating fast again as it had done while making her escape from the bakery. What if he were not here? She reached one end of the room without seeing him and was obliged to turn around and walk back the way she had come. She espied the table of gentlemen all watching her with leers on their faces and as she came close again, one cried out:

'Sit with us a while, young lady, and provide us with some entertainment! Thou looks a most comely companion.'

A hand grabbed her arm and began pulling her down to the bench. Another gripped her waist and she fell into a man's lap as the laughter around her erupted.

'She's keen for sport!' cried one and she saw an ugly

face lean over her, the grinning lips wet with wine.

Suddenly the face jerked violently to the side as another man's hand pulled her up to her feet roughly.

'How dare you treat my kinswoman so!' Joseph Fairtree shouted. 'I have a mind to thrash every one of you.'

'Ah, 'tis just friendly play, Joseph, do not take on so,' called one of the men. 'We knew not of your connection. 'Twas a harmless game.'

'Take a care your harmless games do not bring you harm,' Fairtree warned and finally looked down at Lily.

'You are not injured, madam?' he asked.

'No,' she said, and in her relief turned to the table and said clearly, 'These gentlemen were merely joshing.' And she bowed her head briefly to them, at which several of them responded in kind.

'You are too civil, madam,' Fairtree muttered, 'but your dignity does you credit. I apologise for not greeting you sooner. My table is over that far corner.'

He threaded his way through the crowded room over to the other side which she had not yet reached. Just beyond the last edge of the bar, around which the crowd of drinkers stood and jostled each other, she saw over his shoulder a wooden partition which led into a small alcove. She followed him in and saw a table with two chairs; in front of one was a plate of meat and a large glass of wine.

'Excuse me,' he said, 'I have begun eating. If I am

frank, I did not expect to have the pleasure of your company.'

She must have looked concerned, because he immediately added:

'And may I say, madam, how much pleasure it gives me that you have chosen to offer it. Will you eat something? Or did you take supper at your master's house?'

She shook her head.

'No, I have not eaten for some time,' she said. ''Tis... 'tis a long story.'

Finally he smiled.

'Then we have plenty of time for the telling of it. Do please take your seat. Robert!' He called over to a large sweaty man wearing a butcher's apron who was passing the open door of the partition. 'Bring my guest some supper. And a glass of your Burgundy wine.'

'You are too kind, sir,' she said. 'You need not provide for me.'

'What of this "sir"?' he said. 'My name, as I told you, is Joseph. 'Twas given me by my mother and should suffice.'

For the first time, she too smiled.

'Very well, Joseph,' she said. 'If truth be known, I could eat, and therefore I shall gratefully accept your kindness.' She extended her hand across the table. 'My name is Lily Cadyman.'

'Lily,' he repeated, shaking her hand gently. 'My late departed friend Nicholas Culpeper knew of the Lily. It

is under the dominion of Mercury, I believe, and gives great strength to the brain. The seeds of that plant will be ripening now upon the fields of the heath at Hampstead.'

'Your knowledge is most broad, Joseph Fairtree – for a soldier.'

He laughed.

'I was a soldier. But our wars were completed. Now I toil as a scrivener' – he pointed to a pile of manuscripts lying on the ground beside the table – 'at Gray's Inn outside of the City walls. The law is now my lance.'

Lily felt once more the lack of her accomplishments but she felt emboldened by his frank demeanour.

'I am ashamed to say I cannot read, Joseph, let alone write. I am in awe of your skills.'

'Nonsense,' he replied. 'It will not take long for a woman of Mercury to learn these skills. We shall start tomorrow.'

Chapter Twelve

It's Thursday morning and Marta is sick. She's been throwing up during the night and now she's too weak to get herself ready for work, so she knows she will be penalised for not turning up at the café in the market. The girls have left for school and Angel is pacing up and down the small area of floorspace in their bedroom while she lies still in bed. They both know it's not a virus or food poisoning or anything like that; Marta is just scared sick.

Angel told her yesterday evening that William Cecil had instructed him to be outside St Paul's Cathedral at 8 o'clock on Saturday evening. He would have a task to perform that night and then all their worries would be over: as a proven Luohan, he would have access to whatever he needed to make sure his family was safe and secure. They would not have to worry about money ever again.

The girls heard them arguing last night but she couldn't help that, she couldn't keep it all in anymore. Where was the Angel she used to know, the Angel back in Bogota who would play music and dance with her in their front room, who ran a steady business looking after other people's accounts, who had plans for them to be a family? The Angel who people looked up to, who she was proud to walk down the street with? Where was he now? Who was this new man, this imposter, who talked crazy talk about fire and attachments and nirvana?

'Nothing is real,' Angel keeps saying, speaking in their native Spanish, as he paces up and down the little room. 'This life is a dream, we must stop dreaming and we must wake up, we must feel our strength. London is a dream which is dreamed by someone else. It is not a dream, it is a nightmare. But it is not our nightmare, Marta. I have woken up and now I am real and London is not real. You will wake up too, I will help you, Mr Cecil he will help you. The girls too. Can't you see? Can't you understand how beautiful our life will be?'

Marta can't understand that. She lies still in bed now, not even looking at her husband, her face pale and damp from sweat. Under the blanket her hands are clasped together and she is blocking out Angel's words by reciting Hail Mary's in her mind, one after the other. Holy Mary Mother of God, pray for us sinners now and at the hour of our death.

Over at Baker Street, William Cecil is walking slowly around the big table in his living room. There is a map spread out over the table, an enlarged map of the City of London. Chan is positioning two table lamps so they illuminate the streets clearly in the gloomy room and over the other side four people are standing in front of the statue, their eyes closed. On the surface of the map stand a number of small brass statues of the Buddha, the kind you get in hippy shops. Cecil has more in his hand.

'Fifteen, Falusah,' he says and places another Buddha on the map. 'Sixteen, Richie.' He scans the streets then places another. 'Seventeen, Poppy.' Another Buddha. 'And our eighteenth Luohan, Angel.' He leans over the map, finds Watling Street and sets the last Buddha down on the paper. He puts his hands behind his back and walks slowly around the table, looking down at the pattern upon the streets made by the eighteen little statues.

'Excellent,' he murmurs and a thin smile appears on the stretched skin of his narrow face. He looks over at the four people in front of the statue and slowly walks towards them.

'Here we are,' he says softly as he gets close to them. 'My four lovelies. My four fine Luohans. You were my first. I am so close to you now. Can you feel how close I am to you?' He delicately touches each one of them as he walks around them, a hand on a shoulder, a finger on a forehead. They react, alert and excited but they keep their eyes closed.

'You have been with me for many months now, my brave ones. You were the first. You have undergone the trials and challenges set by the Buddha more than the others, you have conquered the fire. You know that. You are my closest ones. Now finally, I will tell you how your training is completed. The others, they will know on Friday. But you, my beautiful ones, you because of your strength, your power, your glory, you will know today. You will know now. Sit down on the floor, keep your eyes closed.'

The four of them shuffle to the floor and sit cross-legged in front of the statue, their arms straight down and resting on their knees as he has taught them. He continues to walk around them and the burning incense sticks continue to give off sweetly fragrant clouds.

'This is what will happen on Saturday,' he begins.

Four miles east, the Stirling Global office is full this Thursday morning, everyone in apart from Henry who's about to have a meeting across the river. Evie took Jade out for a coffee first thing and told her that she was leaving the company. Jade continued to surprise her by giving her a hug and telling her she was really happy for her. Evie, forever wanting to feel in control of these things, put it down to what she assumed to be Jade's contentment with Darren. She has no idea that Jade hasn't given Darren a moment's thought ever since she stepped onto that motor boat last Saturday morning. She has absolutely no idea why Jade is looking so fine, joyful even.

So when earlier, over her bowl of muesli in Wapping, Evie had speculated that Jade would react badly to her announcement about her departure, was that just her doing what she'd been doing to everyone, for years, worrying that they needed her around when in fact they were perfectly fine without her?

Now in the office everyone knew. Jean was sulky, Rufus and Jimmy were surprised but not particularly interested, Darren was intrigued.

'So where's that come from, Evie?' he asks and for the first time in weeks she realised he was being quite sincere, wanted to understand her state of mind. Even before Jade had come on the scene she had largely written Darren off as a superficial lothario; now she looks at his open, enquiring face and feels a warmth towards him – he and she had always been the best performers at the company anyway.

'Oh, I don't know, I suppose it's been building up. I've been doing this longer than you, you know,' she says and smiles at him.

'That's true,' he says and looks thoughtful. 'Do you think there's a time limit on this stuff' – he waved his hand to indicate the office – 'do you think there's only so much selling you can do?'

'Oh God no, I can't wait to get properly stuck in!' Rufus interrupts.

Darren ignores him. 'I mean,' he says, still looking at Evie, 'do you end up thinking all the time about how to manipulate people, how to make them do what you want rather than what they want? Does that end up with you having a false perspective on people all the time? I wonder about that.'

'Maybe,' she says, nodding. Maybe he is right, maybe the last ten years, since she left Ibiza, maybe that's all she's been doing. Constantly overcompensating with Joy and Jade, lecturing her mum and dad about this that and the other, managing Henry's psyche. It suddenly feels to her that she hasn't thought about what she wants for years. 'Maybe that's it,' she continues, 'maybe I want my life back.'

'Good on you,' he says and she feels a rush of emotion. 'I'm envious of you,' he continues. 'I haven't worked all that out yet. Tell me what it's like on the outside.' He grins at her and she smiles back at him.

Henry's not happy at the moment. He's standing outside the entrance of the Shard, just south of the river by London Bridge station. He's supposed to be meeting Felix here but all Felix said in the text was, *Meet me at the Shard at 11.30* and now he's been hanging around outside the main entrance for ten minutes and he's getting ratty.

The Shard, of course, is the ultimate icon of London

these days. It represents everything about what London is becoming and nothing about what it was. Despite myself, I like it. When you drive along the Embankment I like the way its splintered glass peak dodges in and out of the tall buildings along the river and, gradually, as you get further east the beautiful steep glass slopes that form such a slender shape begin to dominate the skyline until when you're not far off the Tower of London you can see the genius of what Renzo Piano created: it really is like a superannuated cathedral spire, it's like all the spiritual aspirations of the world combined into one alchemical structure, a synthesis of Egyptian pyramids, Spanish cathedrals, Gothic towers. It's absolutely beautiful.

And that's the problem. The Shard is a symbol of belief in a city that has forgotten how to believe. I don't know anything about this Piano guy but sometimes when I'm staring at the Shard I imagine him as a pure, idealistic spiritual being who was imprisoned by a bunch of capitalist thugs and forced to work night and day otherwise they'd chop off his wife's hands. Something like that. And we ended up with this building which in another era we would gather at to worship some God or other but today is just the subject of dumb debate between people like that idiot son of the Queen and half-arsed journalists with copy to file.

It stands there, the Shard, when you're close up to it like Henry is now, a little forlorn, as though it can't quite work out what it's doing there with all these humans wandering around it clutching coffees and smartphones and talking shit. The big empty ground floor is lined with receptionists processing these humans to go up to different floors to conduct whatever footling business they have to and another entrance whisks tourists up to the breathtakingly expensive restaurants at the top. If a building could cry, the Shard probably would.

Henry's not close to crying but he's irritated. He's about to phone Felix when he sees him walking towards him speaking on his iPhone. He comes up to Henry, nods and shakes his hand and makes a raised eyebrow gesture while continuing to talk. Finally he says, 'Sure OK, 2.30. See you there.'

He breathes out, looks around him then back at Henry.

'JP Morgan,' he says. 'They're good guys, but they need a lot of pressure on them. They're not used to getting their hands dirty like you and me, Henry.'

'Americans,' says Henry.

'Exactly. Now, let's get some coffee. They keep a table for me at Aqua on the 31st floor.'

He leads Henry towards the lifts, says 'Morning, how are you today?' to the uniformed doorman, and soon they are both stepping out into the restaurant. Henry's heels click on the brown wooden floor as he follows Felix who is heading straight to a table by the window. The windows are huge and give out onto the same kind of views that Evie saw when she was up in that tower at dawn with Jade. All around, London wrestles with itself down below in the persistent heat but up here it's cool modernism and brown leather chairs and tinkling jazz.

A waiter comes over and Felix says, 'Roberto, give me my usual green tea and my guest will have?'

'Cappuccino,' Henry says automatically.

'Chocolate on top?' the waiter asks casually.

'As it comes,' Henry replies.

'So, Henry, fill me in. You've got the guys at Stirling World pumped up, I guess? They're excited?'

'Pretty much so, yes.'

'Come on Henry, no need to be coy with me. They know you've got them into the big time, right?'

'Yes, of course. Just got a couple of questions, Felix.'

'Questions are good, Henry. Questions bring answers. Give me a second.' He starts typing on his iPhone and Henry's chubby fingers grip the edge of the glass table. The sun is bathing the city down below in so much light the buildings look bleached.

After a minute, Felix puts his phone down on the table again, sighs and says:

'My guys are really driving me on this one, it's fantastic. They've got ownership, you know what I mean? It really pumped them up having Stirling World on board and they're looking to issue the first Spanish franchise this week.'

'I thought you already had most of Europe signed up?'

'Totally. Just dotting i's and crossing t's. Where were we? Oh hold on, here's our drinks.'

The waiter sets their cups down on the glass table and fidgets with the sugar bowl for a second then leaves them.

'I've got this girl in the office,' says Henry. 'She's started recently and she's young so she does all that bloody googling –'

'Tell me about it. Their brains are wired differently to ours, Henry, but they're good kids. I'm excited about this generation.'

'Anyway, she couldn't seem to find out anything about the guys in Florida, the guys who developed the Gener8 formula at NASA.'

Felix looks straight at Henry, surprise in his eyes.

'Well of course she couldn't, Henry. Why do you think that is?'

'Well, I –'

'It's top secret, Henry. The guy who actually isolated the eight nutrients has been given a safe house by the CIA. He's had to change his identity, everything. He's this brilliant scientist and they can't afford him to fall into the hands of those ISIS crazies.'

'ISIS?'

'Come on Henry, think what would happen if those

guys out in Syria got hold of the formula. I'm not even mentioning Iran.'

'So the US government is actively involved in Gener8?'

'Actively involved? It's the most important American government initiative since Franklin D. Roosevelt's New Deal of 1933.'

Felix shakes his head. His thin, slightly-too-dark hair is carefully slicked back over his head and his eyebrows need some attention. He leans into the table.

'Henry,' he whispers, taking a moment to look left and right, 'it even took me three months to get through the full Pentagon security check. They rang up people I went to school with. They even tried to ask my old mum some questions but the poor old dear is past all that now. The Americans take it very, very seriously. That's all I can tell you – you're not authorised to my level yet.'

Henry picks up his cappuccino and takes a sip. His upper lip is sweaty again and now a thin line of aerated milk decorates it.

'I understand, Felix,' he says. 'Obviously I realised it was something like that but you know, I need to keep the guys informed.'

'Of course. And when I kick in my people to deliver the training they'll get a lot more to chew on.'

'When does the training start?'

'Well, you'll need to have at least five regional reps in place before it will be worth bringing my guys in, it's a pretty forensic course. How are you doing on recruiting?'

'We're starting to make contact with people through our network. Bristol, Leeds, Manchester, Birmingham, you know.'

Felix nods. 'That's good. Big cities. Lot of kiddies in those cities. Smart work, Henry. When you've got five ready, tell me and I can estimate the cost of the training for you.'

'There's a cost to it?'

'Of course. I mentioned that to you. This is a big operation Henry and I'm covering a lot of overheads. It won't be much, don't even think about it. You'll be recouping it by the end of the month.'

Henry wipes the sleeve of his pin-striped suit across his face and the milk line disappears. His left eye is twitching slightly.

'And we'll get the first batch of product in soon? I've still just got the one packet, I've locked it in the drawer of my desk.'

'Absolutely. The Gener8 logistics guys are just sorting out the global distribution routes, you'll get the first ten boxes ASAP. You can have more if you want but I assume you'll want to keep a handle on costs in the initial stages.'

'I forgot, we need to pay upfront for the samples.'

A sheen of sweat is now visible on Henry's creased brow.

'And then you're cooking with gas,' Felix exclaims triumphantly. 'Imagine it, Henry: when this thing hits the Daily Mail, Breakfast TV, Woman's Hour...' He shakes his head again, his eyes closing this time almost in wonder. 'It's going to be absolutely mega and you'll be the guy at the front of the queue. I actually can't wait.'

As Henry smiles weakly, his fingers gripping the glass edge again, I know what you're thinking. You're thinking, what a schmuck. How can he believe this stuff? Evie and Darren knew it was bollocks right from the off. But Henry has to believe it and as we leave him there in Felix's grip and we look out across the big showy glass restaurant and down towards the streets filled with cars and people and noise and this relentless heatwave, don't you realise this conversation is going on all over this city? Everywhere. The kid who's loaded up with student loan debt trying to save money from his underpaid job to build up a deposit on a flat whose value will plummet when the shit finally hits the fan; the couple who've moved out east to get cheaper rent and are shelling out four times what they were before just to commute back into town to work all day in ununionised jobs; the Council which sells off another batch of public land to a bunch of spivs who are promising green fields and public housing but in reality will just put up another block which they'll market at the next Hong Kong property show; the Big Issue woman on Oxford Street who's putting her earnings into safe accommodation so she can survive when really all she wants to do is make her way back north and away from this steaming cauldron: they're all doing it, we're all doing it, we're emptying our pockets and chucking our ducats at the fat man and closing our eyes and hoping for the best.

Lily pushed her empty plate away from her.

'A healthy appetite indeed,' Fairtree smiled.

She had told him how she had once more been denied supper at home but she hadn't gone any further. Now she looked at him.

'I have left,' she said.

'What do you mean?'

'Master Farriner's. This evening.' She reached down to the floor and picked up the light canvas bag. 'These are my possessions. All of them. I am not going back.'

'They permitted you?' Fairtree looked concerned.

'They know not,' she replied. 'They think me either praying or asleep in my room. I crept out while they caroused in the kitchen. They did not hear me leave and they will never see me again.'

At this she glared so fiercely at him that he started for a second, then burst out laughing.

'I knew there was the rebel about you when first I spied you in these parts,' he said. 'By Goodness you would have made a boon comrade in our recent wars, young lady.' Then he stopped chuckling. 'I mean no disrespect,' he said.

'None taken.'

271

'But you have somewhere to stay?'

At this she faltered slightly. 'I...I will go to my mother's tonight in Spital Field. Then I will take her back home to where she was born. Away from this City.'

'And where is that?'

"Tis called Eye − I always thought that a strange name for a village. She told me once, it is near the city of Cambridge. The women are lacemakers there, my mother knows that trade, she can work there and I can apprentice.'

'But you told me your mother is sick.'

At this Lily was silent and looked down at the table.

'How sick is she, Lily?'

She remained silent for a moment, then looked up.

'It is all I can think of,' she said. 'Where else can I go?'

'Your mother has kinsmen in Eye?'

'I don't know. She used to tell me about it, when I was a girl. She said it was a pretty place of fields and streams.'

'It is handsome in those parts,' Fairtree said. 'But Lily, you must let me help you.' He pointed down to his manuscripts. 'It is my trade. Let me write to the aldermen of Eye and ask after your mother's family. We will know soon enough.'

'You have been kind enough already,' she said, pointing at her empty plate. 'I shall not be a burden upon you.'

Now he looked irritated.

'Bah,' he said. 'You may be as proud as you like, Lily Cadyman, but I talk sense. If your mother is ill, you will not serve her well by appearing tonight unexpected and so alarm her more. I will accompany you to her tomorrow as we spoke and if I can help the poor soul, I will. This city has been so filled with the suffering of the pestilence these last few years, it is a curse, I sometimes think.'

She began to speak but he interrupted her.

'I will brook no argument,' he said. 'I am a practical man, Lily, like all soldiers. You will stay in my lodgings tonight and have no fear, you will be looked after by my housekeeper, a woman of such fierce and unbending authority that even I stand in fear of her. She will make you up a bed in her quarters and tomorrow we will step out as planned to Spital Field and we will put your good mother's health in the hands of the Lord our God and the wizardry of my dear departed friend Culpeper.'

Chapter Thirteen

Friday morning arrives no different to every other heatwave morning: bright skies, buildings picked out with Californian clarity by the early day sunshine, the pavements already warm, the cars' exhausts giving the still air an acrid edge. London reels around in this heat like an old dog, trying to find a comfortable position for itself but getting up and pacing around every few minutes then having another go. Linda ties the laces of her training shoes on the steps of her apartment building then sets off at a steady pace, dropping down towards the towpath which will take her on a run along the canal up to Camden and back. Angel sits at the narrow kitchen table in his flat and listens to the sounds of his two girls getting ready for school; he's so exhausted by the lack of sleep this week he can hardly focus on anything but he recognises one still emotion inside of him: fear. Jade is making a pot of tea in the kitchen of William Cecil's apartment and thinking about the probation meeting she's got to go to this morning; she's going to get there early so she can get back to Chiltern Court because there seems to be a lot going on today. William has asked her to take the day off work to help out and already it just seems normal that she's here, she's part of his family.

Evie is on the tube heading in to work already because she wants to get in before Jean and have a look through the contracts file to find the contact information for their new cleaner; now she's made the decision to quit, everything seems much clearer to her and she's started to worry about the strange conversation she had with him the other evening. It's all linked in with William Cecil and she plans to ring Cecil today too, just to give herself the satisfaction of telling him she's back in control of her life. That she's not the loser which he appeared to enjoy telling her she was. But she's got this niggling concern about what the Colombian man said and about how something was going to happen; he seemed so strange about it.

Henry is already in the office when she gets there. She's surprised to see him, as normally he's in at 9.30, even on Fridays when he heads off early to get the 2pm train from Paddington back down to the West Country.

'Oh, hello,' she says as she shuts the door behind her. 'You're early.'

'Catching the worm,' he says without looking up from his computer screen.

She puts her bag down on her desk and heads off to the kitchen to make coffee. She comes back in with two cups and puts one down on his desk. He grunts something vaguely thankful and she goes to Jean's desk to look for the office file. After rifling through it in the silent office for a while, she finds the cleaning contract and sees a name – Angel Hernandez – and a mobile contact number. She puts it into her phone and goes back to her own desk and starts her computer.

For a while they sit in silence, working. Evie is drawing up an Excel sheet of her clients and putting in notes against each one so she can pass them all over to Henry for him to allocate to either Darren or Jimmy. She decided yesterday that she didn't want anything more to do with them so she's not going to try and negotiate any continued commissions with Henry – she's walking away. And she plans to leave in a week.

It was so liberating when she realised she could do that. She told Linda about her plan on the tube in from Edmonton. Linda asked if she could afford just to give up any commissions which might be due to her going forwards – practical again, Linda. So that evening back at her flat, Evie had worked out exactly how much money she had saved in various deposit accounts and ISAs and so on and she reckoned she could take six months off work without seriously eating into her savings. After that, well, life would take her somewhere.

'What you doing?'

Evie looks up and sees that Henry is sitting back in his chair holding his cup of coffee and staring at her.

'Just what I said I'd do: doing notes on all my clients so I can hand them over to you.'

'You don't have to,' he says.

'I do, Henry, we've been through it.'

'No, think about it: nothing's going to happen with any of those clients for the next few weeks, just leave it and take off somewhere for a bit. When you get back, the clients will still be there and I'll have got us started on Gener8. I'm appointing my first rep today, this guy up in Leeds. He loves it. And I'm staying up in London again this weekend to keep on top of it. I tell you, it's big, Evie.'

'Henry...'

'Hear me out. I know you're fed up. I'm not very good at saying things like this, you know me, but I don't want you to burn any bridges. Just go and lie on a beach in Ibiza for a few weeks. I can manage everything here and if you do decide then that you might want to give it another go, I'll have set up Gener8 so it's a business you and me can grow together. We can build it, I know we can, we can make a bloody fortune.'

'Henry...'

'I was with Felix yesterday. The whole thing is much bigger than I thought. We'll be making much more money than we ever did with that bloody Malawi rubbish. Think about it, that's all I'm saying, just think about it. It could be like it used to be.'

She gets up and walks around her desk over to his and draws up a chair. She leans over his desk and takes his hand.

'It's not going to be like it used to be, Henry,' she says softly, a sad smile on her face. 'I've tried to tell you.'

He grips her hand and leans forward.

'But why just chuck it all away? Why not give me a chance?'

'Because it's not about you,' she says. 'It's about me. It's about my whole life, everything I've ever done. I've done two go's in Holloway, Henry: do you realise that?'

'That second one was my fault.'

'No it wasn't. I've just been stupid and I don't want to be stupid any more. I don't want to do all this stuff' – she waved her arm to take in the office – 'I want something different. I don't know what it is. But I'll find out.'

She stands up and walks over to the window which

looks down on Watling Street.

'So what are you going to do?' he asks, sullenly.

'Oh I don't know,' she sighs. 'I'm going to spend a bit of time helping my dad with his business, his paperwork is a mess.'

'Going back to Daddy.'

She turns round.

'Don't sneer at me, Henry. I'm going to help him out for a bit because I can. Then I don't know what I'll do. I'll do something. And you know what? You know what I think you should do? You should tear up that bloody contract you signed with that crook and go back to Totnes. Give it up, Henry. It's over.'

'Oh, just fuck off, will you?' he mutters and put his head in his hands. She watches him for a moment then the door opens and Jimmy walks in.

'Morning,' he says.

'Morning, Jimmy,' Evie says. She goes back to her desk and picks her phone up.

'I've just got to go outside and make a call. Back in a bit.'

She leaves the office and walks slowly up Watling Street. Even here in the City, there are men in shorts walking at the same slow pace as her and most of the women are in skirts and skimpy tops. Some more traditional types still bluster on in dark suits, sweat glinting on their brows under the morning sun. She goes into a chain coffee bar, orders an Americano and takes it outside to one of the tables on the pavement.

She spends a while composing a text to Angel, and when she finally sends it, it reads: 'Hi. This is Evie Sangster from Stirling Global. I met you in our office the other evening. I'm sorry if I annoyed you but I was just interested when you said you also knew William Cecil. You seemed a bit upset about it. Feel free to give me a ring to chat about it any time if you want. Best wishes, ES.'

She sits sipping her coffee for a while then she phones William Cecil. After a few rings, Chan answers.

'Hello,' she says. 'This is Evie Sangster. I wonder if I could speak to Mr Cecil.'

'Mr Cecil is very busy.'

'Oh.'

A pause.

'I will ask him.'

She waits for a couple of minutes and then:

'Hello.' William Cecil's voice is curt.

'Mr Cecil, this is Evie Sangster. I hope I'm not disturbing you.'

'You are but I believe I invited you to contact me so the fault is mine.'

'I just wanted to tell you something.'

He doesn't respond so she continues.

'I just wanted to tell you that I've worked some things out for myself and I've left my job. I wanted to thank you for making me think properly about it.'

'Why do you believe you have thought properly? Did I not explain, the Buddha gave instructions to his people in order to train them to think properly and he expected them to work for years even to achieve some basic improvement. It is inconceivable therefore that, as you claim, you are thinking properly.'

'Well, I think I am. Anyway, I just wanted to thank you for the prompt.'

'My dear Miss Sangster, your thanks mean nothing to me. Was there anything else?'

'Yes, I just wanted to tell you about a strange coincidence. The man who cleans the office where I'm currently working is called Angel Hernandez and he knows you too. He seemed quite agitated about something that was going to happen at the end of this week. I just thought it seemed like a strange coincidence.'

Cecil is silent for a moment. Then he clears his throat.

'Mr Hernandez gets very confused. His English is not so good. He has recently begun the Eightfold Path and is receiving instruction like many of the Londoners whom I help. He meant four years; I only told him recently that he could expect to see significant changes in his circumstances and mental health if he adopted the Path properly for four years. You see, Miss Sangster, thinking properly is not a whim of the moment. Goodbye.'

With that, he hangs up on her.

'Pompous arse,' Evie says aloud. She finishes her coffee and heads back to the office. When she gets in, Henry is briefing Jimmy on Gener8.

'I'm not heading home this weekend, Jimmy, I'm staying up here to work on it. And I want you fully on board.'

Ten minutes later, Angel's phone rings. He is still in the kitchen, sitting dazed at the table. The girls left for school half an hour ago and Marta is in the shower. He slowly picks up the phone and sees the name 'William Cecil', as he knew he would. As soon as he lifts the phone to his ear, Cecil begins screaming at him. He screams invective at him and Angel sits very still, the noise of the shower still coming through from the bathroom and tears gathering at the corners of his eyes. The screaming goes on for another minute and then finally, William Cecil stops to gather his breath and then says, in a quieter, threatening tone:

'You had better come here now, Angel. Immediately. Do not tell your wife. Do not speak to anyone. I expect you here within the hour.' And with that he ended the conversation.

As if sleepwalking, Angel stands up, puts his phone in his pocket and steps softly towards the front door. He opens it, the noise of the shower still going on behind him, then he walks out and shuts the door behind him.

Angel heads to Seven Sisters tube station. He's wiped

the tears from his eyes and he now just walks steadily, not aware of other people passing him on the pavement or the lorries revving up at traffic lights along West Green Road. As he's been doing in recent days, he blocks out the terror inside him by trying to remember the phrases he has learned from William Cecil, and he mumbles them to himself, his lips moving:

'The noble truth of the reality of Dhukka...Buddha Nature...a flame above a flower...the path of transformation...'

He doesn't really know what any of these phrases mean but he has been convinced that they contain powers beyond his ability to comprehend and so he repeats them as though they have some sacred quality. Five years ago, in Bogota, Angel would have been contemptuous of anyone who said something like 'Foster wholeness through Samma-Vayama' and he would have shaken his head and smiled and turned back to analysing the profit and loss account of the business he was auditing and he would have looked forward to getting home to see his wife and their little girls and eating supper with them in their apartment looking out over the river.

Now he presses his Oyster card onto the yellow circle at the entrance gates in the station and waits for the lift to open. He chants silently with his eyes closed as people gather around him in the bright metal lift: 'Infinite life, infinite beauty, infinite life, eternal flame, infinite beauty...'

By repeating phrases to himself he blocks out the terrible words of William Cecil on the phone half an hour ago. At Kings Cross he passively joins the mass of people threading through the fluorescent tunnels and eventually gets on a Bakerloo line train. At Baker Street he climbs the final steps out of the station, turns right and on the corner heads into Chiltern Court. The concierge recognises him and says, 'For Mr Cecil?' but Angel just pads softly ahead to the lift, his lips moving as he focuses as hard as he can on the phrases he can remember.

Chan lets him in and directs him to the same front room. Inside, Angel can see four of the other Luohans all sitting at a table which is covered with a large map. William Cecil is standing behind them.

'Stand over there,' Cecil says immediately and Angel moves in front of the statue and stands still. 'Close your eyes.' Soon Angel can feel William Cecil's presence although he has not heard him as he walked quietly over the carpet towards him but he can sense his breath now and he tries to still his beating heart and he clenches his eyes tightly shut and his hands are balled up in sweat and tension.

'I am disappointed in you,' William Cecil whispers. 'I am very disappointed in you.' Angel can feel him walking slowly around him and he tries not to wobble.

'You have spoken to someone. How many times did

I tell every single Luohan that our work is for us alone, there can be no talk to outsiders? Did I not make myself clear?'

Angel is too scared to speak. He tries to open his mouth but nothing comes out.

'You know I must punish you,' Cecil continues very quietly. 'I must bring you back to the Path. You have been weak and I must teach you strength. What must I do, Angel?'

'Punish,' Angel stutters. 'Must punish.'

'Yes.'

The room is hot and dark and the incense burns sickly sweet at the foot of the statue. Then suddenly William Cecil slaps Angel's face hard and the noise fills the room like an explosion. Angel falls to his knees and puts his hand up to his face which is already smarting red and as the tears begin to fall from his eyes again, Cecil gesticulates at one of the other Luohans who gets up from his chair, strides over and kicks Angel in the stomach, jolting him around the carpet, kicking him in his back, his legs, even his head until Cecil puts his hand up and he stops.

The room is still again, filled now with sobs from Angel on the floor and the heavy breathing of the man who attacked him. William Cecil waves him to return to his seat and then he leans over Angel, who has blood coming out of his ear.

'Never betray either me or your fellow Luohans ever

again,' he says quietly. Chan has appeared again at the door and Cecil summons him over.

'Take him to the bathroom and clean him up,' he says. 'Then put him in the small room. He will stay here today.' He reaches down and puts his hand into Angel's pocket and pulls out his phone. 'I will keep this,' he says.

Then Cecil leans over Angel and tenderly strokes his forehead.

'Do not fear, Angel. Do not fear. The path of the Buddha is hard, you are new to it but your heart is good. Do not fear. I trust you.'

The front door of the apartment is heard to open then slam shut again and a few seconds later, Jade appears at the open doorway behind Chan.

'I'm back,' she smiles.

Cecil beams at her and beckons her over. She walks over to him, doesn't look at Angel lying on the floor, and folds her head into his chest. Then he lifts her face up and kisses her on the lips. No-one says anything, apart from a slight whimpering from Angel.

'Now, my beautiful girl,' Cecil says. 'Our friend Angel has had an accident. Stay with him for a while, won't you? You know what he needs.'

Jade smiles and turns to help Chan lift Angel up, and they both put an arm under his and slowly shuffle the crying man out of the room.

The day goes by in one almost final burst of heat:

the weathermen are predicting storms in a couple of days to bring this blaze to an end. In Watling Street the day grinds slowly on with that sense of slow-motion uselessness which offices have in the height of summer and Evie leaves early after she's finished filling in the columns of her Excel sheet.

Then it's Friday night in the city and there's a real sense, after weeks of this heatwave and the news that it's soon to end, of an abandonment, a throwing off of care. No-one's worried tonight about their mortgage payments or their Instagram feed or the new boss who's just come in from America and looks like she might fire you. There's a speakeasy loucheness to tonight, a hot pavement circus feel to the narrow streets within the triangle of Shoreditch and people are carrying drinks out of bars and off down the road and Uber drivers are pulling up everywhere to let more people out into the carnival and more than ever there's this sense that everything could blow at any moment; London is bathing its people in alcohol and sweat and desire.

Linda is up for it. She's had two days off and isn't back on shift until Saturday evening. She's walking down Rivington Street heading for Callooh Callay. It's a bit old school but what the hell, she wants to toast Evie's escape tonight and you've got to start with a cocktail bar when it's thirty degrees in London on a Friday night. She's wearing jeans and a black and gold Desiguel top and she's got Puma street shoes on. She's so toned, Linda, she walks with that lightfooted roll and she's wearing lipstick tonight, a subtle pink which does enough to pick out the strong lines of her lips. She's smiling, in fact everyone's smiling tonight and everyone's already dipping on and off the pavement and the cars are doing that slow summer evening cruise and Linda's thinking, this is exactly where I want to be.

The cocktail bar is humming and she's led to the little metal table with two chairs which she booked yesterday. She looks through the cocktail list then sits back and looks around the room which is thudding with a bass line and all the tables are filled and everyone's showing their teeth and talking loud and making extravagant hand gestures. She watches a waitress with a tight red mini skirt thread her way through the crowd and sees her legs are raised up on three inch stillettos. She looks back over towards the door and then she sees Evie talking to one of the door staff and she waves at her.

'Never been here,' Evie says after they've kissed on the cheek and she's sat down. She's wearing a red cotton dress with a brown leather belt and flats. Her brown hair is lush and looks like she might have added a curl into it tonight. She's wearing a bit more mascara than she does during the week.

'What can I get you?' Linda asks, passing her the

cocktail list.

Evie laughs.

'You choose,' she says.

Linda raises her eyebrows, then takes back the list, scans it and calls the waitress with the red skirt over.

'We'll have two San Giovanni's,' she says.

The waitress leaves and Evie sits back in her chair, smiling.

'So go on, tell me: how many hours have you done in the gym today?'

'None actually. I went for a run this morning on the towpath though.'

'Of course you did. In this heat.'

'Don't tell me you sat in one of those horrible wine bars at lunchtime?' says Linda.

'No, no, I've been a good girl today. Into the office early, argument first thing with Henry, then I left at lunchtime and went home. I was even thinking of going for a swim this afternoon but I think I just fell asleep instead.'

'Why are you arguing with that guy? I thought you'd chucked it in.'

Evie sighs and settles back in her chair.

'Oh I have but you know, it doesn't mean I don't want him to be happy. He's got himself involved in another really stupid scheme and he can't seem to see that it's all crap. I just want him to move on, give it all up, go back to his wife in the country.'

'Doesn't sound that attractive when you put it like that.'

Evie laughs.

'It doesn't, does it? Well, it's his life. I'm out.'

'That's more like it.'

The drinks arrive and Linda raises her glass.

'To your freedom,' she says and they clink glasses and smile. They drink their drinks and Evie looks around the crowded bar.

'So have you had any more thoughts about what's next?' Linda asks.

'Not really. I'm going to help my dad out a bit with his accounts over the next few weeks. It will be nice doing that. Then I don't know. I suppose what I have worked out is that I need to stop thinking about fixing everyone else. I've spent too long getting people to do things, making them do what I think they should do and maybe I should just cut all that out.'

'You mean think about what you want to do rather than what everyone else could do?'

'Yes, that's it I suppose. I'm quite good at getting people to do what I want. I've always been like that. Getting junkies to buy forged prescriptions, pulling punters into Space in Ibiza, taking over people's financial stuff...it's all the same.'

'Do you think you could make me do what you want?' Linda asks, sipping her drink.

Evie laughs. 'I'm not sure. You might be a bit of a

hard case.'

Linda raises her eyebrows and looks at Evie over the rim of her glass.

'Well, you know, you just seem very...sorted out,' Evie continues and she feels a little bit of heat in her cheeks. 'I don't mean...'

'It's OK,' Linda says. 'Everyone says that about me. But I might not be quite as tough as you all think.'

'Is that what they think about you at work?'

'In the Brigade? No, you don't get any of that stuff there. It's too intense. Everyone relies on each other too much, you couldn't operate if you had those kind of feelings. I'm just the same as everyone else.'

'So why do you think you're not as tough as we all seem to think?'

Linda smiles.

'Who's "we"?' she says.

'I don't know. You're the one who said it.'

'Ah. She's sharp tonight, Miss Sangster is. Well, you know, I'm not stupid: I've got this whole thing going on in people's eyes' – she waves her hand across her body – 'you know, the black firefighter, the boxing, the tragic past, the gay thing. It can be a bit intimidating. That's part of the reason I love the Brigade so much, nobody cares about all that. But it doesn't mean I don't get my heart broken like everyone else.'

Evie raises her eyebrows.

'A year ago,' Linda says. 'She was younger than

me. She went back to her old boyfriend and now she's getting married, the silly cow.'

Evie laughs, then stops herself.

'Sorry,' she says. 'That must have hurt.'

'It did.' Linda shrugs. 'So there you go.'

They sip their drinks for a moment, then Evie says:

'What is it with young people? They spend all this time trying to be cool and funky and dead fashionable when really all they want to do is move out to Essex and have a sodding family.'

Linda snorts a laugh into her drink and then they clink glasses.

'You know what I think, sometimes?' Evie continues. 'Sometimes I think when I'm with people and everyone's having a cool time and doing things they probably shouldn't do, sometimes I think those people are just taking a holiday from their real lives and after a while they'll remember their respectable lives and back they'll trot and I'll just be left here as usual, holding the fort, wondering where everyone went.'

'That's interesting. Maybe that's how I felt last year. I thought she loved me but maybe she just loved her idea of me.'

'There's a song in that.'

'Buy me another drink.'

'*N*ow, we are fed and watered and therefore ready to march. 'Tis forty minutes from here, we pass through the City gates and on to the fields which belong to my Lord Hatton. I myself arranged the lease he gave for the building of houses upon his gardens, and I took one myself. It is comfortable enough and close to Gray's Inn. My redoubtable housekeeper will be awake to receive you. Shall we commence?'

Lily looked nervously at him. He smiled and adopted a gentler tone.

'Do not show fear at this time, Lily,' he said. 'An old soldier's maxim: never offer fear a seat. You have done your bravery today, you have struck out against those who so cruelly treated you. Not many would have had your strength to do so and I delight in being the one to have witnessed it. Now a new moon lights your path and a new life awaits you. 'Tis a thing of glory.'

She bit her lip.

'No-one has ever spoken such words to me,' she said softly.

'Then I am proud to be the first. I predict a fine future for you, Lily Cadyman.'

'How can I thank −'

He interrupted her.

'We have a contract, you and I,' he said gravely. 'A contract which I myself have drafted. Whatever obligations I undertake to be of assistance to you shall never at any point be recompensed by any form of thanks. The onus upon you, Lily, is to profit from the opportunity you yourself created by your own deeds. If necessary, I shall write out such terms and seal the arrangement and lodge the document within the safe at Gray's Inn. Are we understood?'

At this she laughed.

'Joseph Fairtree, you are a rare kind of scrivener.'

'It takes a hawk to scan the field,' he said, 'and your sight is most keen. Shall we go?'

They stood up, pushed their way through the crowded tavern and out of the front door. The wind was strong now, gusting through the lanes and they pulled their coats tight as they began walking up towards Great Eastcheap.

Back in Pudding Lane, Mistress Hannah slurred a drunken goodnight to her friend after a link boy finally turned up with a lamp to escort her to her home two streets away. As she closed the door and bolted it, her father staggered past her and up the stairs to his room.

'You'll check on that oven, daughter?' he muttered as he passed.

'You have no need to be supervising my work, Father,' she retorted. ''Tis others in this house you need to concern

yourself with.'

She went over to the corner and pulled open the oven door. Inside, a few last embers glowed in the centre of the brick. She yanked a shovel from its stand, scooped up the remains and dropped them into the iron bucket on the floor, closing the lid down on top of it with a clumsy clang.

As she muttered oaths — 'That filthy wretch sleeps upstairs whilst I still labour' — she didn't notice one glowing cylindrical piece fail to hit the target of the bucket and instead roll silently across the floor to rest under the rack which held the wrapping papers for the ship's biscuits.

Hannah straightened up, snorted, burped, then followed her father up the stairs.

Chapter Fourteen

At nine o'clock in the evening on Saturday 1st September, a small white van with a hire company logo on the side draws up on the corner of Bread Street and Watling Street. The driver gets out and motions to one of the people sitting in the rear seat. A passenger door opens and Angel steps out. In the hot summer evening dusklight the brown skin of his face is marked with cuts and bruises. He walks round to the back of the van where the driver is already unloading two cardboard boxes tied up with string. Several other boxes of the same size are left inside the van as the driver then hands a much smaller package to Angel, this time passing it over with more care.

'Remember,' the man says, 'be very careful with this. Put it in your jacket pocket now. Do not drop it.'

Angel nods blankly and puts the package in his pocket. The man looks at him, then he leans forward and embraces him.

'Tonight,' he whispers passionately into Angel's ear, 'tonight we are become Luohans.'

The man stands back and Angel feels a tear prick the corner of his eye. He wipes it away. The man smiles, turns back to close the van doors then gets back in and reverses the car back down Bread Street. Angel leans down and grips the string tying each box then lifts them up and sets off down Watling Street. After a little while, he stops outside the green door, puts the boxes down on the ground, jabs the code into the metal box on the wall then lets himself in.

The boxes are obviously heavy as Angel struggles a little to carry them up the steep stairs inside the building. Finally he is outside the door of Stirling Global and he uses a key to get in.

The lights inside are on and Henry is sitting at his desk, writing notes on a pad with his black Mont Blanc pen. An empty wine bottle stands next to a glass which is still half full of red wine. He looks up as Angel stands in the doorway.

'And who the hell are you?' Henry barks, starting to get up.

'Cleaner,' Angel stutters and picks the boxes up. 'Bring more cleaning material.'

'Oh, I'm so sorry, lad,' Henry says. 'Of course. Here, let me help you.' He starts to come around the table but Angel moves quickly over behind Jean's desk and lays the boxes down.

'Is fine,' he says, stretching up.

'Fair do's,' says Henry, sitting back down. 'Working on a Saturday night. I like it. You could teach my lot a thing or two.' He picks up his glass as Angel stares at him, drains what is left. 'I was finishing up anyway,' he says. 'I'll leave you to it. Thanks for your hard work.'

He gets up, shoves his papers into his briefcase, tucks his checked shirt into the belt of his jeans and walks to the door.

'I'll wish you good evening,' he says, nods and leaves.

Angel slumps down in Jean's chair and looks down at the two boxes. Then he thinks of something and carefully pulls out the package from his jacket pocket and lays it on the desk. He looks between the package and the two boxes, sweat on his forehead. He grips the edge of the desk with both hands.

'Life is illusion,' he mutters. 'Life is illusion.'

Four hundred yards away, the white van is doing a three-point turn in Laurence Poutney Lane. A figure is walking up the hill carrying two boxes just like the ones Angel has, as the van drives quietly back down towards Upper Thames Street. It waits at the junction as a cyclist passes on the cycle highway – Linda glances up at the driver as she sweeps by, then looks back up ahead. On the right is Dowgate Fire Station. Her shift is due to start at 9.30.

Up in Edmonton, Joy is watching reruns of *Strictly*

Come Dancing. She is sorry that Jade isn't spending any time at home at the moment, but she can tell how changed, how vibrant her daughter seems every time she phones her. Something must be going right with that fellow with the dress, she thinks, smiling and lighting up another cigarette.

While she smiles in front of the TV with a cup of tea, Dennis is brushing his teeth in the bathroom of his flat the other side of Fore Street from Joy's block. He's thinking about his daughter – she's back on shift this evening and he's imagining her cycling down the cycle highway which he's never seen but which she's told him about. Then he remembers how he and a friend stole a bicycle when they were kids in Ghana and how they took turns to ride it while the other balanced on the handlebars.

Darren is looking at himself in the full-length mirror in his bathroom. He's carefully touching his hair, turning his head left and right to look at the angles: tonight he's heading out to a fetish party in Mayfair. Jimmy is at home in Hounslow, sneaking a cigarette in the garden while his wife marshalls the children through bathtime. Rufus is sitting at the bar of a pub in Chelsea, braying at a trust fund blonde.

Henry is striding past St Paul's on the way to Holborn Viaduct. He fancies a couple of pints of Timothy Taylors and the Mitre in Ely Place will satisfy that. He stops for a moment outside the cathedral and pulls out his phone; as he does so, another white van with the same rental company logo on the side turns right ahead of him and pulls into a side street. The driver gets out, opens the back door and pulls out two of the same cardboard boxes and hands them to one of the passengers who has stepped out of the van. Henry doesn't pay any attention: he's texting Evie.

'Just finished up in the office. Got another sales guy lined up for Gener8 in Scotland. I'm not giving up. I only stopped cos the cleaner turned up.'

Over in Shoreditch, an event is taking place. Across the street from the American Car Wash in Great Eastern Street, Chan and Jade are finishing pasting up a huge white poster onto the chipboard covering of a new building development. They've had to use ladders to put it up as it's about thirty feet high, maybe fifteen feet wide. Now they're packing up the extending ladders and the pots of paste into the back of another of those small white vans which is parked just round the corner. Chan comes back out and sets up a low podium on the pavement in front of the poster. There's a small group of Saturday-nighters hanging around on the pavement taking pictures and a few people have stopped to read the words on the poster. There's a young woman who's already had a few mojitos and she's laughing, pointing at the poster and reading the words out to her friends.

'God, London is so cool, I love it when this shit

happens!' she shrieks and they all laugh.

At the top of the poster, in bold red Helvetica capitals, the poster reads:

'LIKE FIRE UNBOUND'

Below it, in large black and white Helvetica type, it reads:

'The events in London of Saturday 1st September 2018 are a deliberate act of Buddhist engagement of mind. They serve to remind the world of the following:

1. London does not exist. It is a fantasy.
2. The strength inherent in a single blade of grass is more powerful than all the buildings of London.
3. Money, work, debt, duty and the entire legal system are imaginary concepts.
4. Through the application of discipline of thought as taught by the Buddha two thousand five hundred years ago, we are freed from these fictions.
5. The fire destroys the fabric of this imaginary city while the strength inherent in each and every one of us remains unbound. London has burned before. Let it burn again.'

A figure emerges from the passenger seat of the white van. William Cecil strides towards the poster carrying a pot of paint with a brush sticking out of it. He passes the bystanders, smiling and saying as he does, 'Excuse me, excuse me', then he stops at the foot of the poster and lifts the brush out of the pot as he turns to look at the gathering crowd of evening revellers. A drunk voice from the other side of the road calls out 'What the fuck is that shit?', then Cecil daubs his name, *William Cecil*, as a form of signature at the foot of the poster in thick black paint. He straightens up as Jade approaches, looks defiantly into the smartphone camera she points at him, and then he begins to speak.

'Good evening, my friends,' he calls out. Jade is videoing now, having taken several still shots of Cecil and the words of the poster. 'Good evening. My name is William Cecil. You do not know me. My name, my existence, are an irrelevance.'

'Love the moustache, mate!' someone calls out to laughter.

Cecil smiles and bows towards the heckler.

'I have come to share with you some information,' he continues. 'I will not take up much of your delightful evening. I simply call upon you, my brothers and sisters, to bear witness to our announcement of this evening's activites.' He looks at his watch. 'In exactly one hour, at 11pm, the fire of 1666, the Great Fire which began at 11pm on Saturday 1ˢᵗ September 1666, will once more manifest itself. While its physical flames were finally extinguished all those centuries ago, the fire itself remained. All we are doing tonight, is once more giving it physical form. Do please feel free to make whatever you wish of the reappearance of the flames: enjoy them, fear them, embrace them, extinguish them. Whatever, as they say, takes your fancy. I wish you courage, I wish you strength, I wish you love and abundance in all that you do.'

With that, he bows briefly, the crowd give some ironic rippling applause amidst jokes and laughter, and Cecil and Jade – still videoing the whole thing on her smartphone, which tomorrow she will upload anonymously to *YouTube* before sending equally untraceable emails to the *BBC*, *The Guardian* and *The Times* – walk back to the van, get in and Chan drives them away.

Evie is lying on her sofa in her flat in Wapping, watching an old Bruce Willis movie and eating a Chinese which she just had delivered. She's heading out to Hadleigh tomorrow for Sunday lunch and today she's just chilled – she and Linda weren't out that late the previous evening, but they did end up dancing in a club which is something Evie hasn't done in a while. This afteroon, she'd wandered around Smithfield market, absently looking at clothes while thinking about her night out. It was obvious that Linda liked her, even though she didn't try anything or even say anything. It felt good, though, she knew that: something definitely felt good.

Her phone bleeps and she picks it up. A text from Henry. She reads it.

'Oh for Christ's sake Henry, give it a break,' she says out loud and throws the phone back on the sofa. Bruce Willis grimaces and pumps someone full of bullets. She picks up the chopsticks again, then puts them down and reaches over for the phone. She reads his text once more.

'I only stopped cos the cleaner turned up.'

What is Angel doing there on a Saturday evening? She'd looked at his contract when she was searching for his number yesterday, and he was supposed to do the five weekdays. There wasn't any mention of weekends. She thinks back to earlier in the week when she encountered Angel after she'd been drinking with Henry. What was that strange thing he said? 'Not long now. Just four days.' Then he got all secretive about it. She looks at her phone diary and works out the week. Tuesday, that would have been. And four days from then means today.

She stands up and walks over to the window. Her flat looks south over the Thames; it is one of those warehouse conversions and the view stretches up river to Big Ben and the London Eye, down river to Canary Wharf. It isn't fully dark yet but the sun has passed beyond the horizon out west and the night is approaching. Lights glitter all along both sides of the river, their shapes dancing on the black river. She looks at her watch: quarter to ten.

Why is Angel in their office on the evening when, he'd told her, something was going to happen? She turns round, switches the volume off on the TV and picks up her phone. She sends Angel a text.

'Are you OK Angel? This is Evie Sangster. x'

In the Stirling Global office, Angel hasn't moved. He's still sitting at Jean's desk, the small package in front of him, the two boxes unopened on the floor beside him. His phone beeps. It would be another text from Marta. He'd found lots of them when William Cecil gave him his phone back this evening before he left with the others. He picks up the phone, reads Evie's text. His hands are shaking. He types a reply:

'I sorry. I was wrong.'

He puts his head in his hands and cries. He stays like that, sprawled over Jean's desk, until the sobs stop. Then Angel sits up, wipes his face with the sleeve of his jacket. He sniffs, shakes himself as though to rid himself of doubt. Then he says out loud, firmly this time:

'Life is illusion.'

He leans forwards and begins carefully to unwrap the package on the desk.

In Wapping, Evie stares at her phone. What does he mean? Nothing about that reply reassures her. What is he wrong about? She paces around the flat, stands by the window again and looks out at the river. Was she doing it again? Was this just what she always did, felt that she had to be in control, sort everyone out? Strangely, the person she'd like to talk to now, to ask for a second opinion, that's Linda. She has a way of thinking more directly, she would know. But Linda will be on her shift now.

'Sod it,' Evie says out loud. She puts the lids back on the half-eaten Chinese and carries them over to the kitchen worktop. She picks up a jacket and her car keys and heads out of the front door.

Just before eleven o'clock that evening, as the bellow of Thomas Farriner's snores shook the house, a paper wrapper slipped down through the slats of the wooden rack and rested on the rough edge of the piece of burned wood which still just glowed in the darkness of the bakery shop. After a few seconds, a thin thread of smoke began to rise from the black smudge where the paper touched the ember and as the smudge spread like ink on parchment, the smoke gathered in weight. Just as the mushroom shape on the paper seemed to be slowing in its growth, a single yellow flame ignited silently and rapidly tore up the outside of the wrapper until it licked the underneath of the whole stack resting within the wooden frame of the rack.

Now smoke began to billow out in a cloud and started to disperse in the still air of the shop. Several flames were visible as the wrappers which were packed in readiness for tomorrow's ships' biscuits caught fire. The wooden struts of the rack were charring here and there in black and soon one of those too was curled in flame. Within a few minutes, the shop was rapidly filling with smoke as, with a gentle thump, the rack collapsed onto the floor and the burning wood and paper spread out, two of the struts resting against the wooden shop counter which immediately took the flame.

Still the room was quiet and the silence was broken by the cryer further up Pudding Lane ringing his bell and calling out: 'Eleven of the hour. A great wind from the east.'

The woollen rug which lay on the street side of the shop floor suddenly erupted, a sheet of flame flashing across its surface and the shop was now brightly illuminated with yellows and reds as the smoke swirled faster and faster within the confines of the room. The wooden door which led upstairs, which Hannah had closed behind her on her way up, began to burn from the bottom and as it did so, the smoke forced its way through the growing gap between the door and its frame and filled the stairway.

The smoke billowed up the narrow stairs and reached the first floor where it gathered outside Farriner's closed door. Still his snoring shuddered through the wooden frame of the house and the smoke, seeking further exit, began to climb the stairs to the second floor where Hannah's room lay. The flames in the ground floor shop could be heard now, a crackle of energy which seemed to be urged on by the strong draft which was coming down from the chimney from the winds outside which by this time were blowing fiercely through the late summer streets.

Smoke slithered under Hannah's door. It crept towards

her bed where she lay on her back, her mouth open and her eyes closed, her sleeping face smeared with potions. Wisps of grey crawled over her bedclothes and caressed her cheeks. Then she coughed in her sleep and her eyes opened. For a second she did nothing but inhaled the noxious smoke and then she screamed.

She lurched out of her bed and seemed to fight the clouds of smoke which were now filling the room.

'Father!' she screamed. 'Father! Fire!' She stamped on the floor to waken him and rushed to open her bedroom door. As she was confronted by a wall of smoke she screamed once more, dashed back into her room and grabbed a towel to cover her mouth.

'Fire by God!' her father shouted from the floor below. 'Hannah! Fire!'

Hannah went back out into the hallway again, the towel covering her mouth, and she looked up the narrow flight of stairs to the attic door, which she could see was still barred from the outside. She hesitated, grimaced, then turned turned to descend down to her father's floor. He stood outside his bedroom, coughing and holding a cloth over his face. The smoke at this first floor level was thicker than upstairs and the noise of the fire down below was frightening.

'We must get out, now!' her father shouted. 'Where is the child?'

'I have woken her,' Hannah shouted back. 'I have told her to hurry. Come, let us make down to the front door.'

'We must wait for the child.'

'There is no time, Father,' Hannah screamed. 'She is young, she will follow us. I must protect you.'

And she pushed her father towards the stairs. They both shuffled down the first few steps but then realised the fire had now consumed the door at the bottom, which had turned into a blazing furnace, impossible even to approach. They climbed back up to the first floor.

'The window,' Hannah shouted. 'Your bedroom window Father, it gives onto the lane.'

'Lily!' her father shouted.

'She will follow us, Father,' Hannah cried as she moved him back through the bedroom door. 'Lily, follow us to the window,' she called out behind her. She stepped past her father and pushed open the window. Outside there was a very narrow lane which just had room for one person to pass and it separated the back of the bakery from another dwelling. Hannah stepped out onto the ledge and called back to her father.

'Give me your hand Father, we can walk along the ledge to safety next door. Quickly!'

The baker heaved himself up after his daughter, then turned and shouted back into the smoke:

'Lily, make haste girl, make haste!'

Hannah grabbed his hand and they stepped gingerly along the ledge. Next door a candle was already alight in the first floor window, and as they approached it opened.

'*Neighbour, let us in!*' *Hannah called.* '*There is a fire in our house. We must call for help.*'

Several minutes later, Hannah and her father were out in Pudding Lane, her father supported by his neighbour who had guided him in through his own bedroom window. Her father was coughing violently. The bakery was a terrifying blaze of flame in front of them and a crowd had now gathered.

'*Are all of the household safe?*' *someone cried.*

'*The girl, Lily,*' *the neighbour replied.* '*She was to follow her master but she remains in the building.*'

'*Poor girl,*' *someone said, shaking his head.* '*That deformity of her limb, it has cost her speed tonight.*'

Chapter Fifteen

Back in 1666, when the fire that started in Thomas Farriner's bakery was encouraged to spread by the strong easterly winds that had picked up on the night of the 1st September, the City of London was effectively a tinderbox: most of the buildings were timber-built, the streets were so narrow that some houses almost touched each other as their upper levels were built out to create more space. Over a five-day period, thirteen thousand houses were destroyed – that's pretty much the entire City, with the old St Paul's being consumed into the bargain. Anyway, you know that: Henry told you.

London's not like that any more. We're a city of stone and metal and glass and with each year there are more and more of these foreign edifices which repel old-fashioned things like fire just as they squeeze the fucking life out of the people who have to troop into them every day. You can't ignite a flame on a sheet of steel.

But that's where William Cecil was so smart. He timed his – what, his performance, his extravaganza? That's how I've always considered it, but it's not how the international warrant for his arrest described it – he timed it to happen at 11pm on Saturday 1st September 2018, exactly the time when it's known that Farriner's bakery first caught fire. And he was smart because where he placed his eighteen Luohans gave their actions the maximum opportunity to allow fires to gain strength while also making the task of the Fire Brigade as difficult as possible. Take Watling Street, where Angel was: it's a single-lane street which is really easy to block if there are roadworks going on to repair cables or something, and most of the buildings are scruffy old places with badly-built office conversions like Henry's. Stirling Global, with its complete lack of fire precautions and its wall of paper correspondence in Jean's ringbinders, was perfect fodder.

Others had to be directed to specific places where the opportunity for fire to take hold was stronger. The Italian translator, for example, Rosalda, she worked in Holborn which, for a perfectionist like Cecil, was obviously outside of the 1666 fire area so he instructed her to target a big refuse wheelie bin outside a MacDonald's by Liverpool Street station.

Annabel, the mixed-up posh girl who was interning at one of those gleaming City law firms, she was sent to Leadenhall Market where she'd used her centuries-old aristocratic lineage to blag her way into an empty upstairs office over a pizza parlour. Tullah was a bit stuck because the office block where he was the night porter was yet another gleaming monolith, but his nightly reading of The Book Of Revelations came in handy and he followed his nose looking for a righteous fire and found a broken lock to a basement store room of an old pub in Ball Court.

So all eighteen of the Luohans were spread out within no more than a square mile, just as Cecil had placed his mini Buddha statues on the map in his room in Chiltern Court. Each of them was somewhere that had a potential vulnerability: difficulty of access for the Fire Brigade, an old building still racked with inflammable materials, collections of refuse built up from the working week. Have you walked around the City of London? You just step off the main drags of Bishopsgate and Cheapside and you're back in a seventeenth century village, with narrow winding lanes. There's a fine irony there: the City was never rebuilt on modern lines after the Great Fire – unlike Paris with its 19th century Haussmann grandeur – because no-one in London could agree who owned what in the smoking debris and so pretty much the same old streets reappeared. Money talked back then too, you see. Now factor in that its Saturday night, and the City of London is closed on weekends – restaurants, bars, shops, offices, nothing opens on Saturday and Sunday. The City streets were empty that last night of the 2018 heatwave, the Shoreditch streets where Cecil gave his speech in front of the poster being the closest centre of human activity.

Evie parks her Audi on a yellow line in Queen Street at about 10.45pm. There's no-one around. She walks down to Queen Victoria Street and takes a right into Watling Street. The air is stifling: surely the thunder will break soon? They'd been forecasting it for the last three days.

Upstairs at Stirling Global, Angel is closing the door behind him as he leaves the office. His hand is shaking, his face and his jacket are drenched in sweat. In the last hour he's carried out the instructions which Chan had given them all. He's opened the two boxes and pulled out both of the 9kg Propane bottles. Chan had told them that they needed to try and position the two bottles where the air wouldn't circulate well, so Angel placed them under Jean's desk and then packed the space around them with clothes that he found in the office: one of Jean's raincoats on the peg, the contents of Darren's gym bag, Evie's swimming towel that she'd left to dry.

Then he'd carefully undone the smaller package which contained a detonator with a digital clock.

The forensics guys afterwards reckoned that Chan must have been ex-Special Forces, maybe Vietnam, because his knowledge of thermobaric bombs was very accurate. The key to their maximum effect was to contain the spread of the gas as much as possible while it mixed itself with the oxygen in the sur- rounding air. The more that mixture could be held together, the more potent the explosion. And the detonator was powerful enough to smash the metal of the gas bottles, so while maybe a third of the Propane escaped into the enclosed air during the five-minute countdown that started when the Luohans pressed the button on the detonator, the bulk of the gas which was suddenly released when the first explo- sion ripped open the metal bottles then created the main fireball.

Angel attached the detonator to one of the bottles with tape so that it was resting on the metal of both. He pressed the button and the red digital reader began to count down from five minutes. He now stands for a second staring underneath Jean's desk, then he turns and leaves the office. He runs down the narrow stairs, opens the front door and starts walking up Watling Street towards St Paul's.

Evie is fifty yards away by then but she doesn't see him because she is texting Henry as she walks: 'Am calling in to check on the office – got a weird feeling about that cleaner being there. Will text you in a bit.' Angel is walking swiftly up the street, checking the time on his watch. After he's checked it for the third time, he turns round to look back and that's when he sees Evie opening the green door.

'No,' he whispers. 'No.' He stands still for a moment, staring back at the now-empty street. He seems transfixed. He looks at his watch again, clutches at his hair. 'No, no.' Then he starts running back.

Evie is outside the second floor door of Stirling Global and is already frowning – what is that smell? She puts her key in the door.

Angel jabs at the numbers on the chrome keypad outside on the street.

Evie gags as she steps into the office – the smell of gas is overpowering.

'Jesus Christ,' she says and covers her mouth. Then she hears heavy steps on the stairs and a voice shouting out:

'Get out! Get out!'

Angel bursts into the office and grabs her arm. She shakes herself free and steps further back into the room.

'Now!' he shouts, grabbing her again.

'Get the fuck off me!' she shouts but he is stronger and drags her to the door. He puts his face close to hers.

'Bomb,' he says.

'What?'

He pushes her roughly out of the room and pulls the office door closed behind him as he keeps forcing her to start taking steps down.

Joy hears the explosions ten miles away up in Edmonton. So does Dennis. Darren hears them as he sits in a cab on the way to Mayfair and the noise is so loud the cab actually rocks. Henry is even closer – he'd finished his third pint of Timothy Taylor's in the Mitre and is on his way to Chancery Lane tube to get the Central line back to Ealing. Everyone has been expecting thunder but there is no doubting what he heard: they were bombs. And in Dowgate Hill Fire Station off Upper Thames Street, everyone including Linda stops talking in the crew room while the massive noise reverberates around them. They are right in between two of the sites, only a hundred yards each way from Angel Lane and Cloak Lane. For a second they are all motionless then, as one, they leap to their feet.

Every one of the eighteen detonators worked; Chan was pretty good at his job. In all the newspaper reports, you could see this almost perfect ring made up of the eighteen locations: Watling Street, Cloak Lane, Ball Court, Leadenhall Market, Adam's Court, St Helen's Place, Pinner's Passage, Great Swan Alley, St Olave's Court, Angel Street, Amen Court, Pilgrim Street, Black Friars Lane, Puddle Dock, Angel Lane, St Dunstans Alley, Bell Inn Yard, St Swithins Lane.

Here, take a look – this is the 1676 map of the City of London drawn up by John Ogilby and William Morgan:

I think every one of those eighteen streets was there at the time of the Great Fire. That's another testament to William Cecil's genius, his attention to detail: it's as though he painted that ring of fire onto the Ogilby and Morgan map and then went about replicating it in real time. Obviously, all that stuff in the press and the TV, the endless self-righteous and self-serving journalists going on about mental health and the iniquities of contemporary capitalism and all that media static – that had its place, like it always does these days. But not many people, I don't think, not many people really admired the sheer beauty of the work. That was what that poster in Shoreditch was all about I reckon: it was the label sitting underneath the work of art, the didactic.

Look, you can see the pattern of the detonation sites here:

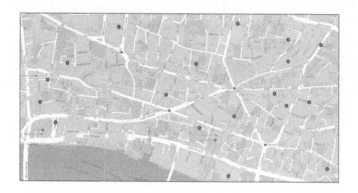

I stare at the map for hours, like lots of people I suppose. That circular grid, it's imprinted on my mind. And Watling Street, of course, sitting right in the middle.

London was never going to burn in 2018 like it did in 1666, Cecil knew that. You can't burn modern cities down, they're just too resistant. But he came as close as you can by choosing from the pattern of the 17th century City and when millions of people in London that night heard the massive roar of the eighteen simultaneous explosions, all within a square mile, most of them thought it was the terrorist attack they had all secretly dreaded for years, the big one. But it wasn't: this was Art.

That's not what Angel thought when the jagged shard of metal from the exploded Propane bottle slammed through the thin partition wall between Stirling Global and the staircase and embedded itself in his thigh. His scream was lost in the huge noise of ignition and he fell on top of Evie and they both tumbled down the narrow stairs as a sheet of flame chased after them.

All the other Luohans got away from their detonation sites as planned within the five-minute countdown. Tullah's ingenious set-up in the basement of the old pub in Ball Court created a raging furnace within minutes which licked up the ancient infrastructure of the building; Annabel's first-floor installation in Leadenhall Market burst through the walls into neighbouring offices and smashed into the pizza parlour below, feeding on the columns of empty cardboard boxes; Poppy actually trotted back up Angel Lane and turned left onto Upper Thames Street and walked past Linda's fire station, about two minutes before 11. The ferocity of the thermobaric combustion of Propane and oxygen and the sheer number of explosion sites made it literally impossible for the Fire Brigade to be able to contain enough of the fires within the first hour and by one o'clock on Sunday morning, the police helicopters that were circling overhead directing their searchlights were engulfed in thick black smoke and even as far away as Hadleigh out east where Frankie and Andy were asleep in bed you could see see the orange glow of fire from the City of London.

Back in Watling Street a few seconds after the explosion, Angel is sprawled over Evie at the foot of the stairs as pieces of ceiling fall all around them. The noise of the fire is deafening and Angel can feel the heat on his back. The pain in his leg is indescribable but he doesn't know at that point that he's also broken several bones when they were hurled downstairs by the blast. Evie is face down and there is blood coming from her head. He shakes her; there is no reaction.

Linda is the first outside Dowgate Hill station onto the street and she can see two very close plumes of smoke from the two nearest explosions. She shouts back into the station just as her Station Manager is on the radio setting up the first Incident Command, and two engines immediately roar into life. As everyone dons kit, three Crew Managers combine dressing with taking notes as the Manager barks out information. Within the first five minutes, they discover there were multiple incidents and that a full-scale terror alert has been announced.

The same activities are taking place simultaneously in Shoreditch, Whitechapel and Shadwell stations and within ten minutes more are being activated: Dockhead, Soho, Euston, Bethnal Green, Deptford. As black columns of smoke now begin to rise into the sky all over the City, sirens begin to sound, more and more of them competing with one another as police cars race into the centre and the fire engines begin to move out.

'Get up, get up!' Angel shouts at Evie above the roar of the flames and as he does so he is hit in the back by a chunk of falling plaster. He looks back up the stairs and sees a wall of fire. He and Evie are caught in a narrow space where the stairs from the second floor reach the first floor landing. He leans down and lifts her head carefully but she doesn't respond. He tries to get up but the pain in his leg is so great he is sick over her back and he passes out.

The first two engines roll out of Dowgate Hill station, one heading round the corner to Angel Lane, one to Cloak Lane. Linda and Steve are in the team readying the third engine to follow when the Station Manager yells over that they are to head instead to Watling Street, where he's just had the third incident close to them radioed in. Once the five-man team is in, the engine heads out.

Linda said later that it didn't occur to her that Watling Street was where she'd first met Evie. 'Your mind's not in that place,' she said and as she sits now in the second row of seats, completing the buckling on her suit as the radio crackles with information and the siren wails, she's going through the checks in her mind, thinking about the stages of preparing the ladders and the hoses, visualising the event before it happens. That's what they're all doing.

Henry has turned around and is walking swiftly back towards the City from Chancery Lane. He's got his phone out, sending Evie a text: 'You OK?' Dennis has turned on his TV and is sitting down in his pyjamas watching BBC News as they start to report a major incident in London.

'Dottie,' he murmurs.

As the thick smoke begins to fill the stairwell, the fumes make Angel cough and he comes to again. There's still no movement from Evie. He rolls onto his back and edges down the last step to the first floor landing, his face creased in pain. He sits up, grabs Evie's hand and tries to pull her with him. Then the jagged piece of metal in his leg catches on the stair bannister and he shrieks with pain, lets go of her hand and falls back on the landing.

Two police cars sweep past Henry as he nears St Paul's tube station, their sirens blaring. Three people run past him and one of them shouts as they pass, 'Get out mate, it's fucked up.' A fire engine roars past and turns left up King Edward Street. He increases his pace.

Linda and Steve's engine noses up Watling Street. Everyone in the cab can see the flames coming out of the second floor window ahead on the right. Their path is blocked by red and white barriers surrounding what looks like newly laid flagstones after some facilities excavation in the one-lane street. Steve jumps out and starts pulling the barriers away until there's enough room and the engine moves on up so it's outside Stirling Global.

One of the team is out with an axe and already smashing at the faded green front door. Linda and one other are fitting their breathing apparatus while the driver is out and beginning the ladder elevation. Steve presses the hydraulic which begins to release the first hose.

There are fire engines outside seven of the eighteen detonation sites now. The fire is really taking hold around where Tullah and Annabel did their work – the blaze inside Leadenhall Market hasn't even been reported yet and it's already forced its way into the next door shop and the market itself is filling with smoke. Tullah's explosion in the basement of the old pub in Ball Court has now created a kind of fireball at the dead end of that narrow little lane and there's not even room for an engine to get in there.

The City is filling up with fire engines and police cars. There's still not many people around in the centre and the police are starting to set up roadblocks to stop any traffic coming in. Up in Edmonton, Dennis can already see a glow of orange from the window of his bedroom which faces down south.

The green door gives way and Linda steps through, another firefighter right behind her. The lobby is already filling with smoke and she makes for the stairs.

Halfway up and she can see a body lying on the floor of the landing.

'Got someone here,' she speaks into the radio inside her breathing apparatus. She gestures to the man behind her.

Linda reaches the first floor landing and assesses the situation. There's one body on the landing, a man, quite overweight – through the haze of smoke she can see there's blood around him. There's another body in the stairwell, face down and legs bent awkwardly. The fire is visible now halfway up the stairs going to the first floor and the carpet is burning.

'Stretcher, now,' she says into the radio and the firefighter behind her heads back down to get them. She looks closer at the body in front of her, he's lying on his back and there's a pool of blood gathering by his leg. Then she sees the shard of metal sticking out. She takes her gloves off, reaches down to take a pulse from his neck and as she touches him, his eyes flicker and he cries out.

'It's OK,' she shouts through the breathing apparatus. 'We're going to get you out.'

Her partner is back up the stairs with the first stretcher and they lay it on the landing floor alongside the man, who's wailing now in pain, coughing and rubbing his eyes. Linda gets behind his head, her colleague puts his hands carefully under the legs and they heave him onto the stretcher as gently as they can, keeping the splinter of metal in view at all times. He's screaming throughout. They carry him down the flight of stairs out into the street where the engine's floodlights have illuminated everything stark white. The ambulance isn't here yet so they leave him on the pavement and head back up.

Linda's in front again. She gets back to the first floor and reaches out for a wrist on the second body. She feels for a pulse then nods back at her colleague. As gently as she can, she manouevres the shoulders round towards the landing floor then goes up to take the legs while her colleague pulls the shoulders down to the head of the stretcher. The fire is almost touching them now and seconds after they start edging back down the stairs with the stretcher, a piece of burning timber crashes down from the second floor just where they were lifting the body.

Once they're back outside the wail of an ambulance can be heard and as they lay the stretcher down on the pavement the ambulance accelerates up the street and stops behind the fire engine. Linda hurries over to brief the medics. While she's explaining to them, shouting above the noise of the engines and the conflagration above them, she notices the wine bar sign behind the vehicles: Jamies. She stares at it, looks back up at the burning building, then runs back to the stretcher they've just lain on the ground. Carefully she pushes the hair away from the face and sees that it's Evie.

'No!' she yells, but one of the medics pulls her away. Linda stands for a few seconds staring down in horror then she hears Steve shout,

'Linda, you're going up second!'

She looks up and sees the ladder is resting against the second-floor wall and one of the firefighters is already on the first steps carrying the hose. She leans back down and asks the medic:

'Is she going to be OK?'

He looks up.

'She's alive.'

Steve shouts: 'Linda – now!'

She climbs up onto the engine and starts following the firefighter in front of her, taking some of the weight of the hose as she climbs. There's a smash of glass as he breaks the second floor window and the foam starts spraying into the building.

Henry finally makes it to Watling Street and he runs towards the commotion, his checked shirt hanging out of his jeans, his face red and sweaty, and he's shouting out: 'Evie! Evie!' But now the police have arrived and he's being held back and even though he's swearing at them, they won't let him through and eventually one of them says, 'Sir, if you carry on like this I'm going to arrest you,' and he just suddenly slumps on the ground and puts his head in his hands and sobs.

Linda looks down from the ladder as she feeds the hose to the firefighter ahead of her. Through the black smoke she can see the A & E team gathering a screen around Evie and at the same time, out in Hadleigh, Andy looks out of the bathroom window where he's padded to for one of his nighttime pees and he sees the orange glow out west in London and he calls out to Frankie, who's still asleep in the bedroom. Dennis is calm and quiet in Edmonton, watching the BBC News channel and glancing out of the windows of his flat. He and his colleagues have been forecasting uprisings in London for years now, maybe this is it? Or is it what the journalists are speculating, an external terror attack? Mostly, he's thinking of Linda, focussing his mind on her strength, her discipline, her survival instinct.

Joy is texting Jade. 'All right love?' she's writing into her phone. 'Something's kicking off. Just tell me you're safe.' And Jade is still in the van with William Cecil and Chan and they're on the motorway already and as she finishes a quick reply – 'Fine Mum, don't worry about me, luv u x' – Cecil leans over and gently takes the phone from her.

'Your mother?' he asks, quite tenderly.

She smiles and nods.

'Good,' he says. 'Now we will need to get rid of these items – Chan will set up up a secure arrangement once we are out of UK jurisdiction. You will be able to speak to your mother tomorrow.'

'She's fine,' Jade grins, and Cecil takes the battery and SIM card out of the phone and drops it all into a bag and hands it to Chan who takes one hand off the wheel to accept it.

About forty minutes later, as Chan guides the van into the entrance of the private airfield at Stapleford out near Epping Forest, the fires are now raging in the Square Mile. Linda's team have got the one in Watling Street under control but there are others which were so cunningly selected that the lack of access for firefighters has meant that several of them are being left to burn while surrounding buildings are being protected. There's a thick pall of black smoke over the City now and the easterly breeze has blown it as far as Berkeley Square where Darren is hoovering up coke in a private house off the square where half the guests are already naked. The TV monitors in all the rooms of this elegant Regency house are showing the fires which seems to be exciting everyone to ever greater excesses.

Joy has joined a group of neighbours out on the patch of grass in front of the block and they're sharing cigarettes and speculating about the fires. Sirens wail regularly in the background. She's lighting up another cigarette when her phone bleeps again and she sees a message from Frankie:

'You all right, love? Trying to get hold of Evie, you

or Jade haven't heard from her have you?' As Joy taps in a reply, Jade straps the belt around her next to William Cecil in the private jet and Chan taxis it over to the grass runway and they prepare to take off, the very last sighting of them anywhere in the world since that night of 1st September.

Linda steps out of the smoking door of the Stirling Global building about twelve thirty. The fire inside is now completely out and they've finished inspecting all the offices to make sure no other people are inside. Her team leader is standing by the fire engine holding a radio.

'Moving out, Linda!' he calls out. 'Got to get over to Leadenhall Market.'

She nods and heads towards the cab. As she passes him, she says:

'The two people here: what's happened to them?'

He looks at her and frowns. 'You OK, Linda?' he asks.

'The woman!' she shouts. 'The woman who was in there!'

'It's OK,' he says, reaching out and gripping her shoulders. 'They've taken both of them to Barts. They've badly injured but they're going to be OK. Tell me: are you all right to continue? Tell me now.'

She bites her lip, nods and gets into the cab. As she's climbing up, a rotund man in jeans and checked shirt she doesn't recognise breaks through the police cordon and races up to the engine.

'Please,' Henry calls out. 'Please, does anyone know what the fuck's going on? Does anyone know where Evie is?'

She looks down out of the window at him. 'Go home, Henry,' she says. 'She's alive.'

London rages for for the next couple of hours and then at quarter to five, just as the dawn begins to gather her strength for another day and as the first of the Luohans, Falusa, is identified by the police from CCTV prior to unmarked squad cars being despatched to Tooting to arrest her (oh, and by the way, the Luohans, they're scattered around various prisons and high-security hospitals now, all still telling journalists that William Cecil will be in touch with them soon, that their place is not in prison but out in the world with him, protecting the reincarnation of the Buddha, and they all still think this even though they've been told that Cecil lied to them when he told them they wouldn't get caught placing the bombs because Chan was going to disable all the CCTVs in the City of London on the night of 1st September, even though none of them has ever heard from Cecil ever again), the thick blanket of black smoke over the City is disrupted as the first flash of lightning hits and finally, finally after all these weeks, finally the rain begins to fall, gently at first and then soon it's hammering down on the pavements and the people who are still up and aren't part of the different response teams but are just up, they're holding their hands out to the sky and the rain is splashing over their lips and eyes and people are crying and up in the Pelican Tower on Bishopsgate, there's a final group of party goers out on the veranda still taking phone pictures of the view over London, even though the management has told everyone the building's got to be evacuated, and they're dancing in the downpour as the City down below them is like a field embroidered with gold, flowers of fire bursting out all over the darkened landscape, the lights of emergency services vehicles criss-crossing the Square Mile like tapestry threads, the sweep of high-power floodlights from the helicopters overhead creating thousands of tiny crystallised rainbows through the rain which is now so deafening that it's all that can be heard.

No word of the fire in Pudding Lane had reached the householders in the homes grouped around the gardens at Hatton by the time Lily and Joseph made it back. As he had promised, a stern and forbidding housekeeper greeted them and, as he went to his rooms to take off his coat, she bustled Lily into the kitchen.

'A young girl like you, he made you walk all this way – and with that leg?' she said, eyeing Lily's gait. But there was kindness in her voice and Lily felt comforted.

'I am used to walking, ma'am,' she said.

'No ma'am's, here, by the Good Lord's Grace,' the woman said. 'We are as we are found. I am Mrs Teign, but Mr Teign is long gone and they call me Elizabeth. That will do for you? You know of Master Fairtree's beliefs?'

'The poorest he that is in England hath a life to lead as the greatest he,' said Lily, instinctively raising her head with pride.

At this the old woman smiled.

'Indeed he does. Come, let us make up a bed for you in my chamber. From all he has told me, you will profit from this opportunity. London consoles those it is about to destroy, they say, and from all I have heard, you have had precious little consolation so far.'

'Mrs Teign ma'am?'

'Elizabeth!' the older woman scolded. 'You'd best get used to your future, girl.'

'Elizabeth,' Lily repeated hesitantly. 'Might I just stand outside the door for a moment before I retire? I would like…I would like to remember this moment for the rest of my life.'

The woman smiled. 'Of course. Go and enjoy your freedom while I prepare your bed. Don't tarry, now.'

Lily walked back to the hall of the house, opened the front door and stood upon the step, looking out at the green fields of Hatton. She could have wept but already she knew that her future was not one where tears could make their home. She smiled at the sight of the moon hanging over the fields and that's when she noticed the smell of smoke in the air. She turned her head to the east and wondered at the orange glow that was now illuminating the night sky of London.

THE END